NEW WORLD

Misfortunes towards Life

MAIYA ELIAB

Brilliant Books Literary
137 Forest Park Lane Thomasville
North Carolina 27360 USA

CHAPTER I

Everyday

Most cases involve ongoing discovery, while those discoveries reveal more cases. "Reiner, please clean the dishes." His mother asked, writing her appointments down in her notepad. The boy quickly gets up from the dining room table, and gathers the utensils and plates from their breakfast feast. "How's your project going by the way?" She wondered.

"It's still in progress…" The freckled brunette was excited about his topics of choice. He had researched multiple articles about quantum physics, and evolution because of his fascination with universal theories.

The tenth grade presentation was required for every sophomore to graduate. The students were to pick a college subcategory (based on insight) for transferred service hours, and references to colleges such as Bradford University, Michelle University, and etc. After cleaning the table and washing the dishes, Reiner collected himself together and walked across the hallway into the bathroom to brush his teeth, and wash. In his room he changed into his school uniform which consists of a long sleeve white blouse in a black uniform suit with the option of a black or red striped tie and black pants. Milford Academy wanted their students to look dashing as always.

Reiner has always been a cute, intelligent and ambitious person who knew exactly how to put a smile on people's faces. The boy soon rushes out the bedroom door upon seeing his mother Kareen chatting, and laughing on the phone with her mother Gabriela…as much of a resentment Reiner felt towards his mother, he still helps her around the house.

"He-He Mr. Strife." Kareen said, pointing her finger in a gunning motion. "I see you're off to school early." She walked towards him pointing at his laptop; he tried detouring his situation as he didn't want his mother going on a tangent about the degrees his project might get him. "Welp, I'll see you when I get back mom." He said in a low cheeky tone.

Within the entrance of the prestigious school he sought the attention of his childhood friend, Vitallin Dubarse. "Hey Vitallin!" He yelled. Vitallin waved as she ran towards him. She was talking to her friends Chrissie, and Megan. "How are you?" She pounced on the boy giving him a big hug. "Good, you?" He replied with a sweet smile.

"Great, I can't wait for the presentations today!" Vitallin was in a bright, and cheery mood today with her long blonde signature braided pigtails, and gorgeous deep blue eyes. She was described as an interestingly clever, happy go lucky kid by most of her peers as had many guys admire her for her quirky charm and looks but never pursued them. "I'll get some of the items out of my locker okay." Vitallin said. "Sure." As the girl searched through her locker she made sure she hadn't lost the materials.

Flashcards, assignments, activity, laptop… "Hey piss head!" A girl laughs crowding Vitallin's locker along with two of her friends. "How's your whoring streak going along?" She taunts. "But then again, it's not like you're able to get a boyfriend anyways with a face like that you ugly piece of shit." *This girl…!* "Want me to give you flashbacks?" Vitallin's demeanor was tense. "As if you could fight me." The girl stuck her tongue out challenging her. *Damn you Erika.*

As the entire class was settling down and taking their turns on what topic to present in class, Vitallin was helping Reiner present. The room was dimly lit, and as the screen was down all eyes were targeted towards the boy's 3D presentation as he began to start. "Vitallin, as of any assistance needed I'm asking for you to be my sub monitor…" She nodded. "Hello, my name is Reiner Strife and I am here to explain how quantum physics, and motions work." Reiners placement background was astronomical, just like a confetti of stars within the solar system.

He then took Mrs. Veiter's wood pointer and began talking about photons and lasers, believing in multiple universes and Schrodinger's theory. "Well class, that was a wonderful presentation." Mrs. Veiter said. "As for any volunteers for next week…?" When Reiner went back to his desk, he saw Brinner walk towards his seat. "Reiner, Reiner." The young man said whilst patting him on the back, his gaze becoming slightly imitating and dark.

Reiner's relationship with Brinner is annoyance at best and downright dreadful at worst. The young man was particularly handsome with long brown lightly mixed curls, and striking facial features. Brinner usually plays Reiner because he knows how to push his buttons and get what he wants out of him, as if he was a puppy dog winding in the wind.

"What's up buddy…" Reiner tried getting the boy's hands off him. "I'm sorry Brinner but why are you near me?" He said in annoyance to challenge him. "Because you're precious to me." He mocked. "Come on kid, we go way back. I could still recall fighting a molester off you when we were little."

It was a sick memory that resonated with Reiner and hasn't gone away since.

The two happen to go way back to elementary school days; coats, scarves, and going all out within the winter "tundras" of the suburbs. They made a promise to always keep each other by their side despite friendly teasing, where suddenly things went downhill. "Don't think I haven't forgotten you shit head…" Brinner whispered into the boy's ear which made Reiner want to slap him in the face. "Brinner if you're willing to fight, take it up with the police, not me. That case is closed now."

Once class was over, Reiner and Vitallin walked over to a pizza shop, and then went over to the boy's house. Two sausage and pepperoni pizza boxes were on the floor at the center of his room. "Hey Reiner," said Vitallin, relaxing on the boy's bed. "How do you think the presentation went?" She tried stirring up a conversation with the boy, but he was too busy glaring at his computer screen working. "Good, but could've been better." He finally spoke.

"Awww…" the girl shifted her attention to a leather diary beneath Reiner's work desk. "Ah!" He turned around in a concerned manner before realizing she was reading it. "Please don't touch that." "Why not?" Vitallin said, teasing and dismaying his request; Reiner was being taken aback to the olden days of bullying, gross memories and his father's death in which he was miserable about it, all he could do was turn towards that diary as those memories came back…

"Put that down!" He raised his voice. "Make me!" Vitallin ran through each and every room causing a chase scene before stumbling against Mrs.

Strife. "Eh, woah!" She stopped the girl from pushing her down. "Why are you running around like this? Aren't you supposed to be in Reiner's room?" Kareen questioned with slight annoyance.

Vitallin showed her the diary. "Bwahaha…I never knew Reiner carried a diary, when did he buy that?" She laughed. "Dammit Vitallin…" Reiner needed to catch his breath first, but Vitallin pats and scruffles through his light brown locks. "I hope you forgive me for taking your diary, but you know most guys in school don't have the guts to ask girls out." "It's not about that," He exclaimed looking away from his own situation.

"Why don't you two go back to the room, and discuss upon it." Mrs. Strife said as the two heeded the woman's instructions. "So…? What's in it?" She said with a sneering smile. "It has all of my battles with assaults," The boy felt insecure inside. "and my father's death." He continued as it was hard for him to say. "You can read it if you want…" Secretly deep down, Reiner didn't want that and was uncomfortable about what he had to sit through.

"Dear dad, you've made such an impact on my life as you've made me see the world in various hues. I know my life is short but you were always the caring person in the house." She continued. "You've taught me many things like Krav Maga, and Martial arts but unfortunately, that didn't stop the man from charging after me as he was three times my size. I wouldn't want to face this world anymore because of what these strange people did to me…"

CHAPTER II

Prelude

"Ahhnnn…" Vitallin began to stretch and reach for the sky, she was sick for the past three weeks off of a strange mold exposure, and her immune system couldn't handle it. "Honey, I've got your pills and thermometer, now say ahhh…" Her mother said. "Blahh…" The girl did what she was told. "Okay, you really are a weird kid." Mrs. Dubarse jokes. "I'm still wanting Reiner to come over…" Vitallin started scuffling under her blanket for support. "Well when you're better you can contact him, but you need to get well." Her mother said before leaving the bedroom.

Buzzz-buzz! Vitallin called the boy to find out where he was. Once he picked up the phone, he was confused about whom it could be as it didn't quite necessarily catch his attention at the moment. "Ah-ha-ha!" A feminine high pitched voice screamed through the air with authentic joy, and cheer. "Reiner, come ride this yellow ride with me!" It was none other than the attractive Erika Marvel, a cheery golden eyed perfectionist sporting her messy bob coupled with her favorite red ribbon hair bow tie. "Ah ha ha, yeah sure!" The scent of food permeated through the air as the sight of vendors were at every corner.

Reiner was pleased despite making sense of the situation. He was at the annual fair with Erika and her group of friends. "Come on, ride this yellow one with me!" The girl said once more, tugging on his sweatshirt. "Erika, I'm about to go after this last one alright?" Said Reiner. "I've had a really fun day by the way." Yes, playing at the fair under the sun was nice; but of course Reiner forgot to check up on Vitallin, even though she called multiple times.

"Ah what's up with this guy, I thought he would have gotten this by now—" Vitallin slowly looked up and saw red liquid dripping from the ceiling onto her bed. *What is this?...* Before judging her situation, a sort of arm emerged from it slowly revealing what appeared to be a black, horrific and boily creature now peeking its head staring at the girl with beaty yellow eyes. *What?!* Vitallin was speechless as to what she was witnessing.

"Get out!" Suddenly, the girl heard her mother cry out. "Mom!" As she peered out the hallway she saw a man with a knife running towards her. "Ahh!" Vitallin tried to hide in her closet but it was too late. "No, stop!" She screamed as the man began stabbing and slashing her over and over. "Ahh!!" Shrieks of pain gripped her voice as she violently hit the man fighting for her life.

No...Reiner, please don't let me die, not without letting me see you! "Vitallin!" Lanet yelled upon hearing the commotion, in pain she crawled to the closet door, grabbed her shotgun and quickly aimed it at the man behind her. Bang! Bang! Two bullets was enough to make him collapse onto the floor. *Vitallin, just hold on I'm coming!*

Lanet mustered her strength to get up and inch her way to the girl's room where she was met with a gruesome surprise.

"Vitallin!" There she saw her daughter slashed and gashed from the head down. Bang! She shoots the man onto the hardwood floor and grabs Vitallin's phone out of her pocket to call nine one one but no one answers. "Vitallin, please don't die!" A pool of blood emerges as her skin hangs and once again the woman calls nine one one, only this time someone finally picks up on the other end. "Nine one one, what's the emergency?"

A stocky voice was heard and Lanet's mind went blank as all she could do was shake in fear, and worry about her daughter. "Send help please! There was a break in and my daughter's injured, please she's dying!" She yelled with hysteria. "Home breached, ok ma'am I'm going to bring the cops and EMS truck over." Lanet was praying for hope, but Vitallin's wounds were too deep, and pronounced.

Meanwhile, it was six-thirty pm and the fair was getting ready to close; friends and classmates were parting ways, photos were being taken, vendors were closing up, and rides were shutting down for next year. Reiner grew close to Erika as a means of friendship, unaware that another would slip away. His phone rings, and apparently it was his mother talking about what had taken place.

At that moment all noise/sound was cut off. "Ha-ha!!" Reiner ran as fast as he could, while tripping over rocks, and branches. "Vitallin!" he cried out. Reiner has always been a passionate person but always hid it ever since he was told to *man up* by a certain thing called life. *Damn, Damn, Damn! This is not good!* He had to run home but kept thinking about time, yes time as the bond between the two was running out.

"Fuck!" He then called Eddy for a ride. "Eddy! I need your help, could I have a ride?" He frantically panted. "Vitallin's at the hospital, and she's in serious critical condition. Please!" Reiner was sobbing hysterically.

You could tell that all he wanted to do was to have someone forgive his mistakes and see her. "He-Hello, who is this?" Eddy said unphased on the other end. "Reiner dammit!" He yelled. "Vitallin needs help, do you have a car? I need you to take me to Northwoods hospital!" "Yeah my mom will be there to give you a ride, just please calm down." Eddy wanted to know what happened. However, he would also be very nonchalant about the entire thing.

Eddy's mother picked up Reiner and took him to the hospital where they met up with Mrs. Dubarse, and his mother Kareen at the front lobby. "Where is she?" Reiner burst through the door, banging his hand on the front counter demanding service. "Young man, If you are going to continue on with these actions I'm gonna have to ask you to leave the building!" The receptionist lady said with an eager face, and a snarky smile. "Now, who are—" "He's with us, please don't mind him." Before she could say anything else, Mrs. Dubarse quickly cut her off. "He wants to see Vitallin. Please let him." "She's inside room two seven three with the intensive care unit." A nurse said.

Reiner rushed down the hallway passing by nearly every number he could possibly see but what if, what if Reiner wasn't ready to see his childhood friend? Would anything else be fine? Meanwhile, as everyone was sitting in the lobby, Eddy's mother queued up the idea of health insurance, and the attack that took place.

"How did they manage to get inside? Was the side door unlocked?" She questioned. "Most likely, though I don't usually leave it unlocked. Someone must've picked it." Lanet wanted to detour the conversation. "Does your shoulder hurt still?" Eddie's mother asks. "My pain is nothing in comparison to Vitallin." She continued. "She was gashed sixteen times and was struggling for her life." Mrs. Dubarse's tone was grim yet sentimental, opposed to her loving nature.

"Doctors and nurse practitioners said that she's susceptible to shock once she wakes up." The girl's mother continued. "She popped a disk in her left spinal cortex and shoulder blade, which now she's gonna need surgery." Mrs. Dubarse was explaining to Eddy's mother as tears ran down her eyes.

As Reiner was vastly approaching the room, he felt his throat tighten up more and more as his vision darkened. He didn't want to lie to himself within his mind because he knew that nothing was fine, and the glimmering hope that he once had was now lingering on a red line. "Vita—"

He slowly approached the dimly lit room and crept the door open. Desperate tears ran down his face as he saw his best friend hooked up to an IV unit and heart monitors. He walked towards the bed and hugged her. "I'm sorry…I'm so fucking sorry." He frantically admits. "I wish I was there sooner, I could've been there for you…protected you, saved you." he said in a low, smooth tone.

"I met up with Erika at the fair, I wished you were there so that you could've met her. She's a really sweet girl." Reiner continued on talking whilst tightly holding onto the girl's hand. "She's in the drama club, and is part of the intel society of Rinfer." Reiner got up as soon as a recent nurse came into the room and told him that visitation time was over.

"Young man." The nurse said. "Visitation hours are over, and Mrs. Dubarse would like to speak with you. Please come out once you're ready." Reiner's heart dropped once he knew he had to leave but before then, he kissed her hand and said "Promise me you wont die."

Once outside the room Reiner stepped foot into the now crowded lobby, people were chatting and minding their business. "How bad is it?" Kareen hesitated to ask. "Scary…I never thought things would get like this." A slight tremble began as the boy covered his eyes in disappointment.

"I should've been there with her, what if she dies?" "It's not your fault so don't feel guilty." Lanet commented as she handed Reiner a journal. "What's this?" He asked, confused. "It's Vitallin's wishes…" *Her wishes?* "If you are her friend I suggest you read it given the situation." The young man could ever wonder what they were and if he could ever fulfill them. The night was long as everyone was sleeping, excluding Reiner who was seen playing with his Rubix cube while studying heat theory when some strange sight caught his eye. *What is that?* He thought to himself, easing in on wonder.

They were light ram horns that looked missing, or lost somewhere within a box of marbles. "When did I buy this?" He touched the fossil-like structure and heard a giggle as the contents within the box moved and one sharp nail began to show. *What the…* This made the boy pretty nervous as he thought he was hallucinating from today's stress. "Whatever you are, please stay away from me!"

He backed himself into a corner feeling nauseated and awed at the same time. *Vitallin's at the hospital and now this?!* He thought to himself. Scared for his life, he turned his head to the side getting close to his desk lamp to shine a light onto the unknown creature. "What are you?" said Reiner. "I don't know, what are you?" The thing replied in an irate tone.

As the creature emerged it's appearance was sorta humanoid like a faun, but a beautiful faun with pale skin, thick horns and curly black hair. In fact it was a ram, a ram named Reece. "Finally…" The creature stood before Reiner in a somewhat dashing way that made him generous and renounced.

"You must be Jeffery's son right?" Before Reiner could respond, Reece licked the boy's cheek slowly then slashed his throat with his nails. "My name's Reece Eatherlove and I've waited years for this." He exclaimed. "Huh? Wha-what the hell are you…?!" Reiner was crouching down putting pressure on his throat to stop the bleeding but it wasn't good enough. "Huh?" The faun like creature said in a mocking tone. "You will know soon enough just how low your father could be." Soon afterward Reece disappeared and left Reiner thinking about the creature's affiliation with Jeffery.

What was that?! He wondered scared out of his mind. *Does that thing know my dad? Is he alive?* The young man wrapped his throat up with gauze he found on his desk and fell to the floor as more and more questions came about. *What the hell's going on?* What's more was about the fact that he saw a talking ram guy in the midst of it all, this encouraged Reiner to go to sleep believing it was all a dream.

Bam! Suddenly a loud crash was heard from outside. It was a car accident which caused the boy to look out the window upon hearing the commotion. Upon the sight were EMS trucks, police cars, and bystanders all gathered around a man with a blue fleece vest on. His head was gashed through, as he hit the upper shield of his Mercedes leaving an atrocious wound resulting in extreme blood loss.

When the man was driving he spun out of control causing him to crash into a quite large woman. "Do you think they have a pulse?" Reece said, startling the boy. "What the hell are you?!" Reiner didn't know whether to fight the odd creature or run. "That is to be disclosed at a later time." The ram said.

Reiner definitely knew he was dreaming and wanted this day to be over. Afterwards, he made his way under the covers. "Do you think I'm done talking to you?" The ram now appeared before the boy's book shelf. Reiner was curious, yet scared as to what he wanted. "Get up!" The creature said "Reece…just in case you won't kill me, let's make a deal," Reiner said, questioning any suspiciousness within the odd *youngman.* "Why?" he said. "You're a monster who…slashed my throat." He continued.

"We should play fair." Reiner found the human ram odd, yet underneath was wanting to learn more about him and his connection to his father as to what he was about. His demeanor was strong and savagely wary. Reiner knew he just had to keep his guard up in case of another attack. "As a deal I'm wanting you to help find my dad and tell me about him since you nearly killed me, let me at least see that hope." Reiner demanded.

"You're lucky I'm somewhat empathetic kid," Reece said with a short sigh. "I'm willing to do whatever it takes to avenge my wife Anri, and get back at this malevolent world!" He continued, "Even if it means hurting people…I am going to find out what happened to her." Reece began to feel disdain towards his outlooks.

"Your father Jeffery Strife, is an investigator." Reece said. Soon after, Reiner grabbed a recorder from his drawer and told the creature to tell him what he knew. "Go on…" "Yeah, he's an investigator under an affiliate group called Hide." He continued. "Hide is a bastardized group that knows no bounds or consequences."

Reece ended his statement there, which made Reiner relaxed yet eager to ask more questions about him as his heart was fluttering so much. "So my father is alive, right?" The boy asked. "Either dead, or alive." Reece told him. "Why is it that important to you?"

"I still believe that he's out there somewhere though he never came back home, I'm wanting him back into my life." Reiner continued. "I believe that whatever people were saying about him were all lies as if he were a threat to them. It made me curious to know that if he was in my life what person would I be? And if so, why would he leave me?"

CHAPTER III

Reveal Thy Truth

It was raining heavily the next morning as Reiner went to school. He made sure to take the umbrella Vitallin gave to him as it was more sturdy than his old one, but something didn't feel right as she wasn't there to walk with him; this would've made Brinner pumped knowing this because he loves torturing Reiner *for fun at least.*

"Hello class my name is Mrs. Kerish, I'm substituting for Mrs. Veiter today, and it seems that she wants you all in a group of three to four members for an activity alright." Eddy, Allen, and Brinner were in one group, while Reiner wasn't in one as he vouched for his independence. "Mrs. Kerish, may I work alone?" The boy asked. "Why?" said Mrs. Kerish. "Because Vitallin isn't here, and everyone else already has three to four people in them so please, I can do the assignment by myself."

He replied, wanting to get what he asked for. *Tsk.* "You ass face retard." Brinner said in a low tone as he got up from Eddy's desk in annoyance and anger. "Why the hell must you care about that weird twat Vitallin, and fucking forget about what you did to my sister!" Brinner had it. "What now Reiner, wait for your precious Vitallin while my Titania is dead?! You really are gonna get payback!" Brinner hissed before throwing a chair at Reiner's face, causing him to stumble and fall amongst the desks.

Soon everyone around him got up and ran to the corners of the room scared yet excited a fight was going down. Reiner staggered on the ground in silence as he tried to catch his breath. He was about to fight back but the level of annoyance and frustration was nothing in comparison as to how he was towards Brinner. "Haven't you noticed by now that it wasnt me?!" "Silence!!" Mrs. Kerish slammed her hand onto the chalkboard. "What would you do if Mrs. Veiter were here?" Soon after Erika raised her hand to answer.

"Well if Mrs. Veiter were here she would—" "Enough!" Mrs. Kerish cut her off for a bit. "You two are gonna learn the hard way!" She then cracked her knuckles and tried to restrain both of them from fighting. "Mrs. Kerish, this fucking twit is a murderer!" Brinner yelled, digging his fingernails into the boy's neck until blood came through. Reiner threw a punch and kicked the young man in the knee.

"Dammit, you two!" Mrs. Kerish slapped both of them on the head. "What's wrong with you guys?! All of you, get back into group work or else you're all suspended!" She then yelled to the class. "Reiner, you can come in my group," Erika said pleasantly. He quickly scrambled around multiple desks on the ground, knocking each and every one in sight. "Thank you." He said politely as the air within the room was tense, and full of strife. While Mrs. Kerish was talking about the assignment, Erika was focused on protecting Reiner.

"Reiner, I hope you're alright. I'm sorry about what happened."

"You're fine, it's not your fault." He said. "I thought you two were friends." Erika wanted to note everything that Brinner did to him, at least from first glance but the boy explained. "When we were kids we used to play alongside their tree house near a hill farm. We were practically inseparable to each other." Reiner continued. "He had a sister named Titania whom he was really protective over, but one day while playing hide and go seek she suddenly died and the rest was unknown on my end."

"Brinner must have thought I killed her as he still held a grudge, and doesn't know who did it." The young man put pressure on his reopened wound. "Do you miss Vitallin?" Erika said as she popped an obvious question. "Huh…um, yeah." Reiner wasn't that focused on it knowing that she was okay, though the girl felt concerned. "It's just, how are you not phased by this? Aren't you afraid she might die?" At that moment, the young man's eyes grew dark.

"Vitallin is tougher than death, so much that even if she's living she knows how to impact. I've never given up on her, nor should you." Erika was stunned and flushed when he said that. *Interesting, why does that dumb girl mean that much to you?* She thought to herself. "I'd only wish you'd look at me better." she mumbled. "What's up, miss Marvel?" A smooth and calming female voice emerged from the crowd. "Oh hi Salina…what brings you here?" The girl greeted as if she didn't want to be bothered.

Salina was an abnormal beauty as she was mysterious and cunning in her own way, even more cunning than a snake. "Ohh nothing, just wanting to get to know Reiner that's all." she continued. "But don't worry, I'm not going to do anything to him. Remember I don't swing that way." The girl then snuck out of the classroom to follow Reiner to art class.

On his way to class Reiner stopped to tie his shoe but when he looked out the window he saw Reece pointing downward signaling to come outside. *What? It's that guy again…* Reiner thought to himself shocked and confused as to why he was there. *This has to be an illusion.* Reiner went outside given the situation. "Don't you know people can see you?" The boy made a point. "These kids are all assuming that I'm in theater drama for lack of better terms, plus I'm wearing one of your uniforms." "Why are you here?" Reiner said in curiosity.

"Just studying." Reece explained as he leaned into the boy's ear. "There's a certain girl here I'd like to meet." He continued. "She's five foot four, has amber eyes, black hair and a hair tie from what I've seen. Her last name is Marvel?" "Erika…" Said Reiner. "Anri's sister." Reece stated. "What would you have to do with her?" "Her sister is my wife," Reece said sternly. "I'm just wanting her to come over for questioning."

Reiner was wary about Reece's questions as he might harm, or has yet to know his true motives. "Reiner!" Salina yelled as she gave Reiner a big hug. "Hey Salina, how's it going these days?" he asked. "Good, good…how's Vitallin, is she out yet?" The girl questioned. "Ah, alright It's been a week since—" "Ooh, are you in the theater arts club?" She cut out Reiner as she caught herself staring at Reece in awe with his curly black hair, coupled with his light green eyes and ram horns. *So cool…*

"I like the ram horns, the group members make pretty great masks too!" "See…" said Reece pointing at the young girl. "I don't have time for this," He said. "I want to see the girl now." Reece was desperate for some answers. "Okay, okay I'll get her." Reiner didn't want to do manual tasks for certain people, especially if it meant interrogations.

"Ah Erika, I have a favor to ask of you." Erika was just done cleaning the room with disinfection wipes. "What's that? I thought you went to the third period." She said. "There's someone from the theater arts division who wants to see you," Reiner said, nearly out of breath from the previous flight of stairs. *Is this bad? Does she even know him?* He thought as to what might happen as they went outside to meet up with Reece, or as if he went to them. "Are you the guy who wanted to see…me?" Erika squinted at Reece. *Light green eyes, pale skin…you remind me of someone?* "Why do you need me?" The girl said, wiping her hands together.

"Your name is Erika Marvel right?" Reece said, anticipating her answer. "Ah, yes how do you—" "Is your sister gone?" He now questioned, "How do you know I have a sister?" Reece smiled sweetly. "That locket of yours, you've held it dearly for years now haven't you?" He said. "Yes, this is like my sister's mini picture frame…she died a few years ago." Reece continued questioning. "You wouldn't know that for certain, Is your sister named Anri Eatherlove?" He asked. "Yes, why are you doing all of this?" "Shhh…" Reece placed a finger on his lips. "I'm not finished yet," He said. "Was your sister married?" This had to be the point. "Yeah March seventh two thousand and twelve, she kept reminding me over and over." She continued.

"She was madly in love yeah, with a man named Reece." The ram patted her on the head before making her flinch back. "I am Reece, Reece Eatherlove." Erika was soon shocked and confused. *That explains why.* "Why did you come to my school? Who let you in?" She leaned in to touch Reece's horns before he slapped her hands away.

Reece's youthful appearance could pass him as a college student. "I came here for information upon finding Anri, maybe she's missing and not dead, this wouldn't be like her." He stated. "Well, I hope so too…I miss her." Erika felt her heavy heart. "Do you know what you're gonna do now?" She asks. "I'm not sure, but either way I have to know."

As school ended, Reiner and Reece walked back together as it was still raining, but they managed to make it home safely in which the ram was ready to talk a storm. "That girl was much older than I remembered. Erika…" He said with a concerned manner. "Why did you need her so much?" Reiner had asked.

"She may hold the answers to Anri's disappearance and I want to see it through one more time." Reece tousled his hair back away from his face. "What was Anri like?" Freckles wondered. This took Reece aback for a minute as he wasn't readily anticipating that sort of question. "Anri Eatherlove was a very magnificent woman; long wavy red hair, and deep amber eyes. She fought alongside me when we were enrolled into the King Tournaments." He continued.

"She found me as her apprentice as she was my mentor who was picked through Simmerton's law." "Simmerton's law?" Reiner questioned. "It's the universal law of ancient sorcerers and familiars." He continued. "It is the strength of one thousand types of statuses that determines a familiar's partner along with a person's abilities and ranking." He sighed. "God I miss her so much it hurts." Reece wasn't the type of person to admit his private feelings upon others. "She was stronger than me so this influenced me to study concentrated to even esper level magic."

Reece continued. "She was also the person who turned me into a ram from a slip up spell." Reiner lifted his arms behind his head. "A magic tournament huh…" He thought with a silly grin. "Yeah, and it's not a game. Some of those tournaments may even give you fame and relevance depending on which region you're in." Reece said. "There's also a chance to win the king's title." "The king's title? What's that?" The young man wondered. "It is an **ultimate** title that allows anyone in said guilds and regions the ability to govern over *all* universes." The ram's tone was serious and with a great purpose as he wanted Reiner to listen and be aware of what's happening.

"Listen, you have to be an eminently powerful mage in order to receive the title." He continued. "The king's title could be given to anyone who survives and wins the day of kings, power is power whether good or bad and if given over to the wrong hands ***we'll know their strength***." "If all of that adds up then could I ask you a question." The boy asked politely. "Why?" Reece gathered his breath for a second as he was tired of talking, along with feeling lightheaded.

"As I recall, I remembered your head coming out of a giant box of marbles." He continued. "Was that an entire world? If so, how is it possible?" Reiner felt dumb for saying that, although he was curious as to where the ram came from. Having a creature coming out of a box was far from reality, yet how he got the box was necessarily far off as well.

Creator...?!

Several years ago, Reiners great great grandmother "passed" due to old age, leaving behind two sons and a daughter. Thomas Douglas Jr. Patrice's eldest son was fond of early aged alchemy in which he made many attempts to transmute objects for *forced immortality* like medicines and food.

One busy day, while walking through the crowds of Ameden town during the dead of winter, Thomas stumbled upon an abandoned shop with a gated door encrusted with jaspers, and rubies. This piqued his curiosity with the place as he wanted materials for his experiments. He knocked on the door. "Hello, Is anyone here?" he said. In a faint ear, he heard banging coming from the side of the shop. Boom! Boom! Boom! As Thomas looked over, the front door swung open.

"Ah Malachi, a customer! A customer!" A strong, yet extremely feminine voice emerged from the gated door. "Ah yes, hello are you the owner?" Thomas wondered. "Nope, assistant." Standing at the door was a five and four-inch woman with shoulder-length blonde hair, sporting a creme green sweater dress.

"What do you want?" The girl asked in a friendly tone of voice. "Do you happen to sell any amethyst, tiger's eye, and a lobster's placenta?" Thomas asked the young girl in a stoic manner. "I'm an alchemist." He explained himself. "And we're wiccans." A tall masculine man with mixed dark hair stepped aside from the young lady.

"Hi, my name's Malachi, if there's anything you want to buy please step inside." The man was assertive and produced an aura so strange that made Thomas nearly choke up with uneasiness. Despite the outside, the shop was surprisingly flourished with couches, chandeliers, cameras, a t.v. and a counter displaying every conceivable gemstone imaginable, along with knives and wands. The two men sat down together while the girl went to another room.

"You said you were an alchemist, correct?" The man questioned. "Ah yes, early age to be exact. I've been thinking about methods of bringing my mother back to life." Thomas explained. "That's good." The man said. "Most of the customers we get here are pretty heinous." Malachi continued. "They mainly use our spells for revenge tactics." "There was once a guy who tried mind-bending spells to keep his loved ones in an infinite loop of insanity which drove them to suicide. Who knew he was that sick?" He told Thomas.

"That's terrible." This gave the man reassurance that he was in the right headspace, as he was only doing this for the greater good; for his loved ones, and possibly for society. After the two exchanged a few prices and stories Malachi led the man downstairs into a dimly lit room.

Inside was a hospital bed, a few glass beakers filled with a dark cloudy substance, deadly potions, a gigantic seventeenth-century old grimoire, and roses all over the place. "This is quite lovely now isn't it?" Thomas sarcastically said to himself as he tipped off his black boater hat in such a sight. While Thomas looked around the room, the young lady from earlier showed up with a plate of red velvet creme filled cupcakes ready to hand out. "Hey Malachi, I made cupcakes."

The young woman delightfully said. "Here, try some." She hands two over to Thomas. "Oh thanks, ah…" unknowingly he didn't quite ask for her name yet which was rather rude, and awkward as it's not like him to not ask for a ladies name since he's such a handsome gentleman. "Um excuse me, may I ask what your name is?"

He straightforwardly asked. "It's Rachel, Rachel Roven." The woman replied. "She's my girlfriend, and an S class sorceress." Malachi stated as he leaned in to kiss her neck teasing her in the process. "She produced most of the potions you see here, some even exclusive and forbidden." Malachi opened the glass counter chest and showed Thomas an array of majestic stones to choose from. "Well, which ones would you want?"

"I need an amethyst." Thomas was unsure whether they sold lobster placenta, but all he needed was to get his hands on some blood for chromosomes purely. "I have three types of amethyst." Malachi continued. "One that negates poison and magic seals, one that alters personalities, and one that creates clones of the one who consumes it." He said. Malachi gives Thomas the second amethyst. "I'm guessing that's the one you're looking for right?"

He said, "Why yes, ah…" Thomas paused for a second as he caught a glimpse of some flashy material through the corner of his eye. It was inside of a giant cardboard box with white linings over the flap marking a symbol of some sort. "What's inside that box?" Thomas pointed. "Oh that?…I'll give it to you for free." Malachi suggested. "What is it?" Thomas wondered as he touched the inside material.

It was gooey and so metallic that it produced an electrical charge from across the room. "It's a special experiment I was working on," Malachi continued. "I could summon up the most powerful familiars I want so they could help with concentrated, and ancient magic like the abnormalities of certain spells." "Since you're an alchemist, I'd figure you should have it." He offered. "Whoa…really?"

Thomas was more than delighted to, yet unsure of what to do with it but took it either way. "I figured you could put your own spin on things," Malachi said. "The lobster is in the deep freezer. Unfortunately, we don't sell tiger's eye, but come upstairs when you're ready to check out."

Thomas grabbed his items, and headed upstairs, he was delighted with the service. "That'll be thirty-seven pounds." Malachi wagered with Thomas as the price was fifty percent off as all he wanted to do was sell something. "Here." Thomas hands over the money. *All right, let's make this work.*

Once he reached his home at six four one Perchmann St. Thomas took off his hat and coat and hung it aside from the bedpost in his room. He began the transmutation sequence right away. He was nervous as he wiped his forehead left to right, then went to the kitchen pantry for a box of salt. *This has to work!* On the ground, Thomas started drawing a salt circle with transmutation symbols inside symbolizing an output: a triangle, square, and inner circle. He then wrote down the items with blood while placing them onto each shape and wrote his desired outcome inside the circle: *immortality*.

Then he placed the items on each shape. The symbols began rotating faster, and faster then it finally stopped. When Tomas looked to the side he saw a potion bottle with dark purple liquid inside of it. "This must be it." He said as he took the bottle, and squeezed a dime sized amount into a petri dish, and fed it to his adult pet tiger, Malik. Soon Malik's fangs turned black as he became really agitated. The tiger hammered its teeth through the side of a closet door, scratching and gnawing off the wood frame.

"Malik, Down!" Thomas yelled. "Stop!" Thomas tried grabbing Malik by the collar, but soon let go once he started growling and foaming from the mouth. As Thomas attempts to step back out the room, Malik rushes towards him digging his eight inch claws through the man's long sleeve shirt onto the right side of his chest. "Ahhh!!" He horrendously screamed in agony, and pain as splotches of blood gushed out.

Thomas had enough strength to maneuver his way to the kitchen, leaking a trail of blood behind. He saw an elixir on top of a cabinet near a pair of fruit baskets. The bottle was an uncrackable mold so it couldn't shatter. In excruciating pain, Thomas looked around for an object that could knock it down.

He picked up a broomstick and carefully swung the item down before him. "Ehh…" Thomas groned trying not to lose much of his energy as he was trying to open it. The man soon took a sip and the bitter sweet taste made him gag a little inside, but he knew he needed it since he didn't have much time.

After drinking the small dosage of microbe elixir felt his arteries strengthen as his wounds slowly started to close. Thomas felt relieved, and oh so grateful for a moment but then saw Malik clawing his own face apart. *Is it hysteria?* This made him realize what his potion does but before changing the idea, he ran to the bedroom to get a remote for Malik's shock collar.

There were six settings, all ranging in severity from a simple shock. Thomas was scared but the situation was dire; he didn't want to die yet he didn't want to watch Malik suffer in a state of insanity. "I love you Malik…" Thomas turned the dial to level four-A, suddenly a blue flash could be seen through the living room. "Hahahng!!" Malik wailed in agony as blood was dripping from his throat.

The tiger tried removing his collar but it wouldn't budge. Once the shocks stopped Malik collapsed on the floor rug, but lucky enough he was still breathing ever so faintly. Thomas ran over to his beloved pet, and started stroking his fur. "Malik." His voice saddened by his decision and promises to bring hope was frail, and loose as he was wanting to invent a potion that would bring his mother back to life along with everyone else's fallen loved ones.

"I will get you back." Thomas cried yet knew what he meant as he caught a glimpse of determination, and hope for his transmutation to work a second time around. After mopping up the blood stained floors, and throwing away the living room rug, Thomas got back into his bedroom where he first started the process of creating the "liquid of healing times wounds" except this time he used the microbe elixir since he found out that the process of artery repair was nearly an instantaneous success.

After rearranging the previous items around in the symbols, Thomas remembered about a crucial item that was missing from before. What was left was the tiger's eye, the one he needed from before to make the entire potion work. "Maybe that's what's missing." He said. A state of shock, and uncertainty came over him as he consciously decided to do the unthinkable.

Thomas walked over to where Malik laid, crouched down beside him and stuck two fingers through one of his eye sockets, pushing the eyelid back by the finger beds causing his eye to pop out in the process. It was dry, and gleaming as if it still had light reflecting from it. Of course Malik was dead but his life still goes on.

Once he got it out he used it for his second transmutation sequence as it wouldn't fail this time, at least he hopes. With the same shape symbols, Thomas once again wrote down every item only now it's including the elixir, and tiger's eye. Once he put the items together, the symbols then again started rotating faster and faster which soon produced a prim bottled potion before him. It was pretty, and beautifully crafted with a white miniature diamond placed on top.

He felt confident this time so he decided to take a sip, but soon felt strange as his nose began bleeding profusely yet his senses felt enhanced by two hundred percent. To test out the potion's new version, Thomas went to the kitchen and grabbed a butcher's knife from it's block holder, then proceeded to cut his arm extremely fast.

He gasped as he took in a large breath, but to his surprise there were no cuts. Thomas tried over, and over yet yielded the same results: no cuts, no blood, no ill mutations. "Remarkable!" He was astounded. *I love you Malik.* Thomas was graciously thankful for everything in his life at that point, as his immortality potion was finished. He told the good news to his younger sister Samantha as she came by to visit him from Delrosa, a fifteen hour drive from the south of Ameden town.

"Wow, really?!" Samantha knew about her brother's inventions and potions, as many of them worked in her favor when she was little; life altering in fact. There was once a mending spell that her brother and their friends made that allows the person who's cast to see the futures of any person they choose, while also being the only one who could stop their extreme decisions as well as taking them away from their preexisting selves whether good, or bad.

"How's my little Gabriela?" Thomas said in a sweet, hazy tone. "She's fine thanks to you and Gerald." She couldn't be more grateful for that spell, as she had her daughter's life to protect in her hands. Samantha was surprised that Thomas was getting her back, she loved her for dear life's sakes; the way she braided and tied her curly, thick long black hair as a child, and how she would usually scold her for climbing through the neighbors fence to get to places.

Their mother was beautiful, and many more; she fed the homeless, and picked up stray kittens along the way for good luck. "Ahh…this could be possible, her funeral is in the next two days so…" Samantha leaned in and whispered into Thomas's ear. "Pfft…hahaha!!" He laughed. "That's hilarious!" "It's amazing isn't it?" Samantha said laughing alongside him with a big smile. "That's great." He said. "I'm sure she wouldn't mind."

CHAPTER V

Reunion

After their chats, Samantha walks into the bathroom and begins taking a shower. As she turned around she saw big, silky, blooming rose bulbs emerging from underneath the tub. "An illusion?" She wondered. Samantha touches the rose bulbs and soon after, the color of the water turns into a shallow light pink. Shocked, and unto her curiosity she sips from the shower head. "Strawberry milk?" Samantha was slightly puzzled yet intrigued. *My favorite.*

She thought this could've been the blessings from the gods due to her foregoing of patience, and kindness throughout her lifetime. She noted to Thomas that she was staying over for two days, so he prepared a room downstairs for her to sleep and hulled the luggage in too. "Thomas, the bath was amazing!" Samantha said in a delighted tone, wearing her signature white robe.

Just before Thomas could say anything, out of mannerisms he ran behind the door pretending he didn't see anything.

"Your shower is made out of milk, did you know that?" She questioned with glee. "No I did not…" Said Thomas talking behind the door. "Please hurry and put your clothes on, as you can see I brought your luggage." "Thank you." His sister replied in favor. The two were planning on taking a night out in the town as Samantha hasn't visited Thomas in months.

After having dinner at The Log Inn, they stopped by the late library to do research. Unfold was the second biggest library in the world, housing nearly four billion books globally with multiple translations. The inside was beautiful, and bright as it has twenty-three brightly lit chandeliers with gold and bronze molded architectural designs; the tables were solid gold, while the chairs were like wooden stumps.

The place was crowded, but luckily Thomas managed to find a computer seat near the window looking out towards the beautiful landscape. He started reading articles about the human anatomy of the deceased, and nonetheless looked up new potions from other alchemists, and sorcerers.

Meanwhile, Samantha was having fun going all around the world with her book ladder; it was at least seventeen feet tall, with over four billion books to spare there were many of them. "Ah…would you mind grabbing that white book that's on the left of you?" It was the voice of a young girl with an Australian accent.

She wore a mid-length pleated skirt, a school vest with a badge that had the words E.V.E.R.G.R.E.E.N embroidered into it, and sported two gigantic red pigtail braids on the sides of her head. "No problem." Samantha said with a smile. The young girl looked shy and reserved, not having any other option for chit-chat at her disposal, just passing by. "Thank you." The girl said, full of nerves.

"You're rude." Samantha said lightly kicking her foot on the ladder. "I can tell you want to talk, but you're just too scared to." She started grinning at the girl in a snaring way, as if she was teasing. "Uhg…leave me alone okay, I'm not awkward or anything so cut it out!" The girl felt irritated and embarrassed, by all means annoyed. "I see you've been bullied recently by a couple of girls at your academy, correct?"

Samantha used her mind bending curse on the little red-headed girl. "You were once so disturbed that that you've attempted suicide twice when they beated you with metal bats, I can see it through you Veronica." She continued. "And once your mother notice all she could do was—"

"Stop right there, dammit!" The girl screamed. "Huh, I'm rude?" She slapped Samantha in the face before she realized, and recoiled. "You're undeniably rude! And how do you know my name, and this stuff about me?" "Arktiki ekrixi." Samantha casted a gust of snow onto the girl causing her ladder to push four feet away from her. "I'm a witch!" The black witch yelled out. "No way~" Veronica said in confusion, and slight amazement as she wheeled her ladder back close to her. "I thought sorcerers were banished, and extinct; that's what my teacher told us." She stated.

"I come from a blood line of wizards, and alchemists. We're early aged." Samantha continued. "Generational blood seeps through each other. You may even have some in your family." Veronica borrowed her head in embarrassment, but was interested in Samantha. "I used my mind-bending sequence on you." She continued. "When I was little my brothers and their friends pulled a prank on me, and got me hexed for life but I used it to my advantage though."

"What's my last name?" Veronica challenged. "Ar-che-bal." The words took a moment to come to her head as the cool witch says with yet another grin. "Wow, you're impressive."

Trying hard not to lie, she was honest and succumbing to belief. There really were still sorcerers amongst them. "How does it feel to see a sorceress first hand?" Samantha asked out of seeing the girl's response. "Show me a trick!" Veronica said in excitement as she was still amazed that she found a witch. "Twilight storm." Samantha whispers. "Look outside." At that moment, midnight quickly switched to daybreak then back as the flower vines started growing rapidly against the windows.

"Wow." Veronica was shocked. "Reconstruction magic." The witch said. "Basic level…" "Samantha!" Thomas called out. She quickly took out a few books from her row, then wheeled the ladder to its holding destination. "We have to hurry back." Thomas was carrying articles of papers beneath him. "Coming!" His sister quickly replied. "See ya around Archebal." She waves as Veronica waved back with a subtle smile.

After their library trip, the two head home in preparation for tomorrow's funeral. "So what books did you buy?" Thomas asked. "The Philosopher's stone by Aveot Pearson" She continued. "My best gift by Jorge Lintuelle, and The sunflower's stare. What did you do?" Now it's his turn. "I printed out magic recitals, and articles of the dead. Hopefully it comes in handy." The next morning, Thomas and Samantha got dressed and headed out to North Brooks cemetery.

It was a day of revival as Thomas brought his immortality elixir; they would only get one shot at this otherwise they would have created a zombie. Thomas wore an ordinary black suit, and Samantha wore an elegant red dress accessorized with silver. The two got looks while walking out as the neighbors thought that Thomas whistled up a lady for dinner. Once they reached the outdoor area of the Mendenhall funeral service, a sermon was speaking. The casket was opened so anything could have been said or thrown into it like flowers, rings, jewelry, money, etc. It was only till then that the two waited for the people to leave for the reception to make their move.

"Our mother was the most perfect person you could've met." They both talked in unison. "She cared for us both, and watched over both of us." They said. "Like the moon, we'll always see your face." People clapped as tears were shed, while others grieved and mourned intensely. As the people left for the reception, Thomas mentioned to one of the pallbearers that he and his sister were going to stay behind for a few minutes to grieve. The man understood their situation, agreed, and went about his way.

Now the moment begins. Thomas pulls out the potion, and pours it into his mother's cold, grayed out mouth. Moments later, her body heat elevated, and skin regenerated to its young, plump pink self. "Ah!" Samantha gasped. "Her chest is rising." "That's because her heart is shocked." He explained.

"The kinetic energy within the lobster placenta's enzymes might have caused it." A few moments later her toes began to wiggle around.

"She's alive." Samantha yelled out once more. "Not yet…" Thomas had a trick up his sleeve.

"Geiomeni psychi!" He yelled out while violently tapping his mother's forehead. Her eyes blinked. Thomas and Samantha's eyes were streaming with tears of joy. "Mother can you hear me?" He wanted to make sure everything was all right. "Ahhh-!" Patrice struggled to make any coherent words as she was abruptly pausing, and slurring her words like a zombie in a light vegetative state. Samantha removed a black piece of straw like hair from Patrice's face and whispered into her ear.

"Pnevmatiko blok." She used a health spell on her which seemed to work as she began to regain consciousness ever so slightly. "Why am I here? Who are you people?" Patrice looked around aimlessly. "Mother, we're here to get you back home." Thomas said with excitement as he hugged her with great emotion, as the process was a success. "We have to hurry and get you back home with us." Samantha said with a slight smile of achievement. "Where do you live?" Their mother questioned, unsure of what was going on. "We're going there soon." Thomas replied.

The three head home to six four one Pechmann St. where the man's large Victorian home was located at. Inside the three sat down together in the living room as Thomas tried jogging her memories. "Um…mother do you know what reconstruction magic is?" He asked. "Yes. Doesn't it invert physics?" She answered. "Sort of, now onto the next question." Samantha spoke.

"What's my name?" She used the old question of amnesia. "Kimber, ah…" "Try again." She smiled. "What was your dog's name as a little girl?" She hinted with that one. "Samantha…" Patrice calmly knew the answer without hesitation. "I'm your beloved daughter." She cheerfully said with genuine honesty. Her brain hasn't aged, just forgotten.

As time went on they all three played board games, and finished each other's sentences. She grew progressively well as her mentality became more aware, and homebound like how she was before. She was quirky, and awfully smart but in the most part nice as she regularly cooked, cleaned, and played the violin all over the entire house. Wearing her white floral dress, and red high heels she was back to her old self again.

One day Thomas shows Patrice the box that was given to him from Malachi. "Thomas stop!" She yelled as she recognised what it was from afar. "Why? I already know what's inside, familiars." He continued. "I reckon that since your magic is stronger and more concentrated you could enchant the beasts, and things within the box." Thomas wanted it made as he was interested in what it's capable of. "That's a Pagan item Thomas." His mother knew based on her dad's teachings of aura sense.

"You could make it better." Thomas tried reasoning with her. "As a new addition, their knowledge could help us out." He stands. "But…" She gives in. "Only to help." Patrice said, lifting her amber colored wand. "Vio ekrixi." She casted a seal spell inside the box which then made the contents voiced, and audible.

Violent words were shouted like darkness, murder, and wars. The filling within the box created a giant black orb within itself, which soon simplified into coal like marbles losing its color over time. "Give the box to Samantha." Patrice demanded. "What, is it not like I should have a servant of my own?" Thomas questioned in disappointment. "It's extremely dangerous especially for you as you can't afford any more losses." She felt sorry for him as she wanted Thomas to go another route with his life after the loss of his second wife. "But me and Samantha are equals."

He tried to convince her once more. "All I'm saying is that your unique magic is better off without familiars." She continued. "You could grow in a different way, Samantha could too." She suggested with a passive intent. "A challenge?" Thomas wondered. "Exactly."

Patrice told Samantha about the box that Thomas kept, and explained to her what her magic stood for. A few years later Samantha gave birth to two daughters named Gabriela, and Camila in which she passed the box over to them. "I'm a familiar." Reece explained. "And there are many others like me. If you're so interested as to where I came from and what's inside then fight me." The ram's eyes grew serious, and unwavering.

Suddenly, Reece kicked Reiner to the ground while pinning his forearms behind the bedpost causing him great pain. "You're so weak." He said putting more pressure onto him. Reiner struggled to fight back but couldn't. "Dammit!" He screamed, but that wasn't enough to stop Reece from forcing pressure over him as his nails dug within the boy's arms. "I'm doing this so that you can have a taste of what's to come." He continues.

"The citizens in my world are all skilled fighters, some even mages. If you even pick a fight with them they'd rip your limbs apart, and even give you over to their guild leader." The boy started bleeding. Despite his situation, Reiner was willing to do whatever it took to find his father whether he's intentionally missing, or hiding something even greater he'd figure that Reece's world had something to do with it.

That box was mysterious after all. "You promised you'd help find—" "Your father…" Reece mocked as he cut him off. "I know but this is *important* right?" The ram said influencing him to go beyond the unknown. "Are you ready to see what's on the other side of the inside?" He unhanded the young man. "Certainly." Reiner said, holding the sides of his neck to stop the bleeding.

CHAPTER VI

Test

"Gnostes pyles!" Suddenly, a golden gate appeared before their eyes. "Hold on tight and hang on for dear life okay?" Reece quickly grabs a hold of Reiner's arm, and teleports through the majestic door. "Wait!" The boy yelled. It was dark, really dark as Reiner couldn't see anything but a bright, red light following behind them. He was scared yet remembered Reece's words clearly.

He wanted to know what was inside for a brief time, so he knew he had to toughen up. Surely Reece had good intentions. From a near sight there was light enveloping them, accompanied with a strong updraft of air. At that moment he knew they were falling, but Reece didn't mind. "Ahh!" He screamed. "We're gonna crash!" The two were falling near a forest overlooking the city. "Pyrovolo oplo!" Reece chanted, suddenly a huge crater formed beneath them as the crust gave away. "There, that's not so bad was it?" He delightfully said, unaware of Reiners distressed countenance.

"Man it feels good to be back! What do you think?" He asked. "Where are we?" The boy choked. His vision was far beyond clear, like every color contrasted perfectly. It was beautiful, yet dangerous as the box itself hosted many familiars, and strong men. "I brought you here to train on my part of the bargain." Reece announced. "If you like this place so much you'd need to fight for it." He said. "We'll be here often." Reece playfully, yet tactfully attacks Reiner from the back stunting him onto the ground.

"I can't move!" He says. "You can move, just try." The ram said, motioning his hands towards himself. "If not then I'll just have to make the first move." He was given enough influence to move his muscles before then. Reece dashed towards Reiner at full speed. "Shit!" The boy tries to get up but only manages to move a few inches away. "Say I didn't warn you." Reece said as he stopped behind him. "Let's see you move after this. Ateleiotes bountroumi!" Reiner blinked once, then blinked again.

"Where am I?" He wondered to himself in the most drowsy sense possible. The place was dark, and cold as the air was dry, and shallow. He felt a sensation of stone beneath his feet. *A dungeon perhaps?* He was correct. It was much easier for him to move since Reece's influence was diminished. Reiner didn't know what he was getting himself into, but he knew he had to get out fast. Tap, tap, tap. He heard someone coming by close, and suddenly a loud bang was heard. "Ahh!" Reiner yelled. He wanted to see what was happening but didn't want to risk getting caught.

"I know where you are!" A loud, gurgling voice of a man hurled through the chamber. "Come out and fight me!" Reiner didn't have time to make out the hidden figure, but he did notice a strange scent. *Rotting flesh?* Bang! A flair blast was seen through the side of the walkway. "Found you~"

The man said with a daunting expression upon his face while licking his lips. As the unknown man walked closer to Reiner, he depressed such a profound scent it almost made the boy gag in his mouth. He was a fat, warted old man with a disastrous intent. "Take this!" Reiner tried sucker punching him, but couldn't succeed. "Nice try, but that's not enough." The man pinned Reiner onto the stone ground while opening his mouth. *Ugh, get off me!*

Reiner's gross memories of his assaults came rushing through. "Ripi." The old man inhaled then blew out a large gust of air at the boy's face. *What?*

Reiner felt the sensation of cuts forming. They were deep, clean and painful. The young man headbutt the old man and managed to wiggle out of his grasp, reverse pinning him in the process. "Diatrito kyma" The man whispered. "Ahh!" At that moment, Reiner felt thousands of hot needles piercing the inside of his skin. "Reece help!" He cried out. "Enough Aericus!" Reece commanded as he appeared out of thin air. "You've got a long road ahead kid."

He was noting the boy's strength, and perseverance in mind. "Let me have him!" Aericus yelled with the serious intent to kill. "I said enough!" Reece sent a daunting glance at Aericus. The old man's mobility stopped as he crouched to the ground clutching his chest. *Damn you Reece!* Blood started coming out of the man's eyes as he was bleeding internally, and soon died. "Diadromi diafygis!"

This proved a way out for Reiner as he quickly ran to the other end of the dungeon. "You're safe, nothing else is coming after you." Reece said, assuring him. "What was that?!" The boy exclaimed in anger. "Why did you put my life in danger?" Reiner was relieved for his life, yet mad he was in this situation. "It was to get you moving." Reece continued. "I'm going to teach you how to fight any way I can." Reece explained in a stern tone. "Why?!" Reiner continued to argue.

"Because you're weak." Reece leveled his voice. "I'm wanting you to fight alongside me as a rep to conquer all of the northern and north-eastern guilds as a start, *then the whole region*." The ram extended his hand out. "Right by my side Reiner we could become kings and take hold of the king's title." He delineated. The magic that Patrice casted sealed the contents, and enabled infamous mysteries within the box. Their partners are able to become stronger towards having the power over both universes even beyond physical existence itself. "So calm your freckled face." He mocked. "We will become the strongest guild alive."

The ram said with cool determination in his voice. "And I'll become a legend." Being king gains obscurity, and obvious knowledge of all things unknown. "You're my familiar?" Reiner said, holding his wounds with great pressure. "I'm not even a sorcerer or anything." He stated. "Your great grandmother, and others were." Reece had knowledge of previous owners and successors before him, as he was one himself.

Once the two made it out of the dungeon they started walking into the nearby woods. "Could I become a sorcerer?" The freckled brunette asked. "There'd have to be a reason, and

I'll have to teach you magic first hand." Reece complained. "Maybe later, I thought you wanted to find your dad?" He tried detouring the situation. "But that could be a reason in itself. He might be in this world. I could locate his soul quickly." Reiner said with a light gleam in his eye. "You could form a contract with me then we'll see." Boom! Boom! The two heard a blast so loud it made half of the forest disappear, and the particles within the air vibrate. "Reiner, we gotta get out of here!" Reece yelled. "What was that?!" Reiner grew increasingly worried as arrows were surrounding them.

They were ambushed by a group of women wearing all white, lace fitted dresses except for one who wore all black; their leader maybe? "You won't get away!" The woman charged at the two with full speed, leaping through the trees, and swinging on branches. They were fast as they were barefoot. "Stop running you bastards!" One of the ladies hollered. "Too weak to fight I suppose."

Tsk! Reece was irritated. "You ugly bitches wanna fight?" He said with a nonchalant tone, running towards the outside plain. "Hold on tight, and don't look down." The ram instructed as he took flight. "Morfi Bala!" Suddenly the ground, trees, and other earth elements took form and compacted into a gigantic ball; engulfing, and crushing the women from behind as they couldn't escape. "Gnostes pyles!" Reece opened a gate to the other side.

After their intense rush back, the two recapped. "Reece what was that?" The boy waited for his adrenalin to go down before he could say another word. "A group of girls wanted to pick a fight." He said thinking of what to do next. "They were probably a part of a guild I suppose." *Sparrow?* "Either way, this is why you have to train." Reece told him. "Like I said, the guilds along with their citizens are extremely skilled fighters." "I know, you've said it over and over." Reiner got childishly annoyed as he grew tired of that line. But knowing that it's true gave him a sense of awareness as he couldn't help but feel concerned, and scared. "Your fight with Aericus was mediocre, and poor."

The ram announced. "Tomorrow I'm gonna teach you magic, but first you'd need to sign this if you're really serious about becoming a sorcerer, or mage of some sort." Reece grabbed a loose sleeve paper, and wrote some form of a contract with blood by slitting his finger. "There." He pointed. "But I know you aren't ready."

He underestimated him. Reiner shook his head. "I'll take the challenge." The boy said. "Good." *Shit, something hurts!* Reiner paid attention to his forearm. "What's this?" It was sort of a tattoo with the word crow carved within his freckled olive skin. *Crow?* "It's like an emblem of our guild." Reece explained as he smiled. "This is the beginning of your new life."

The next morning, the two trained outside on site by the recreational center. "A baseball field?" Reiner was surprised as it was a rainy day and they were on the wet, grassy playing field. Either way, he knew he was determined to train as he was excited to learn magic first hand. "Voitheia machis." Reece pointed towards the dreary, cloudy gray skies as weapons like maces, swords, and steel balls fell from above.

It was as cold as the base of a freezer, but that wasn't enough to extinguish Reiners flame. "Grab a weapon." Reece commanded. "Let's fight." Reiner grabbed a spiked ball. It was slightly heavier than imagined, but he could manage. Reece crouched down. "Ready, set…" As Reiner gripped the iron ball as tightly as he could, he felt the chilling air inside his lungs fervently dancing within himself. He let it all out in one breath, then charged. "Go!" Reece yelled. Reiner began swinging the spiked ball towards a pole adding force along the way as it managed to scratch the ram pretty badly. "Cheirovomvida!" Reeces aim was all over as fire bombs blew up everywhere except its target. "Run as fast as you can!" His familiar said as he cast another spell.

"Xechasmeno asteri!" Suddenly, black stars appeared behind the boy's footsteps while purple chains came from the ground up entangling him. "Ahh!" It stung as his legs became numb as ice. "Try taking them off, they're poisonous." Reece said while watching him struggle. He untangled himself fast enough to grasp an opportunity to tackle the faun onto the ground. From there Reiner began punching Reece in the face over and over again. "All right!" He coughed as he forfeited defeat. "At least you were better now than before. Here's the antidote." Reiner quickly grabbed the bottle from the ram's hand then took a swig of the bitter liquid.

He applauded the young man for his efforts. Both of them got up from the ground as they saw that a quarter of the baseball field was demolished. "I happen to mention—" Reiner felt unsure of saying this, but he wanted to understand. "What language were you saying?" "My mother tongue Italic Greek." Reece calmly replied. "Many mages and sorcerers chant their spells in their Hellenic mother language. I can teach you some." He obliged. "Go for it." "Mystiki apostrangisi." The ram extracted the poison out of Reiner, and immediately felt better as he did not intentionally kill him.

"Give me your palm." He ordered next. "Look into the creases and chant these words; Pyar-ka-ga vomva." The boy stedly waved his hands, then chanted. "P-Pyar-Pyarkaga vomva!" Reiner said quickly as he managed to create flames amongst the shallow, cold spritz of rain. "That's perfect Reiner, even on your first try!" Reece was impressed, as he couldn't believe he would give out his all like that. "Do you love anyone Reiner?" Reece asked. "Wha-What?! Why?" Reiner was baffled, and confused with that question as his cheeks turned as red as a freshly cracked pomegranate fruit. "Either way, It's none of your business!" He retaliated quickly, focusing solely on learning magic. "Calm down…" Reece said.

"Imagine your drive, and will to protect them." He continued to make a point. "The stakes are in your hands, you would have control of their futures. Least she falls." *Vitallin…* The young man thought to himself. That blonde girl has been with Reiner through thick, and thin being childhood friends for fifteen years of course. He's there for her right? "You're going to get stronger Reiner, your perseverance shows that." Reece planted an approving smile upon his face.

That morning Reiner washed, changed into his school uniform, and walked off onto the schoolyard. Milford Academy was in a mellow, yet fun mood today as classes were slow and today was their ice cream social. Things were starting off well. "Ah, Reiner!" Erika called out to him as he caught her eye walking pass fixing his black tie. "What's up?" He asks, feeling chipper than ever. "Where are you headed?"

She wonders, noting that he wouldn't be in any trouble. "Second period biology, why?" Reiner questioned with good intentions in mind. "Could you help me mix the ice cream for this afternoon social?" "The teachers could let you skip." She said with loving excitement in her voice, wanting him to stay. "I'm sorry." Reiner declined. "I have a mid-term assessment to take, it's a huge portion of my grades you know." He mocked her since she earned an average score being the perfectionist she is. Reiner knew Erika liked him so he playfully teases her. He was capable of love yet wasn't interested as it never seemed to meet him with the same eye. Reiner valued every relationship with trustworthiness, loyalty, and happiness but he was never treated with that respect.

The love never necessarily needed to be romantic or platonic, it just needed to be shown with sincerity and heart. While in class paper planes were being thrown in the amiss of boredom; jets, battleships, gliders, and even balloons. Friends in class were chatting about who's the hottest amongst their classes which soon turned to the relevancy of homework, and college. Some even decided to drop out.

"Alright class, settle down." Mrs. Brookes said, trying to gather their attention. "Do you all have your homework? If so, pass it up front." One by one students got up from their desks to the front end of the classroom. Reiner slowly made his way up front before noticing something coming within the classroom. *"Wha—?"* He thought. It was sturdy with large wheels, footrests, and wheel locks. *A wheelchair maybe?*

He assumed the obvious. *Could it be?* He looked at the motion device, then towards the person's feet. It was a female because she was wearing flower printed lace stockings. His eyes looked further up. *Blonde hair in a messy bun...* "Why hello Vitallin." Mrs. Brookes greeted. "I see you're out of the hospital." At that moment, Reiner's eyes filled with sadness, yet relief as slight tears welled up inside of him. "Hi Reiner." Vitallin smiled weakly in her normal manner; a half-based grin which made the young man even more sad. He ran to go hug her before she could even move the wheels to come inside. "I love you too, Reiner." Vitallin started rubbing his head back and forth as classmates started coming up to her asking countless amounts of questions like, "How did you survive?" or "How many fingers am I holding up?".

Some students even cried, as they were all treated like family there since the entire school knew each other. "Vitallin, you can take my seat." A boy sitting next to Reiner obliged. "Thank you." Her voice turned nazely as if she was sick. Her face was still pink yet flushed, and she had bandages up her forearms where she'd been cut. All Reiner could think about was how happy, and relieved that she was alive.

Once the period was over, the social was about. The entire ninth through eleventh grade had options to go to eight homeroom classes, each containing an ice cream content such as: game room/prizes, history, hangout parlor, ice cream building ect. Reiner, and Vitallin choose history with boxes of ice cream sandwiches they lugged along with them.

He wheeled his friend inside the room and sat near the front so they could exit easily. "You like this place huh, Reiner?" Vitallin asked with a smile as sensual as the moon. The dimly lit room was decorated with a signature chocolate styled theme; each table had edible treats on it like frosted filled eclairs, and cold chocolate drizzled paddle pops. It was a smooth delight for the eyes.

"How are you still breathing?" He concerningly said, wanting to know how in the world she survived all this time. "It's a bit focused although I'm getting better." She explained. "One of the nurses said I shouldn't go to school today. I figured I'd be taken out of the roster if I didn't, so I needed to come back eventually." Her innocence started to glow like freshly picked peaches from a farmer's market. "Yeah, you've missed quite a number of days." Reiner grabbed her hands, and cupped them into his. "I've missed you so much." He said squeezing ever so gently. "You'll always be my best friend." Reiner continued.

"It shattered me how I found you in the hospital." He had apologized to her about his day with Erika, saying that he could have stopped the attackers if he chose to be there with her. She was relieved to know he was sorry. "But it all happened out of nowhere…you couldn't have because they were too strong." She saw Reiner's eyes gleaming with sadness, and shame. "If you died, all of our memories would've been gone, everything…would've been gone." He hugged her tightly. "Reiner stop, you're hurting me." She said. "Ah sorry, I just miss you."

Tears started forming from Vitallin's eyes, beautiful tears as she suddenly grabbed him, and kissed him on the lips. The strangely sweet spark of love was felt between the two as Reiner understood what she was feeling. He motioned his hands to her head and received something unexplainable, yet sound deep within his heart. "I love you Reiner, ever since we've met you've been such an amazing friend to me and I wasn't ready to lose you." She smiled widely as she was happy to be back.

CHAPTER VII

Grow

After the social, everyone went home for the night. Reiner began wheeling Vitallin to his house. "So, what did I miss?" She asked curiously, wanting him to surprise her. "Welp, a bunch of homework that's for sure." He joked. "Hmm…" Vitallin decided. "Not much then." "No, there's more." Reiner quickly proved. "I almost got into a fight with Brinner because of you." "Really? Who won?" She laughingly replied. "No, no, no it wasn't necessarily like that." Reiner tried rephrasing as he continued his story. "It was about the past with his little sister Titania." "What happened to her?" She had to wonder.

"As kids, we were all playing hide and seek when Titania was mysteriously found dead at the scene by a nearby shed." The boy sighed with slight grief. "Brinner thought it was me playing a sick game." "That's terrible." Vitallin responded.

When the two reached the house they were greeted by Kareen at the door holding a lit cigarette in hand, and what seemed to be an uncooked cherry pie in the other. "Oh hey Reiner and—" The words were rolling off the tip of her tongue yet she couldn't quite remember the face. "Vitallin Mrs. Strife." The girl politely smiles. "Oh…wait…Vitallin?!" She screamed in shock.

"Oh my gosh! When did you get discharged?" Kareen pondered. "The last two days." She replied. "Well come on in, Reiner could take you from there." She said motioning towards the door as he wheels her inside, and picks her up. "You're quite heavier than I imagined." He said in a light tone trying his best not to offend. "I ate nothing but soup while in that facility." She murmured in embarrassment as she searched for an explanation. "They had a variety."

He took her to the living room as it wasn't far from the steps. "I almost forgot how your living room looked." She says as she fastens her hair scrunchie. "Yeah not much has changed, I just rearranged a little." He stated. The mood was familiar, and comfortable where anything could be said. "Do you want anything to drink?" Reiner asked, breaking the silence. "Cranberry juice please." She knew he had some because it's his favorite, he wouldn't have chosen any other juice.

"Here." He hands the glass over to her. "Thanks." Breaking the silence even further, Reiner decides to talk about Erika Marvel. Even her name grasped Vitallin's attention. "Hey, you know Erika from school right?" He questioned. "Ha, yeah why?" She said slightly laughing in a mocking tone. Believe it or not, the two *were* friends back in middle school before Erika gained new friends and started bullying Vitallin and her friends relentlessly.

"When the school fair started, she asked me to join her drama and photography club in the hopes of her getting closer to me. I assumed she was trying to humiliate the other students so I declined." "Wow she's that mean, who would have thought?" Vitallin sarcastically interrupted.

"She started talking about you too…" He continued. "Saying that I shouldn't get that close to you, and that you were a slut." He was honest. "I don't know what you two have against each other but I'd back out of it all together." This made her snark. "That wench was a whore prancing around every guy she saw who looked good." It was clear that Vitallin was irritated. "Yeah, it was obvious she liked me." Reiner said, trying to relax the situation and drama surrounding her.

"If she confesses, decline." Vitallin demanded. "If she saw you hanging out with me, something bad might happen to me again." Nonchalantly, Vitallin tries ending on that note but unfortunately Reiner was curious to know more.

"What was she like in middle school?" He had to ask that question. "Erika used to be so kind to me when we were in middle school; her mother gave me rides home only because the district route was too complicated for the bus driver." She twinkled the glass with her fingers to where the light shined towards the ceiling. "But things changed once she gained friends and kept bullying, and harrassing mine." The girl continued.

"Erika started talking badly about my friend's dead brother which pissed me off, she was evil." Vitallin took a sip from her glass, then set it on the coaster. "We then fought by the side of the school afterwards." She turned to the side to show Reiner the deep scars across her neck. He was in awe that she could be this rude, and violent.

"Could I spend the night over?" Vitallin asked. "Sure." He said. The next morning, Vitallin got dressed and left for school. She covered for Reiner as he had multiple mock homework, and projects to complete. Meanwhile at home, Reiner was walking through the tinted hallways once he stumbled upon something shiny, and smooth. It was a ruby red marble which led towards a trail of them; one after another until he found a pile sitting near the living room.

This must be Reece's doing. He thought. Digging through the surface he found a suspicious note along with a toy crown. *What was this man up to?* "Reiner, what are you doing?! What is all this?" Kareen yelled demanding an accurate explanation upon seeing the sight of it all. "It's gonna take ages to clean this…" She grumbled with annoyance. "I'm giving you a fair day for not going to school but please do your work." Reiner went back to his room, and closed the door.

To his mother's curiosity she stares at the pile of marbles before looking inside. "What the hell?" To her surprise she saw the same thing as Reiner. Mrs. Strife picks up the note and examines the back of it. "To Kareen…?" She felt confused as if some lover, or anyone was playing a prank on her, but that wasn't the case. "What are you doing?"

A familiar voice echoed through the boy's ears, undoubtedly it was Reece; his low, husky tone was perfectly sound and clear. "Work, what's up with the red marbles?" "It's a little present to your mother, I want to see her." Reece said. "What? Why my mom?" The boy couldn't understand why.

"She'd realize the truth." Reece was adamant upon meeting Kareen, as it was his personal business. "I have a few words for her." He said. "What truth?" Reiner butted in. "The fact that your mother could've been my victor instead of you..." He chuckled in disbelief. "My mother?" Reiner had to question. "What would she have to do with *you*?" "Since she rejected me as her familiar, I was given to you instead." He continued. "Just watch, let me see her and you'll see." With Reiner's permission he walks out the room.

Reece began levitating through the hallway trying to make as little noise as possible. Kareen noticed a slight cold front behind her as the air felt weird. "Hello, Kareen." Reece grinned with an unwelcoming taste as he placed his hands upon her shoulders. "What the hell!" Kareen quickly threw a marble at Reece's face before having it disintegrate in mid air.

She couldn't grasp any words to say at the moment as they couldn't describe the amount of shock she was in. "It can't be!" She said as tears welled up within her eyes. Reiner tried getting a good view of the entire situation so he sat outside his room from afar. "Remember me, Kareen?" Reece knew how she felt deep down and didn't want to waste any moment of it. "Reece, get off me!" Kareen tried upper cutting him in the face before having her arm jerked away. "Hmph..." Reece landed a quick blow to the face. "Shit!" She screams as she lands on the floor rug in pain. "Mom!" Reiner screamed in a frantic tone. "Reece! What are you doing?!" He yelled at the top of his lungs.

"Stay out of this Reiner, she's tougher than she looks." Reece said as he looked upon her bruised face. "Ha, he's right son..." Kareen panted on the floor trying to catch her breath.

"Stay out of this." Reece then grabs her by the neck putting pressure towards the ground.

"If I had you, I could've been the victor of the northern guilds much sooner…" He continued. "Why wouldn't you join me?" Their relations were strong by the looks of their unsettled past. *How could she have possibly known him, and for how long? When? Why couldn't she have told me this stuff from the start?* Many unanswered questions raced through the young man's head. "Parallilo choro!" Reiner's mother teleported and dropped kicked Reece on the back of his neck.

She was a witch, a pretty nice one too. "Enough!" He choked her as he lifted her up from the floor. "I had a goal and stuck to it through and through!" In a dire attempt for his mother's survival, Reiner tackled the ram to the ground. "Will you stop it!" He yelled. "What do you have against my mother?" The boy tried ending the situation, and he did. "It was my decision to reject fighting and winning the title entirely." Kareen stated as she crawled away from him. "My mother specifically wanted my children to be taught and have that glory, not me."

She felt saddened, but full of faith for Reiner. "That kid definitely can't fight as well as you." Reece complimented while trying to reason with her. "There are other mages out there who are stronger than me." She continued. "I'm sure you're going to conquer the region someday." Kareen started giving him insight. "I want it all." He demanded. "Yeah, just don't let it go to your head." She replied. "Reiner can be taught but trust me, he's a fast learner." She continued. "I'm sorry I couldn't have been your partner, but I'm sure he'll make up for any holes left out." The two looked at the boy wishing they were on the same page. "We'll see about that." Reece was bleeding from his neck down. "I'm surprised I've got to see you one last time." She continued to speak.

"It's been years." Looking at the ram's face brought back hard memories for Kareen as she wished they would disappear. "Train Reiner." She said. "He would be of better use than I could've been." Kareen passed out on the hard marbled floor of the living room. Reece soon grabs Reiner's arm and opens a door to the otherside. "Gnostes pyles!" The two were transported inside. "Wait, mom!" "She's fine." Reece reassured. "What the hell was all of that for huh?" Reiner was between furiated, and confused.

"Calm down, calm down." Reece said trying to collect his cool demeanor as he was increasingly annoyed. "I'm taking you to see Mrs. Marlyn Moon." The ram tried explaining to the young man. "Who?!" Reiner yelled while still feeling mad. "And how do you know my mother? She never told me about this so why would she keep this from me?" He asked Reece what he wanted to hear, as things were still new to him. "I met Kareen because she was the next successor of mages I was assigned to partner up with within the world." He continued his story. "But since she rejected the contract, I was set free for the next successor; you…"

He wasn't necessarily disappointed, he just knew he would have made it farther if it was her by his side. "Despite her hot temper, I saw her train from a very young age. She learned spells, and potions that other wizards and sorcerers couldn't have reached in nearly ten years." He exclaimed. "This isn't just about governing guilds, it's about synthesizing power throughout the entire world both yours, and mine."

Reece ended his terse statement there. "So this is about mages, and wizards battling all over the country." The boy understood. "World." But Reece corrected for emphasis. "It's been past generations, and time. That's why the king's title is widely sought out for. People's ancestors only proclaimed stories about it, which are half true as they only wished for it." The two stopped talking as they made their way towards a small town by the Southern guild plain; Ariel Town.

"Welcome to Ariel Town, home of the southern guild Gorgona turf!" A paperboy yelled out onto the streets. It was crowded as vendors and shops were packed with customers they haven't had in years. "Welcome to Ariel Town, a place filled with the most smuggest assholes alive." The man grew into a slump as he felt that the town's economic state, and people were unjust and conceited. *Vouching for Marxism maybe?*

"So this is the place where Madam Moon stays?" Reiner wondered. "Yup." Replied Reece. While the two were getting near the mansion, they overheard someone gossiping about them. "Eww, who are those guys?" A young woman rudely asked. She was wearing a pleated mini-skirt and blouse as if she just got back from a preparatory school. "They look like thieves, hide!" Another girl replied. This stirred concern within the group so they tried getting help. "Collin!" The girls ran to see him. "Collin! Collin!" They yelled louder. "You have to help us, those two weirdos over there tried molesting us!" The three pointed at Reece, and Reiner's direction.

"Hold on, let me handle it." Collin was amongst one of the most admirable men in town. He was loved by citizens, and ogled at by most of the women around. A B-class sorcerer at best. He had dark brown tousled hair and wore a gray sweater with classic dark pants and sneakers.

"You three, stay back and stay out of trouble." The mage commanded. "Please marry me~" The ladies responded as they lusted. Reece bought an apple from the vendors. "Drop the merchandise!" Collin commanded as he pulled out his amber wand. The man dashed around Reiner, and grabbed Reece's arm pinning it against his back.

"Get off, you flimsy shit weasel!" He insulted, struggling to slip away. "Thilia." *Shit!* Reece's hands were electrocuted as Collin gripped tighter. "Is that the best you've got?" He smiled through the pain, laughing under the stinging sensations. He was strong. "Who are you?" Collin was demanding an explanation. "Enklovizo ekstasi." Reiner let out a few snakes coming from the girls hair. "Co-Collin help!" They yelled as the man rushed to help them out.

The two clearly had no time for fights. "That'll settle it." Reece was impressed by Reiner's development of magical abilities. "You memorized new spells?" He asked. "We're here to train aren't we?" Sassy. "I took some pages from your spellbook, it had everything written down. I've been learning to perfect my abilities ever since." *I see...* "We'll meet Mrs. Moon first." Reece confirmed. They were at least twelve miles away.

She lives in a mansion that cost more than twenty-four million shekels in assets. "Who *is* Mrs. Moon by the way?"

The ever so humble brunette asked. "She's an elder witch who is homebound." Reece continued. "I'm taking you there to talk with her, then train." He was unimpressed by Reece's actions as he has done so much for him now.

CHAPTER VIII

Learn Now Boy

"Where here!" Reece said, waving his arms around signaling their arrival. "Visitors! Visitors!" A woman's voice was heard through a mini intercom by the side of the gate. The mansion was white with rose gold trimmings. "This is beautiful." Reiner said, feeling the outside of the mansion. Creeeak…The front door creaks open. "Hello." Mrs. Moon greeted at the door with a hint of subtlety in her voice as she knew why they were there. "Please come in."

Despite her old age, Madam Moon was quite beautiful; she had long, aged out silver hair, wore a knee-length black skin hugging skirt, and a red off shoulder shirt. She was still fashionable. "This place is massively beautiful." Reiner said mannerfully. "Thank you." She replied. "Would you like some gingerbread tea?" Mrs. Moon suggested. "Um, yeah—" Before the boy could say anything else, the freshly brewed tea teleported onto his lap. *How did that…?* He thought.

"It's time matter magic; an enchantment spell." Reece explained with a straight face. "Correct." Mrs. Moon confirmed. "I'm able to appear, and disappear objects at will." She continued. "Shrinking, and growing matter material in size, and density." Her powers were phenomenal. "Now boy, tell me about yourself." She grinned, sipping her tea. "My name is Reiner Strife, I used to live a normal life…before Reece took me here." The young man continued. "I was wanting to find my father Jeffery Strife." He says. "Jeffery Strife huh?" Mrs. Moon arched a brow. "So you are the investigator's son." She said. "Yeah, you know him?" The young man assumed. "Shuttman's men are dedicated to pushing their agendas for a perfect world. It only makes us fight back more, especially if we aren't a part of it." She told him. "Your dad sucks Reiner." Reece butted in.

"Think of Hide like a head organization formed for the methods of autocracy and facism." Mrs. Moon leaned comfortably in her oversized cushion chair. "They slaughter sorcerers and familiars, and extract their magic for weapons, warfare, and governmental tests for the other world." She said with a dreadful, serious tone.

"They are wanting to exterminate our magic, and life for their benefits and superiority. It's cruel, and unjust…" She wanted to wage a deal with Reiner. "I'll let you stay, and train for three days only if you understand what you're in for." Reiner felt concerned. "Will I die?" "Pfft!" Suddenly, Reece's laughter broke the suspense. "Probably." She says. "You are a sorcerer now, learn to be strong and die with purpose and dignity." She gave conscious words. "Try to live, and good luck. We start tomorrow."

This was an ordeal. An ordeal that the cute freckled face young man wasn't prepared for, but alas, an ordeal that would uncover something greater. "Welp, I guess we're staying here tonight." Reece said, fixing his tousled black hair. Reiner tried feeling comfortable, but was scared as he was afraid of what Mrs. Moon would do to him. He didn't know whether she was helping, or harming. His stomach knotted inwards.

"Here's your room Reece." Mrs. Moon said as she opened the door to a large guest room showcasing swords, and grimoires; a recent edition. The bed was huge, for better words ginormous as it was at least seventy-two by eighty-four inches wide and had brown blankets, and white body-length pillows. "Alright!" He was more than delighted to stay for the night, not even coming out for dinner. "Reiner, I'll help you with your room next." She was happy to oblige.

As they walked down the hallway, all Reiner could smell were honeysuckles and oranges lightly wafting his face no matter which way he turnt. It was a pleasant scent as it took away the tension of the atmosphere. "What's the matter?" Mrs. Moon looked at the young boy worryingly. "Could we change the outgoal?" He asked. "Since this is life or death, could the deal be secrets of Gorgona's turf?" The young man wagered.

"Sure, what would you like to know?" She accepted a little revision. "Umm…" Reiner couldn't make out what to say. "Who's the guild leader, and about the king's title, what are the hints to beating the other guilds." He wanted to know what his situation was coming to, whether he stepped into it or it chose him. He didn't want to go into the unknown, as he didn't want to fight what he did not understand. "A secret is a secret, but only if you stay alive then I might tell you." She says in a rhythmic melody. "Don't worry this is a challenge." She continued to lift him up.

"I know you'll have what it takes." Her response was cold as she opened the door. "Here's your room." Reiner fell asleep on his cashmere bed thinking about tomorrow. *What are the other guilds like? Was my father really that bad?* He let these questions swurve through his mind while he rested.

The next morning was breathtaking as the scent of peppered eggs, heaps of smoke filled bacon, and buttery croissants filled through the hallways, and into the rooms. The boy had to wear his same attire, but luckily he did manage to take a hot shower. "Reiner! Reece! When you're finished, come meet me downstairs for breakfast." The head yelled loudly. There were fresh scrambled eggs, spicy hot sausage, crispy golden hash browns, salad and orange juice all set upon the dining room table.

"Help yourselves." She says while clinging her glass with silverware. "This is great!" Reece complimented, as he was stuffing his face with egg salad, and hashbrowns. Meanwhile, Reiner couldn't think of what to say as he was getting anxious by the minute because he knew he had to fight her soon. Was this to be his final meal? Mrs. Moon picks up her napkin and wipes her face. "When the two of you are finished, please meet me outside at the back." She directed. The boy knew he had to suck it up, and focus on combat, as he was unsure of what came next.

"Don't fret Reiner." Reece idly patted him on the back. "I believe in your future." This hit home for him, as all he was trying to understand was his future and life. "Thanks." He gestures. The two head outside the back of the mansion. There was a lawned area with two blue lines in the middle. "Reece, you'll be Reiner's aid." She points. "What?!" He wanted to watch the fight, not work. "Fine…" Reiner was relieved, but only momentarily. "Here are the rules!" The lady yelled loud enough so they could listen. "You are to check his pulse, and if he forfeits by any means, he loses the deal." Mrs. Moon looked at Reiner with an impending stare as if she could see right through him. "Ready boy?" She asks while taking a stance. "Yes ma'am!"

He had to let all his fears go to the hot stone they were standing on. "I'm ready…go!" Reiner dashed at Mrs. Moon dodging her electricity. Before catching him she kicks him in the stomach. "Guahh!" He vomits onto the ground. "I'm going all out on you, so be prepared." Mrs. Moon says with a straight face. The boy got up and tried uppercutting her from the side. He manages to land a hit before she grabs and throws him across the area.

"Get up Reiner!" Reece yelled cheering him on. The boy was out of breath and felt confused, as this took the entire cake but he had to see his deal through whether he lived or not. "Avyssos!" The boy yelled. Soon Mrs. Moon did not shift well as she was sinking. "What is this?" She smiled impressed by Reiner's abilities. The stone cratered through the ground spewing out lava, melting Mrs. Moon's skin. Unfortunately, she took advantage. "Pidaka Nero!"

She jetted underneath the ground leaving an uprooted trail of soil behind. Reiner took notice of this, and tried running away as fast as he could but he wasn't fast enough. "No way." He exclaimed in shock. *Gotcha!* Mrs. Moon grabbed the boy's ankles, and pulls him under. Dirt was everywhere; in his eyes, nose, and mouth. The lava burned his skin, and quickly dehydrated him putting his body into a state of cardiogenic shock. "Teleport!" The two suddenly teleported above the surface, into mid-air. Mrs. Moon started punching Reiner until the blood started rushing to his head. "Gio-Gio." They both changed space as they got closer to one another. "Push me." Mrs. Moon says, encouraging Reiner to knock her to the ground. "Pyrovolitis!" Reiner lets out a large blast that was seen from afar, raying all over Mrs. Moon causing her to crash onto the ground.

"Ugh…" She seemed bruised, and vastly out of breath. "I give up, you win but this is only for today." She smirks. "Huh." Reiner felt as if he wasn't given a fair chance despite wanting to get it over with. The last two days have passed, and unfortunately Reiner had a taste of what real brutality, and strength meant during that time. "Reece!" She yells. "I'm on it!" Reece grabbed pieces of color coded candy from his pouch.

It gives the consumer the ability to regenerate their body from flesh wounds, to skeletal structure: red for muscle, green for flesh, and blue for bone reconstruction. He places the candy inside the boy's mouth at once. The taste was as sweet as yellow cake with bouts of frosting. Soon after, his flesh started regenerating as muscles began pulsating; red blood cells were functional again. "He's alive, Mrs. Moon." Reiner wiggled his fingers amongst the ground, and slowly yet cautiously opened his eyes. "I'm not dead?" He said softly. "I gave you regeneration candy." The ram stated. He was ever so grateful; Mrs. Moon gave him flesh wounds, and second degree burns.

"Thank you Reiner for giving it your all." She continued. "This was a wonderful fight, as it was a test of strength. You've shown amazing combat, but unfortunately I can only tell you half of our deal." *Half?* Reiner thought as he looked at her from afar. "Reece! Carry the boy inside, would you?" She commanded. "Yes ma'am—" Inside, the two sat down in the living room. The burnt and bruised boy was resting, but kept a faint ear on their deal. "Hungh…" The lady stretched. "If you don't mind me asking, what was Reiner's deal again?" Reece asked. "He changed it." Mrs. Moon said. "He was wanting to know about beating the other guilds, and the secrets of Gorgona Turf."

"Really now…" Reece was interested, as it was what he needed to hear. "Gorgona Turf's castle has custom radiation sensors built inside detecting who's one of them." She continued. "They're also highly skilled wizards, who have an array of skill sets in combat, in which they can't use flame spells because of their low body temperatures." Mrs. Moon felt ashamed for ranting out her own leaders.

"Logan, Mason, and Athena are head of Gorgona, all others are subordinates and members." She continued. "This is Mason's second year entering the king's tournament. He was chosen as a president." She tried being as honest as she could. "Oh, I remember Mason." Reece spoke. "That guy with the long frizzy hair, shitty eyeliner, and bumpy wand. He looked pretty cool." He felt his ego give away. "Mason, and Logan are powerful fighters, while Athena is their subordinate whom is strong, and worthy enough to be near them. Fighting the guild is tricky as they're extremely strategic, and secretive. Preferring to ambush or assassinate most of their opponents ahead of time." She finished her exposition.

"Thanks for the tip." Reiner awoke from his rest. "What makes you think you could beat them?" Mrs. Moon snide. "I let you win the first match, but you have perseverance." She saw the same thing Reece saw in him. "You wouldn't last against them. Start training with friends." She was telling the truth. "Try not to feel scared, you need to grow out of that and fight." The boy took those words to heart, as they were true. "So I'm not strong enough?" He wanted an answer. "Certainly." She gave it to him. "But I'm here anytime you need advice."

Mrs. Moon got up from her chair to wave goodbye, whilst the two headed out. "She's great isn't she?" Reece wanted to influence his mood. "Great but tough in a way." Reiner replied. "What made her say that stuff? Why did you change the deal?" "For our sake." The young man was weak willed, yet he knew how to use his head as he picked up a little precedence from someone. "Nice job." Reece applauded. "We needed that."

He continued, but his contentment soon faded away. "But the fact that she let you win the first time wasn't." He knew that Mrs. Moon wasn't easy. "I've tried my hardest, and nearly gotten melted alive if her hand wasn't keeping me stable." The boy protested. "You're still weak." Reece responded with an overall description of what he could have become, or will be. The two bypassed the crowd, and away from Ariel Town where they saw a crevasse of light peering from a far out area.

"Wanna explore some more?" Reece didn't want to go yet. "Where are you taking me?" "Carousel Land." Reece was gleaming with satisfaction once he said that. "What's that?" Reiner wondered. "It's a place where me and my buddies hung out a few years back." He started to reminisce. "It happened as one by one came along Aiden, Jack, and of course Anri all ended up here out of fate." The ram continued.

"They were the few friends I had before a generational war broke out due to scornment of a treaty within the previous guilds Nightingale and Heathcliff. I got their backs, and they have mine." He was still confident in their friendship, as they were loyal as could be.

"How old are you?" Reiner looked at him ruffling through his hair. "Biologically I'm twenty, but chronologically I'm a hundred and ninety-two years given the fact that I'm a familiar, and a ram." He proudly announced with a smile so bright it made his insides healthy. "What makes you think your friends are still there?" The boy questioned.

"They aren't, but it's a coincidence if one shows up. I'm only there for the sights. There's something magical about that place." He says as he looks up towards the clear blue sky. "Race ya!" Reece ran as Reiner just took notice. "No fair, you got a head start!" He yelled in excitement. The two guys ran their way through the forest towards Carousel Land; passing lakes, streams, and animals nearby. Stumbling upon stumps, rocks, tree barks, and gravel along the way; they ran faster, and faster without breaking a sweat.

The cool air blasted their faces with a gust of wind. "We're almost there!" Reece said as Reiner caught up to him. "Look at the sign!" A 'Welcome to Carterville' sign was advertised along the riverbed. It was a large floating banner that stood out floating above the water. "It's inside Carterville." Reece laughed. "It tricked ya, didn't it?" "Yeah!" Reiner yelled out.

As they approached Carousel Land, they saw an abandoned amusement park covered in loads of sand. "Let's stop here." Reece stretched. "Ugh…" The boy quickly caught his breath. Despite the appearance, some of the rides were functional, but dangerous. "You guys hung out at an amusement park?" "It was Aiden's. His family owns the place, as it was our hideout during the war, no one noticed." Reiner hopped onto a bullet shaped ride with rocket jets on it. "It doesn't work." "That's why it's abandoned." Reece pointed out. "So…how do you all know each other, except Anri of course." Reiner started to chat to pass the time.

"Within the period of the previous generational war, Jack and Aiden were preteens and babies of their home guilds yet found each other." He continued. "They were too young to fight, and serve so they got information about each other's guilds like what magic they used, strengths and weaknesses, and plans. They would report here and place bets to see which group of noblemen get slaughtered. Bets ranging from money, to snacks and food."

"Wow, so they were like pin pals." Reiner was fascinated. "You could say that." Reece replyingly agreed. "They spotted me when I was showing Anri this place, it was like an amusement park so I figured why not? Plus we were twelve so it felt like another adventure." Reece continued the story. "The boys didn't want anyone on their terrain so Anri came up with a deal, have us play here or turn them over to each other's leaders." *So she's that cunning huh?*

The area was quiet, but brought vividly bright memories like happiness out of a spring morning full of blooming honeysuckles, and dandelions. "Well look who's here." A grungy males voice was heard as Reiner looked around. "Reece, is that you?" "Yup, who are you?" He replied. "Jack, Jack Lester." His combat boots stamped onto the ground. "Long time no see."

He was a lightly-mixed blonde who wore a strapping leather vest, with a plain dark-tee, and jeans. The man was with his long time buddies from his home guild Siren. Reece was even more happy to see him. "Hey Jack, you've grown taller over the years." He said, trying to find a way to make a compliment. "Yeah, It's been about seven years since we last saw each other. How's it been?"

Jack was delightfully interested. "Alright, I've entered the kings tournament with my president, and is now training with my partner." "Hi, I'm Reiner St—" The boy didn't want to give away his full name knowing that his dad had an infamous reputation, yet couldn't understand why on his behalf. "Hey Reiner I'm Jack, a member of the Siren guild." He extends his hand to greet in honor.

"It's nice that Reece is training you. He's extremely strong, you'll do well." He smiled. "The kings tournament allows you to pre-examine other guild leaders, and subordinates. He's fit enough to have made it in along with Anri." Jack was always optimistic in his ways, even if introduced to a potential enemy of Siren.

"We're here because I wanted to train, and show him the sights around this place." Reece stated. "Well we're here for the same thing." Jack looked at his posse. They were dressed up in lightweight athletic attire-a simple hoodie, long sleeve tee, boxing shorts, and weight gloves. One was even hulling around a gigantic tire attached to a thick rope ready to be used. "You guys can follow us." He obliged with a gesture. "Thanks, will do." Reece replied.

CHAPTER IX

Experiences

Carousel Land had many areas like an amusement park. Jack led Reece and the guys to the far back of the area called Sharpe route. "Alright men, let's do this." Jack decided to take advantage of the situation as the abandoned place had so many construction pieces that they got creative. The group of guys made a training maze, training weights, and weapons out of the scraps they collected. "This is an awkward place to come by." Reiner said, admitting his honesty. "You're right." Reece agreed.

"But we didn't come here to judge, pick up a weapon." The boy picks up a coal piece of sharp steel. "Where do you think Anri is?" He said as he took his stance. "Well I know she isn't dead, she'd even fake it for reasons." *That slick woman.* Reece didn't feel like talking about her. "She's either kidnapped, or held captive." He continued. "She's the type of person to get into trouble for fun, even if it meant assaulting other guilds.

She's too manipulative when it comes to getting information." Reece shook his head in annoyance. "My wife…"

His palms were sweaty upon his thick green fur. "She's still alive, and could fend for herself." She was *his* teacher after all. Through the end of their training Reiner decided to go home as he couldn't sit still to watch Jack's fight; the restlessness, and time was getting to him. "Leaving already?" The blonde man said with disappointment in his voice. "Yeah, sorry."

Reiner shook his hand while Reece hugged a farewell. "Nice meeting ya Reiner." Jack waved. Onto the light we go as the two makes it to Reiner's room "Temetafora!" by magic. The young man felt a strange feeling of euphoria for the ram. "That place was marvelous." He said. "Mmhmm." Reiner unwinded, and cleaned up his room.

"What happens if a familiar, or anyone from your world comes here?" He questions. "They'd wreck havoc, and slaughter everyone on sight." The man bluntly explained. "Reason be is because they are wanting to become the most powerful, whether that meant taking out humans, or anyone who happens to stand in their way."

"I'm talking about unchained familiars. They have no partner, conscience, or morals; it's extremely dangerous and worse if they target you or any loved ones." Reece wiped his palms on his leg fur once more. His world was extremely beautiful, yet fatal. "Humans are vulnerable, and I'm leaving you at that. Just don't get too soft." He decided to drop the conversation at that and move on as he felt that Reiner was getting an iffy idea. "Reiner, come eat your dinner! I bought take out!"

Kareen yelled across the hallway. "Coming!" He replied swiftly as he packed away his clothes in his wardrobe closet. Plates of sweet, sticky yellow rice with jumbo sweet and sour chicken were presented on the dining room table. The savory aroma filled the entire upstairs rooms. While enjoying their meal, the two spoke out with a question at the same time. "Why…ahh." "You first dear." Kareen tried to break the unison of words. "Are you a witch?" Reiner waited for long, clear cut answers as he's been wanting to know if she was keeping secrets from him.

"Um, kind of. But from my side your aunt Martha and grandmother Gabriela are as well." She said with an open mind as she placed her fork down. "I was offered a position as a sorceress at a young age of five. Reece was to become my familiar, but since I declined him and wanted to raise a normal family, I'm not quite as useful as I was back then." She continued as she took a bite from her food. "My mother even tested out on me, and saw I had high potential to become a mage." "How did you and Jeffery meet?" The young man spoke as this question alone took her aback. "Your father and I meet at an advanced preparatory academy similar to yours which specializes in math and economics." She continued. "He was a real womanizer with a dashing aura, and a handsome face; he knew how to talk his way into any woman's heart." His mother slowly felt the melancholic atmosphere then downed her head against the table. "Jeffery was a beautiful man inside, and out. He was also playful, and easy going at best."

"I was a caribbean and he was a german, who'd know we'd collide with each other. Every morning he'd come by my class and we'd talk about the most serious of things like religion, books, and even the changes of genocide as it affected his great great grandfather." She noted. "Either way, he turned out to be an amazing husband…most of the time." Reiner tried keeping a straight face through the entire story, though he couldn't understand why Jeffery worked for Hide? "He's alive you know…" Reiner hoped, wondered and believed. "We don't know for sure."

Kareen said, questioning. "He's been missing for years now and would've been dead." "Believe in me and him at least, he's alive." The boy was eager for his mother's wishes, and hopes. "Wow, I wasn't invited to eat?" Reece peered his way into the dining room where he was playing in Kareen's big, curly highlighted afro. "Reece, stop!" She yells. "You've done enough damage you goat, and stop messing with my hair you're acting creepy." "I don't take orders from strangers." He mocked. "Well help with the dishes." Reiner commanded. "Sure, I guess." The next day while in class, Vitallin was seen sleeping along with her friends near the center stage of the room. "Vitallin, Chrissie, and Megan! Wake up!" Mr. Mountgomery slammed his ruler hard on the chalkboard. "I don't get paid to babysit." He said with a hint of frustration. "You either learn the material now for this week's test, or fail. Whichever one suits you." "Ah, sorry…" She apologized with a drowsy, worn out look on her face that made everyone turn around the three and start snickering.

After the lessons were taught a few kids in the class decided to have a study session; they played games, questionnaires, and even studied normally for the first time in groups outside the rambunctious classroom. "I'm so sleepy." Vitallin said, yawning away. "Well why don't you skip school tomorrow, and stay home? We'll cover the test material, and homework for you." Megan suggested. She was always helpful when it came to that stuff. *Yeah.*

Vitallin thought to herself. *Reiner always skips out on school, but what does he really do?* She wondered. "Thanks." Vitallin says as Megan handed half of her notes to her. "I felt pretty drowsy this morning too." She said, "You might have a fever, that's a perfect reason for a note." Chrissie responded as she cunningly smiled.

Whilst the school day ended, everybody went home. It was strange for Vitallin to be sitting behind as Reiner would normally wheel her, he had walked ahead of her some minutes ago. "Reiner!" She softly yelled, but he didn't hear so she resorted to wheeling herself home instead.

"Oh honey! How was school?" Mrs. Dubarse was just done baking a quiche pie for dinner. "Alright, same as usual." She wheeled through the front door. "Can I skip school tomorrow?" Vitallin asked. "Why?" Her mother wondered. "I felt drowsy, and hot all day today. I also feel asleep in class." The girl felt sorry for her excuse. "Take some medicine and go to bed early, I'm sure you'll feel well enough tomorrow." Lanet tried to help her out in some way as a mother could.

After taking her medicine, she wheeled past the hallway, and into her room where she slipped out of her uniform and into her silk, black pajamas. Soon after she plops on the side of the bed, and falls asleep. The room was getting colder, and colder by the hour, yet she managed to sleep tight. It would've been a shame if her fever spells were true as she's already been out of school for weeks.

Vitallin started feeling uncomfortable by all the pressures, and worries that the day brought her. "What's this?" She was soaked as she found herself sitting in a crater of some sort of liquid inside what looks to be a massive cave. It was raining outside, acid rain to be exact which smelled like sulfur eating away metal as it was seeping through the mud, rocks, and dirt. "What is this place?!"

The girl yelled wanting a reply from anyone, or thing as a sound echoed through. Hiss~ Hiss~ Loud hissing noises were heard from afar.

"Dear Vitallin." A woman called out towards her. "Come closer." She said, leering her head from the side. Vitallin did as she was told when suddenly the woman jumped out and bit her neck. "Ahhh! Stop!" Vitallin screamed as the woman continued gnawing her neck, tearing her way through every layer of skin.

The woman revealed herself as a large, naked, long black mamba snake with slimy scales that looked as if it could shed any minute. "Hold still girl!" The snake lady hissed. "It'll be over before you know it." In desperate pain, Vitallin wrestled with the woman trying her hardest to escape the gripping coil. "Get off me!" She screamed in agony as the venom was boiling hot.

"Your blood is mine!" The woman squeezed tighter, and tighter as she looked dead into the girl's eyes. "You'll be dead before you know it!" The lady said before letting out the most horrifying hiss imaginable. Vitallin pinned the snake's head by the side of the cave then ran in the hope of scraping off the woman's head; alas, she succeeded. As the woman's face bruised and swelled up, her tail stopped wagging before it shed itself into a hard yet flexible piece of steel. "Are you dead yet?!" Vitallin yelled in anger with as much expression as she could as the venom was taking over.

"You've indeed killed her." A mysterious voice of a man butted into her situation. It was both sweet, and smooth sounding. "Now quickly eat the scales, it works as the only antidote." He assured her. Vitallin took a piece of the woman's shed scales and ate it, it was salty and metallic as the texture could be compared to that of hard taffy…with no flavor. "Who are you?" She asked, trying not to feel frightened after what happened to her.

She saw a tall, young faced man with light blonde curly hair. "My name is Xan, I'm a guild investigator working with Hide as an associate." He continued. "We kill familiars, or anyone who produces magic in that manner." "Famili, family-airs?" She tried pronouncing, but couldn't quite get it. "They are the companions of witches, and sorcerers." The man explained. "What you killed just now was a demon, they'll harm the lives of others as we protect them ma'am." Xan explained as he wore a blue uniform to prove it. "My name is Vitallin Dubarse." She waved as a fellow greeting.

The man stepped towards Vitallin and planted a kiss on the lips causing her to suddenly wake from her sleep. "What?" She said confusedly as she looked at her arms and shoulders for bites, and blood; none were present.

Vitallin looked around the room, then decided to strip her blanket set apart. "But it all seemed too real…" She said to herself as nothing was out of the ordinary. *What happened to me?* The girl checked her forehead, and to her surprise she was sweating like a condensed ice cream jar left out in the sun. The young girl slowly took a deep breath, then exhaled. *dammit.* She touched her neck for any wounds. "Familiars huh…"

Meanwhile, Reiner pushed in his desk chair as he stood up to go to the bathroom. When he passed his bedroom mirror he noticed that the scar across his neck healed. "Why would Reece do such a thing?" He said to himself as he touched it halfway. "Mom!" He yelled. "I'm going out!" "Sure thing!" She replied. Reiner decided to head out for a walk in the park. It was a beautiful, yet cloudy day outside.

He stops by the Bates recreational center; it was a youth organization with loads of gym equipment that was coupled with a thirty-two mile trail outside. The Bates center also hosts after school clubs for children as well. *Let's go!* With his sweatpants and long white tee on, Reiner takes the thirty-two mile challenge and walks the trail. The walk proved a way to calm his head as the atmosphere around him was calm, and reserved. *What's so special about the weapons Hide were making, and what's so special about them?* These questions made him understand a bit, but not entirely. *Can't they fuel their own magic? Do they bring weapons here?*

He soon shook his head and continued walking as he didn't want to break the fifth mark. "Can I walk with you?" A little girl asked. Her face looked red as if she just ran over here. She was a young vietnamese girl wearing a frilled green blouse, denim shorts, and white sneakers. "Um sure." Reiner said whilst looking around to see if anyone was nearby assuming if she were in after school care. "Um…If you don't mind me asking, where are your parents?"

The girl squeezed Reiner's hand tightly. "They're dead." She said nonchalantly as Reiner could feel the saddened, pained expression across her face as they walked together. "My name is Cammie." The little girl spoke. "Hey…Cammie." Reiner felt odd with his greeting, as he didn't know what to say to the young child. "My mother was a pediatric nurse, and my father a carpenter." Cammie said with a bright smile. "Unfortunately, they died from a car accident." Her smile soon faded as she looked down at the graveled trail. Reiner crouched down to meet her level.

"I'm searching for my father." He said trying to reason the mood. "Just know they're in a better place, and never give up on them." He wanted to cheer both of them up. "I know." Cammie nodded her head in a sincere fashion. "They used to bring me here everyday to play." She said. "Now I come alone. What was your life like?" The girl asked. "It was nice when I had my father around." Reiner continued.

"I had someone whom I could learn from. He was a former professional fighter who taught me krav maga." "What's that?" Cammie wondered. "It's Isralian martial arts." He explained. "My father trained me when I was little, he said always take use of your advantages. Just because you're civil, doesn't mean you have to close your mind." Says Reiner. "He was the best fighter around." This made him proud of himself. "Wow, you can't take that for granted." The little girl replied. "My father used to teach me archery when I was seven growing up. It made him happy." She continued.

"We used to participate in area competitions like here, and apply to grand tournaments like the I.Y.A.A they held theirs annually." Cammie smiled with gleams in her eyes. "So you shoot bows, huh?" The boy interestingly commented. "Yeah, I could teach you sometime." She wagered. "Only if you teach me Krav Maga…" Despite Cammie's young age, she was way beyond her years when it came to intellect, and manual talent.

"By the way, what's your name?" She asked. "Reiner…" He addressed. "Renear." The girl half jokingly pronounced. "Great! Teach me martial arts, and I'll grant you the power of archery." Cammie was excited. "Sure." He delightfully replied. "Meet me here this evening around eight, and I'll teach you all you need to know." It's a deal.

Before they knew it, Cammie and Reiner finished their walk at around twenty-two miles. He felt happy that he made someone else's day, especially someone similar to him. After the walk Reiner heads back home to prepare for his training with the young girl. *Cammie.* He thought. *How could such a little girl like you be so strong willed?*

CHAPTER X

Prove (Part I)

Reiner takes off his shoes, and heads to his room where he cleans up and does at least twenty sit-ups. It was awfully funny that he made a deal with a little girl, but nice since they seem to have a common history with their upbringing. The boy heads right back outside around eight twenty. He managed to bypass his mother as she was sleeping near the other end of her bedroom.

Creeak, click-click. Off he went as he shut, and locked the door behind him. While walking closer to the Bates recreational center he saw Cammie wave. "Renear! Renear!" She was still pronouncing it wrong. The girl changed into a gray sweatshirt, and sweatpants as it was colder around midnight and it matched the large, trusty archery bow hanging around her back.

"Nice bow." Reiner said. "Thanks, I like your compression gloves." She replied. "Ready to use em'?" he joked. "Yup." "Teach me archery first." He said. "Fine." Cammie sighed as she wanted to have it her way. She handed a wooden bow to

Reiner. "This is a traditional bow. She said while holding one up to her hands. "You take your aim and—" Fwwshh!!

The tinted arrow cut through the wind like an angry sparrow, then landed near a target tree. "Shit that was fast!" The boy was impressed as it was like looking at an after-image. "I wanna see what you can do." She pointed. "Twelve gold metals, and eight trophies." She could even use flame arrows if she wanted to. Proud girl.

Reiner held up his bow, and tried practicing without an arrow. "Your aim will be slightly lower than the actual target." She explained. His grip on the bow wasn't quite subtle as he kept lowering it to his knees. "Use your forearm strength." She tried helping behind him as she motioned his arm. "Steady now and…let go!" They were in perfect sync. "You would've hit your max speed like that, now try with an arrow."

The girl handed Reiner a black arrow. "Cool." He said looking at how thick the piece of structure was. He prepared his stance, then reared the bow back all the way. "Nice, now let go." Cammie directed. Fwwshh! The arrow was tremendously light and elegant, but Reiner's speed couldn't compare to Cammie's. "Practice more and you'll get the hang of it."

Nonetheless he was good. As with each arrow Reiner grew faster, and faster; his agility and speed was credited by his competence. He's gotten used to this. "It's that simple, just aim and shoot. I could even do a flaming one if I wanted too." The girl boasted. "Great, now I can teach you MMA, and Krav Maga." The boy joked. "I'm excited." Cammie always wanted to learn martial arts, it would've been another staple to her many talents.

He handed the girl some compression gloves. "Wow, they're so soft." Cammie knew things were getting serious. "Put them on." Reiner instructed. "Sure thing." They stood within the forest of trees where Reiner was training earlier. "Watch me." The young man began punching the tree with massive strength, causing the outer bark to chip off. "Amazing!" Cammie was in shock at how strong he was. "Pfft!…"

He laughed with honesty. "Anyone can break a wooden board, you try." Cammie gives her all in one punch. "Ughh…" "Pfft!" The young man burst with laughter. "Use the palm of your hand to push, while your fist tears away." The young man explained.

"Act like you're pulling a rope. Find its pressure point and—" Crack! A piece of bark was hanging from the edge. "Congratulations." Reiner clapped. "I…I did it!" The girl was astonished, but soon found herself being tackled onto the ground. "What the heck, get off me!" She screamed. "You gotta think fast, anyone could attack you." He said while easing his weight off of the girl as she was struggling to get free.

"No fair, I'm like a hundred and twelve pounds." She said. "Try grappling me." Reiner replied. "Pin my arms behind me, and try to get on top." The boy instructed. The little girl wiggled, and struggled her way upfront then did what she was told. As Reiner was acting like an opponent forcing her down, Cammie grabbed his right arm and pinned it behind his back, while going around his entire body with her left thigh rolling him onto his back while trying to pop his shoulder muscles.

"I give, I give." He said joking through the pain as he tapped on the ground three times as if they were inside of a ring. "You're gonna learn fast." He complimented her strength.

"Don't tackle me out of the blue like that!" She said with an annoyed tone of voice. "You could've told me we were doing another lesson." "You may come across people who may assault you out of the blue like that." Reiner stated. "You have to decide which move to make and fast. Your parents aren't there to protect you anymore." He wanted to choose a better choice of words that would get his point across. "Don't bring my parents into this Renear!" The little girl yelled. "This is between me and you, got that! I'm fine by myself!" Cammie learned how to become independent ever since her parents died. She used her abilities to credit her worth for survival. Innovating ways for herself along the way as she grew up.

"My name is Reiner, Rei-ner." He pronounced as he grew tired of her saying it incorrectly. "Whatever!" Cammie pouted. "If you're so mad, then come at me…" Without pressing any further, the girl charges directly towards him at full speed. "This is for bringing up my parents!" Before she could throw a punch to the face, Reiner grabs her wrist, and twists it behind her. "Oww!" She screamed as he drop kicks her onto the wet ground.

"It can't be that bad…" Reiner said, stretching his body in a twisting motion. "It's moderate…" Cammie replied. "That was just a sweep kick." "Correct." He stated. "Now, try kicking me at the core as hard as you can while throwing me to the ground." The boy instructed her just that as she quickly knocked him to the ground, and clasped his arm between her thigh muscles. "Shit, okay!"

Reiner cried tapping the ground once more trying to be freed. "This is punishment for twisting my arm." She said as she pulled more, and more locking her hand upon his wrist; it's terrifyingly remarkable that a ten year-old could be this strong. Cammie wanted to feel in control, as if she were a queen in battle. "I'll let go now." She knew he was in pain. "Juji Gatame…" Reiner struggled to catch his breath as he pronounced.

"That's the move?" She questioned. "Yes, but be careful it'll dislocate an arm, or even cause death to the victim." Reiner continued. "Only use it when necessary. Thanks for teaching me archery." He added. "Thank you for teaching me MMA, are you sure you could walk home?" She was delighted, yet wanted to make sure he was okay. "I'm fine." The young man replied. As Cammie, and Reiner parted ways they were neither strangers, nor long time friends, but they were similar. The things they took with them were strength, and intuition as they both have unforgettable ties to their parents, and skills they can harness once they come across different people.

Once Reiner made it home, he slipped off his shoes, and crept through the house trying not to wake Kareen up. Lucky for him he managed to get into his bedroom unannounced as he saw Reece sleeping, and levitating near the corner of the room. *Did he always sleep like this?* He wondered to himself as he crashed onto his bed fast asleep. Goodnight, and sleep tight.

Meanwhile. "No! This can't be!" A voice broke down in disbelief. "Gazelda, my daughter!" He shrieks in horror. "Who would've done this?!" The old king hugs his bloodied daughter's body in agony. "Silece! Guards!" As the dreadful situation unfolds, the moon cried blood and waged war. "Sir what—" The guards were scattered, and mortified once they saw Gazelda dead, lying in her blood soaked bed. This only led one question to arise, *"Who did this?"* Magnum's guild king was furiate, and unforgiving. "I want them interrogated." He demanded. "Search the entire kingdom inside, and out. Bring them to me!"

Gates were locked, and sirens were off waking up nearly everyone inside the town. King Meurium saw a note underneath his daughter's blanket which read **Magnum will be overthrown!** This led him to believe it was one of the eight guilds at the time, or even worse all. "Stop right there!" One of the guards caught something running in their view from afar, they tried catching up but the heavy snowfall was distancing them further and further. "They're onto us Lee!" The girlish, squeaky voice of a little girl cried out. "I'm on it!"

A man replied. "Kratira Pagou!" He yelled as ice craters formed around the guards. "This is an order!" They quickly hurtled their spears towards the two as they fell from above surrounding them at full speed. "Ahh!" The girl screamed in shock as one of the spears impaled straight through her neck causing her to bleed out fast. "Lex!" The six foot two raven yelled as he came to her rescue. "Don't die on me please!…" He frantically removed her red scarf. "Stay back!" Lee commanded as a few Magnum guards were catching up to them, ready to capture.

"We know what you did!" They said in unison. "Under Meurium's orders, stop right now and follow us!" The guards were hesitant of any further movement. "We didn't do anything !" Lee proclaimed as he pressured Lex's wound. "Just stay away!" The man was in distress, as he didn't want to see his partner die in front of him. "Lee, do as they say and calm down…I'll be fine, I promise."

The girl heard her voice give away as she knew she didn't have much time. "Please let me go…" The little girl said as the man sighed and gave in. He placed her onto the snowy ground, and quickly yanked the rod out of her neck, worsening the wound by spilling out more and more liters of blood thus causing her decease. Piling snow upon her body, Lee surrenders and follows the guards back to the guild.

On their way back to the kingdom, Lee could only think about how they failed their mission. "Who am I going to see?" He asked as he tucked his hands into his black denim jeans. "We're holding you to the courtroom until king Meurium arrives, then we'll know what to do with you." With that being said, Lee could only want to glimpse at what his future would look like.

The king walks into the courtroom, and instantly orders Lee into the incarceration holding cell for further questioning. "Your majesty." The guards pardoned. "You've done enough, thank you for your help." Meurium said kindly. The next morning, Reiner woke up ready to take on the day as Reece kept hitting the ceiling (He was a hard sleeper). He took a shower, changed into his uniform, and headed off to school when suddenly he received a call from Vitallin.

"Hello?" He answered. "Hey Reiner…" She said as she sounded off, uneasy in fact. "I'm not coming to class today." "Why?" The young man wondered as his eyebrow squinched in suspicion. "I can't move." She shudders. "What?" Reiner found her situation to be played off as a joke, or just plain ridiculous. "I'm serious, please help. There's a gigantic, creepy, scary black monster hanging from my closet door." The girl continued. "It told me that if I moved in the slightest, I would die." The low shallow tone within her voice was nearly about to crack. "It's staring me down…" She wasn't kidding.

Reiner soon grabs his backpack, slings it over his shoulder and races towards Vitallin's house. He rang the doorbell multiple times but no one answered so in desperate measures to get to his friend, he elbows through the glass of the front door, and unlocks it from the inside. Reiner dropped his backpack and ran upstairs. He smelled something out of the ordinary as fear of the unknown gripped his throat, causing him to feel as nervous as ever. "Vitallin!" Reiner yelled. "I'm here!"

She signaled as he scampered through the hallway searching through every room, then finally into hers. "What the hell is that?" His entire body froze as he was greeted with huge, stalking yellow eyes that looked as if they were about to pop out of their sockets any minute. The creature was ginormous, scary, and grotesquely fuzzy, just like how she described. Terrifying.

"Help me…" Vitallin said, holding her breath. Once he snapped out of it, Reiner grabbed a stick fan from the corner of the room, and slough both of its eyes out. The monster then let out a jarring shriek before attacking the boy. "Vitallin run!" He yelled while fighting the creature back. "No." Instead she decides to fight out of revenge. Vitallin goes to the hall closet and grabs a gun from the lockbox. "Reiner, fight it!" He puts up a struggle against the monster, throwing it onto the ground whilst ripping its purplish-black fur in the process. Bang! Bang! Her aim was perfect.

The smell of sulfur and blood emminated throughout the house, so deadly that they had to leave immediately. Fortunately, Mrs. Dubarse wasn't home. "You broke the door?" Vitallin exclaimed. "There was no other way." Reiner said as he was carrying her outside. At least they made it out safely. "What was that?" Reiner asked, still shaken and disgusted by what he saw. "I'm surprised you believed me…" She said as she felt some reassurance in herself.

"I need to tell you about this dream I had yesterday." The girl continued. "There was this snake lady who tried to kill me, I fended myself off by scraping her head off the side of a cave." "Wow, really?" He sounded interested. "I then met a man named Xan who worked for an investigative group called Hide." "What?" The name sparked familiarity with Reiner. "Hide." She repeated once more. *How could she have known about this?* "It was a dream, correct?" He paid attention to the story but had to ask. "Mmmhmm…" Vitallin nodded her head in reply.

He believed in her, so now it's time for her to do the same. "That monster we just killed was real wasn't it?" He tried reasoning with her. "Yeah, the entire thing was scary, and bizarre." She continued. "You were there too. The thing was fucking hideous." He wanted her to believe. "I'm a sorcerer!"

The young man blurted out. "And there's a talking faun living in my house…" Her face told it all as she lifted a brow concerned for his well being. *Are you for real?* She thought. "Hahahah!" Vitallin began laughing. "I'm serious, it's true."

Reiner decided the best thing to do now was show her. "Come to my house." He looked at her silk, black pajamas. "You can also wear my clothes." He obliged. Reiner headed onto school, while Vitallin went opposite to his house. Ring-ring! "Hey Vitallin!" Kareen greeted at the door with open arms. "Hey, Reiner told me to come over here…may I come inside?" She confidently asked.

"Sure, but why are you in your pajamas?" Kareen was confused. "Aren't you supposed to be in school?" "It's a long story…" The girl explained herself. "I'll call my mom and tell her I'm here." The young girl puts her gray, soft slippers aside as Mrs. Strife helps her upstairs. While sitting down on their black couch, she thought about what Reiner said and if any of it were true. What more could he be hiding from her? "May I go wash my face?" Vitallin asked, as Mrs. Strife put down the washed dishes to help the girl up the steps. "Yeah that's fine, by all means do as you wish…"

Kareen was the type of person who was really laid back, and respectful at the same time. She was willing to help out in the long run as she was like family to her. "You can also stay in the squirts room if you'd like…" She suggested. "Okay." Vitallin checks herself in the mirror as she messes with her blonde hair, and touches her plush, rosy-red cheeks. "Looks fine…" Despite her appearance, she felt hot and anxiety ridden after what happened several minutes ago.

After rinsing her face with cold water, she decides to head into Reiner's bedroom.

Creeak… She peers through the door looking around to notice anything suspicious. Vitallin started having a little fun snooping through Reiner's things: playing his video games, reading his books, playing darts, and tampering with his message board. "Ahahaha!" It was as if she was at a sleepover, but her fun soon came to an end once she turned around. "Oh my god!"

She jumped back, and slammed onto Reiner's closet door. "What the hell…who are you?!" She pointed. "Who are *you*?" Reece said with a confused face, and book in hand trying to read in peace without disturbance. *A total stranger is in their house.* She thought to herself as she was scared to call for help. "Who are you, and what's with the horns? This isn't a theater…" She commented. "Well come over here and see if you could take 'em off for me." Reece grew annoyed with the girl.

Vitallin sought it as a challenge, so she leaned over and touched his ram horns. "Ahh!" She screamed as blisters, and cuts started forming on her hands. "What the hell did you do?!" She panicked. "Explain yourself and I'll give you the antidote, normal healing creams wont work it's poison." "Poison?!" Her panicking soon turned into hysteria. "Explain!" Reece yelled in a straightforward tone. "There was a gigantic creature in my room trying to kill me so Reiner helped me out, and told me to meet him here after he's done with class."

She said at the speed of a runaway gazelle. "Whoever you are, please don't kill me!" Vitallin crouched beneath where Reece was sitting. She then realized that wasn't all he told her, and soon began to see that everything Reiner told her was true. "Here, drink this." Reece sets his book down, and hands her a bright yellow potion bottle containing the antidote. "So Reiner sent you?"

He questioned. "Yes…" She gently replied, trying to reason with him. "Um…If you don't mind me asking, what's your connection with him?" She had to ask, but did not want to. "I'm his familiar, or he would be my partner to be frank." Reece messed with the chained pouch around his fur. The little blonde girl was bewildered out of her mind, so many questions arose.

CHAPTER XI

Prove (Part II)

"Mom, I'm home!" Reiner entered through the door in a delightful mood. He dropped his backpack near the closet door, across from the marbled kitchen. "Did you buy any food?" Reiner looked through the pantry, and cabinets for new groceries as he was wanting to cook a cuisine style stuffed chicken with broccoli rice. "I'll go to the store later on, I have stuff to take care of right now."

His mother replied. Left feeling hungry, Reiner heads to his room. "Vitallin, are you there?" He knocks. "Yeah…" She said, doting the forthcoming mood. He opens the door and notices Reece awake sitting on his bed. "Yo." The ram greeted in his usual nonchalant manner. "Is this your girlfriend?" He insisted on bringing that situation up based on how he dealt with her so far. "That's not the case, she's only a friend." Reiner replied. "I brought her here because it was dangerous for her to be at home, we've killed a monster hanging from her closet and now it's releasing toxins." He continued. "If she moved, she could've died." He told Reece the truth, like Vitallin as well.

"That seems about right." It took a few minutes to settle down the familiar, yet strange atmosphere around them as Vitallin finally opened her mouth to curiosity. "So you really are a sorcerer." She said, gearing the attention towards him. "So you believed." Reiner replied. "He is." Reece butted in. "And you're a talking goat man." The girl pointed at the strange man knowingly. "Yup…oneiros kremas." Suddenly an ice cream sundae, and full rows of donuts appeared on the boy's work desk. "Wha-?" Vitallin was in shock to see such a thing appear. "Was that a spell?" She wondered in amazement. "Yes, It's for you." He offered. "Thanks." She takes a bite from her churro flavored sundae, and creme filled donut.

"Mmmm." The sweet treat swished inside her mouth as if they were singing together in perfect pitch, and harmony. "I can cast magic too." Reiner noted. "I believed in everything you said up till now." Vitallin said. She was still in shock that her best friend was a wizard. *How long were you keeping this from me and how did it happen?* She thought. *We've been friends for fifteen years.* "Pyrina louloudion."

He chanted as huge, blooming roses enveloped her blonde locks. She touches them gently. "Could I learn magic?" She questioned the possibilities. "It's only through generational witches and wizards." Reece explained. "Their ancestors, and new generations were chosen for particular paths." He continued. "There would be no need for regulars." She felt disappointed. "So what can I do?" "Live your normal life." Reece insulted with irony.

"But that's so boring…can't you take me on…whatever you guys do?" Reece looked at Reiner with great contempt. *Remember what I told you.* He thought. *They might come out to get her, along with everyone else.* "Ah, no that's not an option…" Reiner said, motioning his hands around. "It's too dangerous, and you might die." He was sure she would catch on to that since she's been in so many dangerous situations in her lifetime. "No fair…" Vitallin pouted. "Are there any other secrets you're hiding from me?" The girl wanted answers. "No, but I promise to get back to you at all costs." A promise he was sure to keep.

"Well could I stay here for the night? I'm too scared to go back to my house…" She asked as it left an open window for an excuse. "Um…" "That's fine." Reece cut him off from speaking. "Thanks." Vitallin was relieved as she really didn't want to go back. "Reiner dinner's ready!…And bring that ram head too!" Kareen yelled as she placed food onto the table. "Care to join us?" Reiner said with a polite tone.

"Sure." The strong scent of chicken breast, and spinach permeated throughout the rooms. Stuffed chicken, and cuban rice was laid out before them, vibrant with color and texture as the creamy cheesy spinach was oozing out of the chicken in such a delicious and delicate manner. "Thanks." The kids said.

The night was peaceful as they ate, compared to the day they had. *So is this normal for them?* Vitallin thought in sound silence. "So Vitallin, how's this semester treating you?" Kareen asked. "So so." She said. "I was in need to catch up on all of my projects, and past homeworks so…" She sighs. "Hopefully you'll get them done." Reiner joked. "We'll see who finishes first." Vitallin chuckles. "I'm finished." Reece said as he finally spoke.

After dinner, the three decided to go to sleep early. Reiner wheeled Vitallin to his room and placed her on the side of the bed. "Thanks." She politely acknowledged. "No problem." Reiner stretched as he slipped onto his side. Throughout the night the three slept well for hours, but soon after Reece awoke. "Reiner." He whispers in a low tone. "We need to go." Reece said as he pointed at the marble box. "But what about—" He hushed him up, placing his finger on his lips. "I got that covered, l'era oneir…"

Reece whispers as he casts a spell onto the girl. "There. She'll enjoy her sleep at least." He assumed. "Epichrysomeni porta!" A door with a crown design appears and opens up. "Let's go." The ram said as they both headed inside. "What did you do to Vi?" The boy said worryingly. "I cast an illusion spell on her." He said. "I don't think she'll be waking up for a while." While stepping their way into Randleman town, the weird stench of blood and carnage lingered within the hot, sunlit air as if they stepped foot into a war zone full of casualties.

Was it a scented mirage? *There's even guards walking around town too?…* Reece looked around the area. Magnum's guild was nobleship, and integrity as king Merium was their leader. Despite his old age, he had the speed, and strength to take down over a thousand opponents at once. He's been chanted as an overlord throughout his lifetime. He's spoken at best, but ruthless and unforgiving at worst.

"Why are we here?" Reiner asked. "To sneak." Reece smiles. "A friend?" "No, information." He put emphasis on information. "I'm wanting to know how Magnum's guild operates; their plans, techniques, and goals." Reece continued. "So when that day comes, we'll be prepared to fight for our title." The man was enthusiastic yet felt weak, as it was his strength vs. the other guilds. "And you're doing that by walking in head on?"

Reiner couldn't quite understand Reece's motives, as it's his way of doing things. "Watch me." The ram replied as he hushed up the conversation between the two. "Who goes there?!" One of the Magnum guards yelled. "These two said they were planning on entering the Magnum guild sir!" A young town woman was eavesdropping on their conversation. "If it's necessary for king Merium to let you in, then do by so, otherwise we'll have no trespassers." The guards were in high demand on instructions as always, so the two thought of a plan to get in.

"Tell your king that we have an additional act in our treaty." Reece was slick. "Are you from another guild?" He asked. "Not necessarily, but I am relevant towards a certain district." "Which one?" The guards continue to press for answers. "This information is to be enclosed with the king." Reece hushed as he knew what he was doing.

"I'll let you talk to king Merium, only if you leave the young man outside." The guard wagered as he looked at Reiner. "That's okay." The boy didn't want to be caught up in Reece's plan, nor "consequential" actions. "See ya." He winks a goodbye to Reiner. He heads towards the castle stumbling through a short forest as he follows a nearby crow with an amulet collar on. *Cute crow.*

Reece thought. *An M for Merium, huh?* Every step closer gave him the urge to defend himself; an excuse to impulsively fight. *I'm close.* The castle wasn't that far off, noting that it was near the town of Iron Blood. Reece felt Merium's presence near the front gate, "Seems strong I suppose…" he said to himself softly as he felt the strength and power within his own heart. He knocked on the door. "Hello! My name is Reece Eatherlove, I've came to deliver a message to the king."

The ram was at ease as he went along with the plan with good intentions of snooping. "Under king Merium's orders, I shall open the gates for you." A guard replied. "Thanks." Reece walked through the kepler chained gate. The castle was massive with nearly thirty-seven rooms both upstairs, and down. He wanted to decide where to go but nothing piqued his interest. "Hello, you're Reece Eatherlove correct?" The king said. His voice was clear, direct and commandful like how a king should be.

"Yes." Reece said. "You're king Merium correct?" "Correct, please take a seat." The king requested. While the two sat down with coffee, they were each examining each other's "senses". Merium was quite strong, and quick to question. "What's your message?" He asked. "There has been an additional act within the Tressfer Declaration."

Reece continued as he was wanting to gear the narrative towards Magnum, and its relations. "It's apart of act three: No guild shall synthesize weapons out of organisms, which includes taking biological properties of a man like eyes, heart or blood." He sets his coffee mug at the side of the table. "Are you harboring any advanced weaponry?"

Reece said this with a straight face. "Are you associated with Hide?" Merium questioned with suspicion. "No." The calm and collected ram replied. "Then yes. Magnum has iron blood infusers that cause manipulation towards the joints, and skin of the subject. They can never get cuts, scrapes, or anything of that matter because it regenerates itself." He continued. "The joints increase jump height, and reduce the aftershock from falls tremendously." *Interesting.*

The tone of the atmosphere grew serious. "Raven trains in groups, does Magnum as well?" "Certainly." He said. "As the captain of the guild, I train with my subordinates Alex, and Christopher." "Are you aware of the king's title?" This was Reece's final question. "Certainly, I'm wanting to prove myself as the greatest king alive." He stated. "Supreme Justice. As ruler, I get to form a legacy others would appreciate, and follow." Each town knew about their leaders ideals, and wishes, and would already respect to a certain extent. *How lame.* The ram thought. Seems as if he wanted to spice things up.

"What would you say if I were to kill one of your members in a fight?" He said wanting to challenge. "Then you'd be victorious, the match would be over." Merium replied, given only a hint of sincerity. "Let's say I conquer Magnum, and take control of your life and loved ones." Reece threatened. "Their life is mine." This provoked the king as tensions were running high, and implications were being used. "If you think you can take control of my guild I'd like to see you try!"

Reece teleported and tried socking Merium in the face before getting thrown across the hall. "Dammit!" Reece hit the ground with sharp pains in his arms and sides. The guy was on edge since Magnum was a northern guild, it was all the more sweeter to kick a district's ass. *Tsk!* "I'll enjoy beating the shit out of you!" That wasn't enough to kill his anger. "You would have already lost the moment you've started boy, If you were planning on scheming like this during the day of kings, then wake up!"

Reece got up from the ground. "Shut up old man!" He yelled. "I'm going to be the ruler of this entire region!" It was his goal, and heart on the line. He charged and clawed through the king's training uniform, exposing his hard abdominal muscles through years of fighting. The ferocious ram managed to throw a punch at him but was ineffective. "Thermiko yama!"

Merium opened his mouth to release a flame so hot it turned whitish-blue. "Ha," Reece was lucky to be quick enough to dodge that by climbing behind the man's back. Merium grabs Reece from behind and slams him onto the ground. "Shit!" Reece had to escape his grasp otherwise he's done for as the king was punching him continuously over, and over. "I will become king!" Merium twisted Reece's lean arm backwards. "Ahh!" He screamed as he squirmed on the ground helplessly.

"I'll slowly rip your limbs apart." It was ruthless. Reece desperately thought of a way to escape, even if it meant using a pathetic move. "Ariantika opla!" He pointed towards the sky as millions of bullets rained down from the ceiling, "Schedio holo…" he could now see more places at once for a chance to escape as he broke out from his grip, and ran into an unknown room. Inside was a jail cell, and a timer clock counting down towards the day of kings. "Whoever's there, don't come near!"

A voice yelled from afar. "Stay back! What more do you want from me?" The estranged man's voice turned into crying. "Huh?…" Reece was unsure who, or what was inside. "I'm going to release you, but after that you gotta run quick!" He commanded. "You might die if he catches you!" The two men both said in unison.

The two men ran towards an exit near the side of the castle before Merium could find them. "What's your name?" The guy asked. "Reece, Reece Eatherlove." He continued. "I'm an independent fighter, and an associate of Crow."

"You are?…" Reece turned the introduction onto him. "Lee, Lee Price." The man continued. "I'm a professional assassin for my home guild Warfall. They took me in and trained me when I was thirteen years old. I was assigned a partner to work with named Lex, but unfortunately she died…" Lee nearly shed a tear. "I failed as an assassin." He mumbled underneath his breath. Lee felt extremely guilty for letting Lex down, yet if she were alive she would've called him a champion. "That's such a hard burden to carry."

The two were nearly out of breath as they ran through the forest, Reece was still in pain after having his arm twisted, and nearly torn off. He knew he had to get to a hospital fast as they were approaching the town. "Reece!" Reiner waved upon catching sight of him. "Who's he?" Lee wondered. "My partner in crime." "You're his familiar?" "Correct." Reece noted. The two meet up with Reiner near a crowded vendor. "So how was the plan?" The boy wondered.

"Could we go to a hospital nearby? I'll tell you later…" Not having any more regeneration candy left Reece felt as if he couldn't go on much longer, Merium's punches really got him good. The Radical Healing Clinic was east of the city, near a nearly deserted town called Farehart. It was quite a walk but they managed to make it in no time. "Hello, welcome to Radical Healing, what can I help you with today?" A bubbly lady at the front desk announced. "I'd like to check into the E.R. it's an emergency." Reece politely said. "Sir, please take a card and go into the rooms two doors down the right." The lady instructed. "Thanks." While in the waiting room, Lee and Reiner talked.

"Hi, my name's Lee Price. Your friend out there saved me." He continues. "I'm a member of the southern guild, Warfall. One of their assassins." Lee whispered in a low tone. *An assassin?!* Reiner thought. "Don't worry I won't harm you. I've been trained into the guild for years. What's your name?" The man extends his hand for a greeting, as he was wanting to be friendly. "Reiner."

"I don't know much about the king's title, but I'm wanting to find my father Jeffery Strife." "The Hide member?" Lee exclaimed. "Yeah and if I were to achieve the king's title, I'd hope he'd at least be proud of me." Reiner was interested in knowing more about Jeffery, especially the bad parts. "Is Jeffery really that bad of a person?" He questioned. "Hide associates are investigators and anti-sorcerers, so in my opinion yeah."

Lee continued. "Their essential goal is to get rid of all sorcerers, and familiars for some reasons." Reiner didn't quite know how to feel about Hide as he doesn't know his role in this world. He ended his statement there as he stretched. Reece walked back into the lobby with what looked to be wrapped up gauze on his right arm for lacerations, and a black brace where Merium twisted his arm.

"Let's go." He said as he signaled the two to hurry up. "What happened with Magnum?" Reiner questioned. "I escaped a fight, but managed to know information about them." Reece said. "You were fighting king Merium?!" Lee exclaimed in confusion. "You're not that strong are you?" "What's that supposed to mean?" The faun got annoyed.

"Once I see that old man again, I'm going to make sure he pledges to me! Least if he's alive." His words stung to the heart as if he got pricked by a bee. "Why would you want the king's title?" Lee asked Reece. "So I'd know that I'm the strongest." He was serious, and unwavering when it came to strength and the level of status for himself.

Throughout his life, Reece has always been a hard worker yet often felt unfaired by the people around him. No matter how hard he tried, he was never given the credits, and opportunities he deserved; whilst the people around him were undeserving as things were not made for them it was out of their range. He felt as if he was a promised king amongst fools. True to an extent. "Your tenacity reminds me of Lex a little."

Lee laughed. "She would've loved to work with you." After their visit to the clinic, Reece and Reiner head back home while Lee returns to his home guild. "Does the room light ever change areas?" The boy asked. "Nope." Reece said. "Well, I don't know…probably." The light was seen glistening above the clouds. "Epistrofi." The ram chanted as they floated towards the sky. *It was never like this before…* Reiner thought to himself. Once inside, the two saw Vitallin awake unbraiding her hair with a brush on her side. "Hi." She smiled widely as if she had a secret to tell.

"What day is it?" Reiner questioned her thought process to see if anything was wrong with her. "Tuesday…" The girl softly replied. "Did you remember me and Reece leaving the other night?" He questioned her once more. "That was two days ago." She was fine, but it seemed as if time speed up. *Really?!* Reiner thought. *Two days?* "The time within my world is different," Reece explained. "The place is slower so days and nights stretch, setting foot within that world gives an illusion especially if you're not from there so anything parallel like this world would've speed up without realizing." Reiner was astounded. "So we've been inside there for two days? It certainly didn't feel that long." "Inside where?" Vitallin asked as his location caught her attention. The boy nearly forgot she was in the room. "In the deep woods, near the east end of the docks there's a certain tree…" He continued. "It's a pathway to my home world, I sometimes take Reiner along." "That sounds stupid…" She said, unbelieving. Reece made up an excuse, their adventures were far beyond reach.

"Aren't you going to school today?" Reiner had asked. "If I could borrow your clothes maybe." Vitallin suggested. "What about your skirt, you don't like it?" "It's lame." She said. "A suit and tie is more grasping than a skirt, no?" Vitallin tried metaphoring. "No?" Reiner replied with uncertainty. "Either way, it's original." After their tangible chat, Vitallin wheeled herself to the bathroom to change clothes.

"So what are you going to do with her?" Reece questioned Reiner's actions with a concerned face. "What do you mean?"

The young man said confusingly. "You know what I'm talking about Reiner, just don't get too attached to her." "Sure, I promise." He declared. "I don't really believe in promises." Reece stated. "You either do, or you don't there's no holding in betweens." Meanwhile once Vitallin was done changing, the two headed off to school. "So how does it feel to wear my clothes?"

Reiner questioned in a funny tone. "Great!" She replied. "I feel as if I could be myself. It fits well." "You look good." He commented. Once they reached the entrance of the school yard, by the corner of their eyes they saw Eddy getting beaten up by a group of boys in which it looked like they were from another school. "Hey tar boy, tell me where Brinner is or else!"

The young man continued punching Eddy in the gut until he spoke up. "He's not coming today!" Eddy screamed in anguish. "I don't know where he is but he's not here, let go of me!" He tried fighting back but it was no use as the group of boys were about twice his size in weight and height, most of all their weapons. "We wouldn't want any limbs hacked off now would we?"

The young man lifts up a knife and proceeds to hack at the kid's legs, and stomach. "Ahh!!" Eddy's gut wrenching screams were torturous. "Help me!" He yelled as blood was spilling out like rain on a field of flowers. It was serious. "Stop!" Reiner cried out, without hesitation Vitallin grabs a mid-sized taser from her bag, and hands it to him while she calls nine one one. "Fight!" She tells him.

"I wanna see how far you can go to protect a life precious to you." She knew whom she was implying.

CHAPTER XII

A Gearing Discovery?

Surprisingly, Reiner wasn't scared as he knew what both of them stood for, strength. Reiner crept up behind the tall, stocky young man and tased him in the neck. "What the—" Once he turned around the boy then sucker punched him in the face as hard as he could. Meanwhile, Eddy winced and cried in pain. The sensations within his legs were so severe he was afraid to move so he stood still on the ground while the police, and ambulance came. "You wanna die now?!" Reiner threatened the group of boys with a menacing face of anger as he slowly walked towards one of the boys grabbing him from behind and forcibly pinning his face towards the cold brick walls of the school.

"Antistre'fo!" Reiner summoned a combustion spell which caused the young man's stomach to bloat up like a balloon as his internal organs began to swell inside. "Ugh…" The delinquent felt nauseous, then began vomiting up blood. "Wha…What's going on?!" He had such an uncomfortable sensation that his skin tore through then burst open like a watermelon. *Shit!* Blood was everywhere as Reiner didn't know what to think. That was his first kill.

The two quickly left the area before the cops arrived, luckly Eddy covered for them and told his side of the story. "I hope Eddy's okay…that fight looked nasty, those assholes." Vitallin nudged Reiner's arm as they looked outside a nearby school door.

"I killed someone." Reiner said softly. "To protect." Vitallin reassured him. "It was either him or Eddy." She said, "This school doesn't need anymore tragedies." *How could you be so calm?* He thought. "I was once brushed with death, remember?" She told him. "Every stabbing sensation got me close to wondering, why is time on the bad guys' side and not on mine? Shouldn't the innocent live a little for having such a cruel fate?" Vitallin continued her speech. "As I layed helplessly on the ground, my situation was unjust; I didn't have time and the killers got away. You did the right thing, freckles." She smiles as she gives Reiner her perspective. "Thanks, coast clear?" He asked. "Yeah." She replied. "I hope you didn't take the act personally, it *was* self defense."

The two went down the now deserted hallway. "What did you think he wanted with Brinner?" The girl asked. "To fight perhaps…or deal drugs." They managed to sneak past geometry class undetected, and unnoticed as they blended with the crowd. "Alright class, take your seats!" Mr. Mountgomery said. "I hope you're all ready for today's quiz." The man said. "It'll be a mock five so be prepared." The class felt more crowded than usual.

"After school, could you show me the hidden world?" Vitallin stealthy whispered. "No." The young man replied as he patted her head. "How lame…I bet that goat guy would." Reiner rolled his eyes. *As if, he would be the least person to.* Despite wanting to let her see, Reiner kept Reece's words to heart as that place was vastly beautiful, yet dangerous; he couldn't afford anymore suffrage, especially after what happened to her.

Once the mock five quiz was completed, all pens and pencils were down. People got up from their seats to stretch while others talked as usual. It wasn't hard to tell that the test was difficult. "All good Vi~?" Chrissie said, hulling the girl's wheelchair back and forth. "Yeah, that stuff was hard." "Well you should've studied harder." Reiner jokingly butted in. *Haha, as if you had any time to…* She thought as she batted an eye towards him. "Fire! Fire!" A young man suddenly shouted across the hallway.

Teachers and students from every class rushed to fill the area as they saw the flames grow louder, and louder. An extremely foul scent stained the air like a crushed stink bug, almost as if it were rotting flesh. "Everyone get back!" The teachers yelled while others called nine one one. Without thinking, Reiner decides to put matters into his own hands.

"Pago koilo…" He muttered underneath his breath. Suddenly, water spills from the hall merged together and formed ice crystals which soon turned into a gigantic sphere enclosing the flames. "Kafsimo!" A random student yelled, it was the voice of a female…a witch? The flames diminished as the sphere combusted. "What the—?" The students, and teachers were boggled out of their minds after what they just saw. "What is going on here?!"

People looked around to see who caused the spellbinding magic, while Reiner wanted to know who finished it. The hallway was left with charred residue as the large group of students opened the janitor's closet. "Oh my god!" Inside they laid their sights upon the body of a decapitated woman, her blood was everywhere; on the containers, cleaning agents, shelves, and mops. "Everyone in the classrooms now!" The teachers screamed while they called nine one one. Reiner and Vitallin were shocked as to who could do such a thing, strangely enough there was a note next to the body reading *From Raven: The new god!*.

"It was a guild member…" A girl said walking up towards the two. She was a fairly tall student with long, brown, wavy frizzed out hair (that almost looked dried in a sense) the girl seemed stuck up in a way, but her emerald green eyes spoke otherwise as they were attentive and friendly. "You were the one who cast that spell, no?" The girl questioned the young man. Reiner didn't know what to say but it was obvious she knew. "You were the one who finished it correct?" *He* now questions her. "I saw the crystals forming from the ground beside you." She continued. "Along with what you said." *She is a witch!* The boy thought. "Well it took action once I heard you finished it." *What guild is she in?*

"I'm able to use parallel magic, I add or take away meaning from other mage's spells. I can also invert attacks as well…" She smirks at Reiner as her eyes grew cold causing Vitallin to hold onto his arm even tighter. "Ha!" The estranged girl laughs. "It seems as if your girlfriend here is frightened." "Leave her out of this!" The young man yelled. "Lay a single hand on her and I'll beat your ass!" Reiner ment it. Behind that sweet exterior was a fighter willing to protect what he had left. "Anyways, Raven's guild leader was behind this."

She said, gearing the attention towards the note. "Someone must've known that wizards were nearby." But who? "My name is Elizabeth Valentine." The girl introduced herself. "And this will possibly be the last time we'll meet, just watch your back." The estranged girl left the scene moments before the cops arrived, while Reiner and Vitallin hid inside the classroom with the other students. *This is bad.* He thought. *Real bad.*

As the incident cleared up, the entire school was sent home early. As to while most students were talking about the gruesome murder, the young man had other things on his mind. *Am I being followed? How was there another wizard in school? What about the box?* "You okay…?" Thankfully his friend snapped him out of it. "Huh? What…"

"What's wrong?" She was serious, and grabbed his attention this time. "You know, that girl." He said. "Elizabeth?" Vitallin replied. "She seems snarky—" "What guild was she from?" Reiner asked. "Guild, What's a guild?" She was confused as she didn't know what he meant as his thoughts slipped out. "A club, like a section within a church." Reiner was so off but he didn't want to lead her on.

"Is that about the different church reformations?" He soon leaned over the wheelchair, and kissed her forehead to shut her up. "Let's just go home." Reiner took the girl to her house, then walked over to his soon after. His day was confusing, and grimm as death was around him. All he wanted to do was get to Reece fast. "Hey—" He zoomed past his mother and went up the stairs towards his room.

The ram was levitating near the corner sleeping. Reiner touched his pale, lean abdomen startling him from his peaceful state. "What?" He grumbles. "There's a situation." He wanted to reveal so much. "Someone from our school was held hostage, and murdered." He continued. "It was a guild member who did it. There must've been another wizard, sorcerer, or mage involved at school." Reiner ended his exclamation there. "Do you know what guild it was?" Reece yawned though he wasn't really attentive.

"Raven." The boy told. "Raven…" he laid on the bed but with slight attentiveness. "It's a really dark, and crafty guild." Reece said. "It's also my wife's home guild." He sighs in misery. "They also dabble in dark magic like forbidden magic in which they can locate any mage, and witch nearby as for any other sorcerer." *Elizabeth…*Reiner thought, though he didn't want to say anything. "How is forbidden magic different from the others?" The boy spoke up. "Forbidden magic casts eternal curses onto anyone subject to it, it's like immortal torture. Despite living forever you'd be in extreme pain or have something latch onto you like having snakes eat away your insides or bearing never ending cuts all while your loved ones die before you." This made the boy worry. "You can defend yourself can't you?" Reece then questioned. "Otherwise, be careful. It's your life, deal, wishes, and the title at risk." The faun soon closed his eyes and went back to sleep. *You're my partner, aren't you supposed to help?* The boy took matters into his own hands yet again. Now understanding the magnitude of his situation, the young man knew how serious things would be as he knew the war for a new world was coming ever so close.

Reiner grabs Reece's spell book from his desk drawer, and figures out how to cast a gateway spell. "Katafygio…" He whispered in a soft tone as he knew the faun could possibly hear him. The boy disintegrated without a trace as he ended up falling mid-air into the eastern plain of Anon. "Ahh!!" He had to find a way to break his fall when suddenly, he heard a voice. "Parino Pitsi!"

A particularly handsome young man, with light blonde hair yelled out to Reiner. "Take flight!" With the whirly gust of wind the boy soon found himself flying next to the young man. The guy had a feminine "good natured" feeling to him with a flawless face, tousled blonde hair, plush pink skin, green eyes, and a birthmark near the corner of his left eye. "Hello." He greeted. "My name's Matthew, what's yours?" The man asked with such an angelic tone within his voice. "Reiner, Reiner Strife…" Reiner started doing tricks as he levitated in front of him. "Reiner…Strife?" The guy tried pronouncing. "Nice ring to it."

"What guild are you from?" Matthew wondered. "I'm not sure what guild I come from." Reiner replied with slight confusion. "I came from the other world." "Are you a sorcerer?" He then asks. "Yes." The boy proudly announced. "Who's your familiar?" "Reece, Reece Eatherlove." He answered a simple question, "The vice leader of Crow…?" that led to a can of worms. "Must feel lucky to be the partner of a head member."

Could this have revealed much? "What's he like?" Matthew asked. "He's really determined, tactful, blunt, and a bit of an asshole." He was honest. "Seems strong." Matthew cited. "A few miles to the left is my home guild, Hawkeye. I've been adopted into the guild at age fourteen." The man pointed south as he continued. "I found my familiar Noulege, after my aunt tragically got murdered." Matthew continued. "He was the one who saved, and raised me since then. We've trained most of our lives together."

This caused Reiner to reassess his meaning of relationship with Reece. Hawkeye was an interesting guild built upon friendship and love; their guild leader Renaldo, had a tragic test of perseverance as all of his friends, and loved ones died at his kingsmanship ceremony. Years later he was met by Mr. Kaillo, his personal mentor who told him to keep living for things to get better, as he would be able to see things through and to have a chance at getting the king's title. Since then, Renaldo trained his hardest with Mr. Kaillo for eighty-two days before getting over his intense state of depression.

Mr. Kaillo soon suggested starting a guild to see his potential fruition, and resolution for his fallen loved ones. "So Reiner, why are you here?" The man questioned. "Raven's guild leader murdered, and held a woman hostage. I've also found out that there are other sorcerers roaming around my school." He explained. "Other people might get killed and—" "So fight." Matthew concluded. "If people attack what's precious to you, what would you do?"

He continued. "Would you stay still and let them take things from you? Or would you prevent, protect, and fight for your beliefs, friends, and family? I'll help you sneak into Raven, only if we become allies…" The young man suggested. "Really?" This was a new challenge for Reiner as he had to face his fears, and fight as it was a means of war, and revenge. "Yeah, it's nice to fight with friends." He smiled, cheering him up. The two head towards the city of Versai, on the way there they stumbled upon a giant, scaley yet furry beast as it bared its ginormous pitch black wings towards the starry sky. "Gahh!"

The creature yelled with the lowest tone imaginable, frightening the two young men. "Woah…" They said petrified as they backed back. It seemed as if the mysteriously horrendous beast was caught within a tight wired net, begging to be freed as it frantically wiggled its neck around. "What should we do?" Reiner asked confusedly, "The only thing we can do, set it free." He replied stating the obvious. He grabs a steel dagger from his pocket and hands it to the young man. "Cut the net." "Right." The wires were four inches thick and patterned. Unfortunately, the dagger was far too dull to cut through so Matthew got innovative. "What are you…?" The boy said upon seeing the sight of Matthew gnawing through the wire with his teeth.

"What are you doing?" Reiner says. "I'm able to melt the wire with my breath." Matthew explained as his fang like teeth turned black, releasing steam. "It's a spell Noulege taught me when I was little." He continued. "I can melt my way through anything: metals, diamonds, etc." Reiner was impressed. There were so many spells that were passed down from multiple generations ago, some aren't even practicable today. "Got it!"

After setting the beast free, it spread its wings again and let out another daunting screech once more. "Gahh-!!"

"What's wrong?" Matthew frantically worried about their safety for a moment. "Gahh! Gaaahhhh!!" The creature continued to screech louder, and louder. "Stop right there!" A voice called out as there were two tall men approaching behind them. "Don't move any further!" One of the two men pointed his musket gun at Reiner's forehead. They wore black combat boots, and baggy uniforms that kind of resembled Hide, but it wasn't. "Gaaaahhhh!!" The creature grew more rampant than before.

"Okra, be quiet!" The other man yelled, calming it down. *Okra?* The boy thought. *Was it their pet?* "Stay still Reiner." Matthew said as he tackled one of the men onto the ground, digging his face into the soil. He then proceeds to gnaw upon the man's neck with his steamy, hot black teeth. "Fuck!" He yelled in excruciating pain. "Seph!" The other man quickly jabs Reiner in the neck with his musket blade, "Fight Reiner!" Matthew hollered as loud as he could. Hazy and blurry, the young man attempts to cast an enchantment spell: bodily enchantment, "To aima urzei" to be exact.

Moments later, the man's blood began to boil creating burns, and blisters as blood was escaping from his eyes, nose, and mouth. "Marco...Seph...down." *Huh?* The creature spoke with a low tone. "It talks?" The two took notice as they saw the thing fly away. "That's amazing, Reiner." Matthew was astonished by the boy's enchantment sequence. "It talked, and flew..." Reiner thought the beast was more important. "Where do you think it went?" He asked his friend. "I dunno, wherever it went it knew these guys." He mentioned as he looked at the two dead men behind them.

"Who are those guys anyways?" The young man asked as he saw Matthew loot through one of their pockets. "I found a key, money, and a locket." He revealed as he lifted up the objects. The strange man had sixty-five shekels in cash, a silver home key, and a guild locket with a photo of his three children inside of it. What was oddly enough about the locket was that it had the letter R, and the name Raven on the bottom of it.

"It's a Raven member!" Matthew said with a hint of laughter hidden in his voice. "They weren't so tough after all." "Hmm…" Reiner was surprised, and alarmed at how vicious he could really be. "Should we head on?" He asked with certainty. "Yeah." The two continued their route towards Versai and before they knew it, they were walking through the town of Bellemere. It was late evening as fireworks were going off, and people could be seen dancing together outside the streets as there was a parade nearby with sweets and fried food like chicken, corn dogs, and vanilla rose cupcakes.

"Hi Bellemere!" A young girl presented herself on the balcony of a large mansion. "Ahahahahah, this is fun!" She said sitting upon the ledge. "Good evening, Madam Maria!" Some of the townspeople called out with glee, and cheers which caught Matthew's attention as she was just a short little girl with chestnut brown hair and gray eyes. She wore a beautifully ruffled, sheer violet dress with glitter all over. What's so special about her?

"Dear citizens of Versai, and travelers!" A stern voice of a fairly thin elderly old man cried throughout the town, silencing the massive onlookers for a moment. "As you could tell, this is a wonderful celebration for my granddaughter, and vice-president of Raven; Maria Ciago." The elderly man continued his speech. "She has conquered many regions, and lands belonging to other guilds in the past, but unfortunately Okra shared some bad news today." He continued. "Two of our members Marco, and Seph have died in a fight..." Surprisingly, given the fact that most of the Raven members are insanely powerful beyond belief.

"We should walk further down." Matthew whispered as he tapped Reiner's shoulder from behind. "That's the vice-president of Raven?" The boy said with disbelief. "Shhh..." He hushed him up as they made their way near the outer side of the large mansion, bypassing the people and familiars around. "Gah, Gaahh!" A recognizable creature was spotted in its gigantic cage, flailing its wings around. "Shit, it's that beast from before!" Okra's eyes were blood-shot red as if someone sprayed lemon juice onto them. "I knew it was their pet." Reiner commented as it yelled louder, and louder.

"Ahhh!!" It screamed. "Murder! Murder!" Reiner quickly devised a way to burst through so they wouldn't get caught. "Falaina ble kanonas!" A large archery bow and arrow formed within his hands as he fired as hard as he could. "Boom!" The freckled plush brunette blasted through the side of the house creating an extremely wide, gaping hole seeing through the downstairs banquet area. "What was that?!" Maria questioned as she ran inside as fast as she could. The blast was so alarming that the people thought it was a terrorist attack.

"Halt! Who are you?!" Multiple butlers surrounded the area with hilarious weapons like glasses, tongs, and hard food in hand. Reiner looked through each room: bedrooms, bathrooms, and gym rooms to see what he could mess up. He started breaking mirrors, ripping photos, tearing clothes, and running the water on to cause a flood. Meanwhile, Matthew was fending off the servants once he heard footsteps. Tap, tap, tap…The sound of high heels were clearly noticed. "Amanio, Staviche, and the rest of you…please stay back!"

Maria grew from annoyed to furiated. "Who are you, and why the hell did you bash through my house?!" She didn't want to pay for all of this. "Answer me!" The girl yelled. *Why is this little shit a vice?* He wondered to himself.

CHAPTER XIII

A Different Venture

Maria grabs Matthew by his collar and begins slapping him around. "IF-THIS-IS-NOT-YOUR-GUILD-THEN-GET-OUT!!" She repeated over, and over. "Shut up!" The man was repulsed by her attitude, so he pulled her by the hair. "What are you doing sending people to kill innocent lives?!" He yelled. "Are you trying to slaughter my race?!" Matthew thought about his time together with Noulege.

"You're not gonna do anything to stop Raven…" Maria said in a menacing tone as she stared him down with pity and mockery. Crash! Bang! Loud noises were heard across the other end of the banquet hall within the upstairs rooms. Maria slowly turned around to see Reiner throwing flower pots onto the ground. "Haaah!" She screamed with every degree of fury, and rage. "What are you doing?! Get out of my room!" Reiner threw a basket at the girl's face before having her melt it with the palm of her hands. "Jasper, Cornell! Sick now!"

Two gray spotted hound dogs ran after the young man, their fangs were foaming and ready to attack. "Ahh!" "Hggrrrr…" They sicked their teeth into Reiner's calves, piercing through his black uniform pants. "Matthew, run!" He threw him an artifact of a monk. "Guards, after him!" She commanded. "I'll deal with you myself kid, just like that woman."

Maria was far beyond livid as the two ruined her birthday parade. "Machairi Chalazi." Knives from all directions came at Reiner at full speed as the boy quickly made his move into another nearby room. "What the hell?!" What he saw was gruesome, as he stumbled upon a cascade of sticked human heads. Among them were the heads of previous fallen guild members whom the girl conquered. Reiner felt as if he were going to throw up, he knew he'd be next if he didnt make it out. "I see you found my trophy room." The girl stepped in to play, and kill. Reiner was sweating bullets as he tried reasoning with her.

"I'm sorry but you murdered innocent lives! It's only right that you get what you deserve!" How rational…He then charges and tackles Maria onto the ground. "Let go, you bastard!" She hollered. "So you're the vice-president, let's see what you can do." Reiner challenged as he had to grow up and focus on the title that holds all, the king's title. "Tiger Roar." Moments later, the house began to shake as the boy started punching Maria over, and over. "It's no use boy. It's over for you." Maria eerily spoke as she grabbed his throat and yelled as loud as she possibly could, like a lion. "HAAAHH!!" Suddenly, Reiner's heart started beating faster and faster. He couldn't breath as he nearly passed out while struggling to stand. "Le…ugh…" The boy didn't want to say anything, as he didn't want to waste his last breath.

Finally, Maria released her grasp on the young man, and threw him onto the ground. "Could you stand now?!" She was annoyed as she got up and crouched beside him. "How did you guys get this far anyways?" She wondered while poking his face. *Is he…?* Maria placed her ear onto Reiner's chest. *He's not rising, there's no beat…he is dead.* She thought to herself. "Seems like this battle is over. Never mess with vice-presidents." She calmly said.

"Reece, where are you going?" Kareen wondered as she noticed him creeping through the halls from the dining room. "I'm going out." He answered. "I need some time to get out more, that room is cramming me." "Pfft!…" Kareen snickers. "I don't think anyone would take you seriously." She imagines the possibilities. "Anyways, don't go causing trouble…you might scare someone." Reece grinned as he exits through the door. "Will do!"

It was a beautiful day today; bright, calm, and sunny. *Where should I head to first…?* The ram thought to himself. After visiting a cake shop away from town, he decided to go to Reiner's school to check out the crime scene. "So this is the place huh?…" He wondered as he walked through. No one was inside as it was past four-thirty, the time where kids usually leave out. The halls within the first floor seemed normal: clean floors, regular slender dark blue lockers, chandeliers, and everyday wooden classroom doors.

Reece felt as if he were the biggest snooper of all time, so he checked the second level too. As he walked up the stairs to the second floor, he saw a girl cleaning the walls. *What is she…?* This interests the ram. Sparking plenty of mischief, he wanted to scare her off so he began pounding on the walls real hard. Bang! Bang! Bang! "Ahh!" She screams. "What the hell are you—" The girl looked at the horns, hooves, dark green leg fur and guild tattoo. "Reece!" She ran in to give a hug. "Reece, what are you doing here?" She was obviously happy to see him.

"And you are?…" He couldn't quite put his finger on it, but was surprised she wasn't scared by him. "It's me, Elizabeth!" The girl smiled widely. "How could you forget your own guild members?" "Hey how are you—" Before he could say anything else, Elizabeth grabbed Reece's arm and rushed into a nearby classroom to sit down. "It's so nice seeing you here." She leaned in across the desk. "There was a murder here today, and I was just staying behind to take in the feeling of the aftermath." Elizabeth cutely told with all her subtle slyness.

"Was it that Raven leader who caused all this?" Reece asked though he already knew. "Yeah, how did you know?" "My partner already told me." "Partner? Who's your partner?" She questioned. "He's a kid within your grade who is a bit passionate, gullible, friendly, and better yet determined." *So it's that kid…*She thought. "He has much power within him though…" The ram told. "If he were to be a sorcerer, I must've seen him today somewhere."

She continued. "Welp, how's Crow doing?" Elizabeth asked. "Mr. vice-president." "Crow's defenses need to be lodged." He continued. "We need to come up with a defense strategy, and draft in more fighters, and skilled sorcerers." He said. "Crow is strong, but isn't certain enough to beat Magnum, nor Hawkeye just yet…" He puts his head onto the desk. "But we have you, and Xavier." Elizabeth said. "Most of all his abilities are forbidden, it's perfect!" She tried rationalizing their situation.

"I lost to Magnum's guild leader, Merium…" He sulked. "Imagine that during the day of kings." Reece was annoyed at the fact. "You're getting ahead of yourself. We aren't there yet as we have a few years left." The girl reassured him. "Years can pass like months, and months like days." Reece replied. "I'm wanting to win this for all of us." After their coincidental meeting, Elizabeth hugged Reece once more as a goodbye. "Thanks for listening to me all that time." He said. "No problem, and thanks for accepting me into the guild…"

Elizabeth tried to kiss Reece on the neck before having him push her away. "No no no." He scolds. "I have a wife, got that?" "I understand but…" Elizabeth's love for Reece was purely out of romantic/lustful feelings for him, in the end she was genuinely happy to see him though. "Nice seeing you Elizabeth." Reece waved as he departed. "Nice seeing you too, vice-president." While leaving Reece took in a scene of the school, as he felt that it would become a hotspot for every battle imaginable. Least to come.

Maybe I should go see Vitallin. He thought while walking near the area. He stepped onto the steps of the front door, and knocked as hard as he could. "Um…hello?" Mrs. Dubarse answered. "Who…Why are you?" She thought she was talking to a guy in theater arts as she was taken aback by his horns, his nails, his fur, and his overall appearance…"Hello ma'am, is Vitallin home?" He was being polite as possible, despite his situation. "Yeah, but please don't come in…I'll get her." She offered as she didnt want him to come in terrorizing her house. Mrs. Dubarse didn't know what he was capable of doing.

"Hi, Reece right…?" The two greeted normally this time around. "Vitallin, I want you to tell me about your relationship with Reiner." He commanded. "Ah…Reiner?" The girl was hesitant to talk. "He has been my best friend for years ever since we were little." Vitallin continued. "Reiner is sweet, kind, and precious to me…I wouldn't have him any other way." "So how was that murder?" He questioned. "If your knight and shining armor died protecting you, how would you feel?" Reece knew where he was getting at. Such tragic intent.

"What?" She felt offended, yet nonchalant about the entire thing. "I wouldn't cry or anything, we've both been through a lot of things as I've been brushed with death, it's only fair that he experienced what I felt." The girl would've held Reiner's life, emotions, and even death with pride only looking at the efforts of their labors.

"I'm assuming that he's trying to fight a guild leader." Reece said. "Huh?" Vitallin was confused, yet heard that word before. "Reiner is fighting a pastor?!" "What are you talking about, a guild is a sect group of magicians, witches, and sorcerers." He shouldn't have said that as this got her excited.

"Can I join?" Vitallin asked with a smile without getting her hopes up. "The only proper way is if you form a contract with a certain familiar. Unfortunately, I can't help you in that department." He continued. "I know he's fighting for his father's sake, but also for your safety so It's best for you to stay put." With that being said, they both ended their conversation there.

What's going on? Where am I?...And why is it so dark? Confusion, and panic shrouded the boy's head. "Help me!" Reiner could see the connected link between his body, and soul withering away ever so slowly. "Help me!" He cried out once more. "Who's there?" A soft voice echoed through the area. It was pure literal light that took away the spatial darkness from corner to corner. "Lift up your hand." Reiner heeded its instructions. "Within the darkest of rooms, your light will always shine through." The voice chanted away.

Suddenly, the whole area was lit up, and he could see where he was. It was a gigantic room which looked like a reception area for a funeral, all of Reiner's friends and loved ones were there crying, and sobbing with excruciating sadness. "What is all this?" He wondered in horror trying to figure out such a thing. "This is your funeral..." The voice itself belongs to a sandish blonde haired man named Galihade. Tall and gentle in stature you'd think he wouldn't have fought in the previous day of kings.

Galihade is one of the current title holders now watching over everyone within both worlds. When someone dies, Galihade reviews their life and shows them crucial parts of their past, present, and future. "What's going on?" He couldn't care less about who he was talking to, all he wanted to do was make sense of his situation. "You're dead, for now." Galihade pressed. "That girl's magic was extremely potent and complex." He continued. "Though there has to be a way I can get your soul back into your body…" "Could that be possible, Maria busted through my arteries." Reiner said.

"I can fix them for you." The man offered. "I use forbidden magic." Galihade smiled with certainty. "So what do I do now?" The young man was feeling uneasy, and nervous by the minute. "Let's go over your life, and we'll wait for your help to arrive, surely someone knows you are here." Reiner's life has impacted his emotional development; he has fought people who've either offended, or wronged him in the past, but is currently improving.

"This is your father Jeffery Strife." Galihade explained. "He's a hard working man, who decided to work for Hide." "Decided to work for Hide?" The boy spoke up. "In the human world, it's hard for this universe to reach out to." Galihade continued. "There was a cursed fortune teller who told Jeffery about a certain leader containing information about an organization that exerts peace for world order." "Like a cult sort of…" The boy guessed.

"I'm assuming he was in a state of depression and grief, so he wanted to lose and help himself at the same time; figuring that humans were helpless, impure, and doomed within themselves. He took up the offer expecting direction, peace, and tranquility." All in all, Jeffery did the deed. "Jeffery Strife works for them in spite of their flaws and corruption. He thought that Shuttman could bring him happiness and escape from his problems with death."

"He was brainwashed to work for them?" Reiner exclaimed. "In a way, though he must've been on board himself." Galihade said. "Why is he with Hide?" "They took him in to extract their plans for a new governmental civilization, superior weaponry etc." Reiner sat next to his cousin Bruce Lanerty; he was always a quiet man who kept his money, and business to himself. *Bruce...* He was crying immensely.

"He deeply cares about you." Galihade said. "But we can change all of this from happening until the time being. Basically, just wait for your help to arrive...In the meantime I can talk to you about magic, and universal rules." He explained. "So why are you really here?..." Vitallin said. "I was just taking a stroll around town, and decided to see you." He felt funny saying that as it would've been the most he ever did for a person. "Thanks, you take care." She waved goodbye.

To even want your loved ones to give their all for you... "Nea Pyli!" He opened a gateway to the other world. *I can sense him.* He knew where the kid was at, and did not press on any further. Meanwhile, Matthew was almost out of Versai, lucky he fought through the guards and assistants. *Why did he throw this...?* He looked at the odd artifact of a monk sitting on a box wearing large prayer beads around its neck. *Could it grant wishes? Is it magical?*

The only way he would know is if he tried it out. "Come on..." He briefly rubbed the relic against the palm of his hand. "One, two, three..." He chanted. Moments later, a cloud of blue smoke appeared and shocked Matthew. "Ah!" The pain was mild, and subtle. "What is your wish?" The artifact talked. *Whoa, so it does grant wishes!* "I would like a replica of Markov's wand, and larger fangs." The man commanded. "Grant accepted!" *Cool...Maybe I should give this back to Reiner.* Matthew thought. Last time he saw the kid, he was fighting Maria and minutes had passed since then.

The cheery young man decided to go back and find him, as he hasn't quite left the massive city. "So this is Versai…Anri~" Reece's mind went on a tangent. *How dare he come to this place without me.* He thought. *It serves him right if he's not worth the challenge…* Reece knew that Raven's guild was difficult to fight. He searched through every area of the western town once he noticed a parade of people. "I wonder what all this is for?" He slowly walked through the crowd of people trying not to be noticed, but what he could notice was a large gaping hole within the side of someone's house.

"Pfft!" He laughed. "Someone had to have caused this." The ram took a peek inside and saw the expensive room demolished as it was flooded with water, dirt, food, and glass all over the place. "Wow, what the hell happened?" Reece crept his way inside, though the place was empty. "Reiner!" He cried out. "Reiner, are you here?!" No reply.

He then searched through each and every room before skipping into the "head" room. "What the fuck?!" His impression was that of Reiner's, the decapitated heads were gruesome, torn, and bruised. "Reiner!" Reece caught a glimpse of the boy, and rushed to his side. He placed two fingers on his wrist…no pulse. *He can't be…* He thought. "He's dead." Maria said. "How do you know him?" She asked.

"I'm his familiar…who are you?" The ram questioned. "The vice-president of Raven." *So you're a vice too?* The mood grew intense. "So what are you going to do about your partner?" Maria asked. "I used an anatomy spell that killed him." She told. "Reconstruction magic huh?" *That vs. esper magic…* Reece wanted revenge. "Ack!" He choked Maria onto the side of the wall. "What…are…you?" "Let's see if I can put your head on one of those stakes!" And revenge he got.

"Pologizo Faira!" Reece pierced through Maria's chest and ripped her heart out, instantly killing her in the process. "I guess you didn't have a heart for those people you've killed." He repulsively jokes. "It seems as if your help arrived!" Galihade smiled. "How do you know?" "I can see through your eyes." He continued. "The people you've met and places you've been to were all sought through your eyes." The man elaborated further.

"I gather information from everyone, and everything all by seeing through them." He said. "Reiner!!" Matthew yelled as he rushed into the house. *Oh great, more noise…* Reece thought to himself. "Who are you two, and how do you know Reiner?" He questioned. "I'm his friend, and this is my familiar Noulege." Noulege was dewy with beautiful dark skin, dreadlocks, and decorated with jewelry. He was a wolf.

"Hello." The man introduced himself. "We're here to rescue your friend, Reiner gave me this artifact that grants wishes." Matthew continued. "I was wanting to give it back." "It might be useful because he's dead." Reece pointed out the fact.

CHAPTER XIV

I Caught You

"So he isn't breathing?" Matthew was sad. "Are you Reece?" He asked. "Yeah, why?" "You must be Reiner's familiar." The young man continued. "He told me all about the vice-president of Crow. Here." The young man hands Reece the artifact. "Rub it onto the palm of your hands three times and make a wish." It was hard for him to believe in it after the first rub, but soon after the third he began to chant something strange. "Anapnoi organou… anapnoi organou." Reiner's organs reconstructed as his body started to rise slowly.

"He's breathing." Matthew smiled. "Yeah from the looks of it…" Reece thought the spell sequence needed improvising. Noulege suggested lighting something near his body. The ram did as told and began chanting another sequence louder, and louder. "Imarimadae kenchiki wo! Imarimadae kenchiki wo!" With flaming hands he quickly clasped his hands together.

"It's moving…" Noulege said noting towards the boy's hands and feet. The young man blinked once, then twice.

"Hi…every…body." Reiner struggled to talk. "Your back!" Matthew hugged tightly causing blood to come from the kids mouth. "Hey Matthew, and—" He turned over to Reece and smiled. *I knew you'd come through.* "Hey Reiner," Matthew said, holding his attention. "I'd like you to meet my familiar Noulege." The boy greeted with a wave. "Hello." Noulege announced himself. "Matthew told me some things about you." He said in a smooth, and polite manner.

"Enough greetings…" Reece said. "We better get out of here before someone questions their leader." He killed Maria. "Alright let's go." The four head out of the mansion and into the evening city of moonlight. There were many buildings, and shops around to go by. "Maybe we should stop by a cafe." the cheery young man suggested. Once they got into the Drunken Raven, the four made their way into the back of the room where they could see everything.

"Hello, welcome to Drunken Raven what would you gentlemen like?" one of the waitresses greeted with bubbliness, and respect. They handed over the menu board. "Thanks, that'll be twenty-six shekels and fifty-two cents please." Matthew hands the lady cash. "Wow…" Their food looked delicious: two scones, six egg sandwiches, three coffees, and three creme custards.

After dinner, the two pairs split ways before having someone catch Reece's attention from afar. *That scent…it has to be.* There was a woman checking out flowers near a bouquet shop; she had long, shiny red hair and wore a flowing black dress with gold jewelry. She was stunning. *It can't be, can it?* "Gah!" Reece placed his hands on the woman's shoulders, startling her to turn around. "Anri!" Without hesitation, Reece pulls the woman into his arms. "I knew I'd find you…" He muffled into her shoulder, and cried.

"Aww, poor Reece…I knew you'd come after me too." The woman said softly as she kissed his cheeks. "You aren't dead." He mumbles. "I'm wanted." She whispered. "I'll tell you more once we're in private." She soon kissed his forehead. "Come with us." Reece offered. She was delighted, yet afraid as it would make matters worse. "Yeah…" Reece was ecstatic. "Thank you." He hugged tightly while the three made it back to Pruitte Dr.

"Reiner, I'd like you to meet my mentor and wife Anri Eatherlove." The boy waved with a hint of familiarity rushing over him. His room was quiet and clean as the way they left it. "Hi." The woman greeted, and waved back as Reece continued to hold her tightly. "Down boy." She motioned him to back off. Reiner was amazed to see his mentor's mentor; it's like noting a grand elder. "So questions…" The kid said, hesitant for answers. "What happened to you?" This took her back as she was afraid to say. "I kidnapped, and murdered some guild members from our allied sector." She continued.

"Their leader broke a peace treaty and held me captive in their prison for about three years, now I have a bounty on my hands, and sparked a new enemy." "So you broke an allied trust?" Reiner asked. "Unfortunately." It was more than she could chew. "Next question. Why did you marry Reece?"

Reiner was curious as to why him in a sense. "Hahaha, what kind of question is that?"

The woman laughed. "Reece was beautiful inside, and out…" Anri continued her story. "He cared about me, and my situation when no one else understood, or was too scared to." She said. "He's the most genuine challenger you'll ever meet, we're perfect for each other." Anri kissed Reece's neck. "I love Reece with all my heart, and I'm sure I'm the same with him. You're grateful to have met him too, right?" She asked.

"Yeah, of course." Reiner replied. "He revived my life." He continued. "There was a guild leader who killed me, but fortunately he was there to cast a spell sequence to resurrect me." Reece smiled. "It was his willingness to help that kept me alive." "See, he's great!" Anri smiled. All of these heartwarming statements were making the ram blush. He was just relieved to see his wife again.

"I love you too, Anri." Reece said back, snuggling up against her. He has never shown this much affection towards anybody before. "You can stay here with us as a refugee, Kareen may understand." He said. "No." She rebuttled. "If I stay here I'll cause trouble for you guys and might have a greater sentence." The woman was in a sticky situation, but had to get him to understand. "I love you, you'll always be mine forever no matter what!" Anri hugged Reece tightly. "I love you too much to let you go again…" He admits. "I promise to come back for you."

They kept it to themselves as they reached a decision. "Mystiko koraki!" Anri opened a portal to her home guild. "This isn't the last goodbye Reece." She gave him hope. Once things were all said and done, the room was silent as she left the scene. "Well that sucks." He was happy, yet felt bummed that his woman was gone. "She murdered an ally." Reiner softly said to himself in thought. "I wonder why." "Possibly for a good reason, allies can backstab first at any moment." Reece made a point. "They *are* the ones closest to their potential *opponent.*"

"Ever think you'll find her again?" The boy questioned with empathy. "Hope so…probably, probably not." He replied. "She was a wish granted." Ring-ring! Reiner's phone rang. "Answer silly." Vitallin said, slightly gritting her teeth together. "Hello?" He answered, but he wasn't silly. "Vitallin I love you." Reiner exclaimed as he now realized what death meant. "What's this about?" She was startled. "I now see how you felt when you were getting stabbed, and I can't live without you."

He genuinely thought about the scenarios of missing her. "Reiner what the hell, what's wrong with you?" She was offended, yet still concerned for him. "If I died, how would you feel?" He wanted honesty. "Dummy, why would you say that?" She could ever wonder why. "Just curious as to what you would do." The young man pointed out. "Bye Reiner." Click! Vitallin hung up unannounced.

I loved what I missed about love… The evening was full of required feelings, and longed love as Reiner proved himself, and Reece found hope in Anri again. Two weeks passed by and Reiner headed off to school. This proved well noting that nothing else happened on school grounds since the murder, but now most students were talking about magic, and the unknown sorcerer. "Hey Reiner." A random kid went up to the boy's desk.

"Who do you think the wizard is around here?" "Huh?" He felt pressed. "You know, that kid who said that spell the other day, the one who diminished the flames." The kid said once more. "Yeah…It was cool right?" He knew he had to lay low. "Um, could you get off my desk." Reiner politely asked. "Sure." Ding-dong! Ding-dong! It was eleven till, and class was about to start.

It was English two hundred and one with Mrs. Brookes, luckily it was one of Reiner's tolerable classes, despite his pressured image of being the boy wizard. "Everyone pass up your homework and get into groups of four." She commanded. "How 'bout it." Elizabeth said scooting next to the young man. "Wanna group up?" *How much effort did you need to say that?* "Yeah sure." Each group was assigned passage cut-outs, the goal is to sort it onto whichever literary que it goes to.

"Could you help instead of talking Elizabeth, we need to finish this." Reiner was super focused. "Yeah, yeah…" *So this is Reece's contract holder…* "So, about that murder…" The girl was interested as to what he did. "What about it?" He questioned. "You told your familiar Reece, didn't you?" *What?* The boy thought to himself. "He already talked to me about it." She continued. "He's the vice-president of my home guild Crow, he's a pretty powerful leader." *So she's from Crow…* "I guess you and I are allies." He motioned trying to influence her.

"Not so fast turtle." She insulted. *Turtle?* "You're not strong enough to be my ally, but you seem like a hard worker." "So you know Reece?" He changed the subject. "Duh he's our vice-president, didn't he tell you?" "No." Reiner replied. "Well you need to ask better questions." Elizabeth said subtly scolding him. *Don't I ask enough?* "Have any of you completed your assignments?" Mrs. Brooks asked. "If not then don't waste time, we've got a lot to do today."

People were rushing pasting passage cut-outs together and their explanations. Once english class was over, Reiner made it to his locker where he heard students gossiping about the unknown sorcerer. *I might need to lay low for a while…* He felt the pressure get to him while walking to his next period, it would've been easier if Vitallin were here. "Yo ho, Reiner!" Elizabeth could be seen trailing behind him.

What do you want now? He tried ignoring her, she was in a cheerful than normal attitude. "I wanna talk to Reece again~" She had her hopes up. "Not today." He waved. "Just go to class." Once school was over everyone packed their things and went home. "Ahh!" A student could be heard a few distances away. "Ahh, get off me!"

It was a female struggling to ward off a black, grotesque, and bizarre looking creature; it was gigantic and slimy like a parasitic worm. "Help me!" The girl cried out in desperation and terror. "What the—?" Other students froze with confusion and fear as the feelings of panic rose upon their faces. "Get the teachers!" They all yelled as they scrambled around the entrance. Reiner was just about to grab things from his locker before hearing the whole commotion.

"What?" Right before his eyes the creature gouged one of the girl's eyes out with its mouth. "AHH!!" Blood spurted out in liters as she tried hanging on to hope any way she could. "Flogovolo!" The boy ran towards the young girl whilst throwing fireballs at the monster before tackling her onto the ground. "Quick, call nine one one!" He yelled.

"My eye!" The girl was in an immense amount of pain. *Why the hell is this happening?!* Reiner had to think of something quick. "Suck on these…" They were regenerating candies he snuck out of Reece's pouch. Moments later, the muscles in the girl's eye healed but formed a blood clot. "Whoa dude…" The students were in shock, and disbelief.

"So there are wizards among us!" Their weeks worth of suspicions diminished. "It's a sorcerer!" Give and take, he knew what he had to do. "Attention everyone!" Reiner yelled. "It's my duty to protect this school!" *Why are these things here?* "No questions out of the ordinary, I'm just a normal person like you." He wanted everyone to calm down and believe in him, so he humbled himself. "I'm here for—"

"Cool so you're magical?" "How long has this been going on?" "What are these monsters?!" One by one, more and more students rushed in for answers pertaining as to what was going on. "Okay everyone what's going on, get on the buses now!" The teachers wondered why the kids were scattered around. "Mrs. Baker, Reiner's a wizard." *You're kidding right…?*

She gave a look of annoyance. "Wizards, and magic aren't real." She stated further. "They are only creative notions of the—" Suddenly, Elizabeth grabbed Reiner and teleported without a trace. "Are my eyes tricking me? Or am I going crazy?" Mrs. Baker said. "Did that girl just disappear?!" Elizabeth teleported the boy to a nearby neighborhood. "What are you doing?!" Reiner exclaimed, feeling rushed. "Don't blow your cover idiot!"

She scolded. "There might be other sorcerers nearby, you should thank me for getting you out of that situation. That school is a hot spot for sure." The girl sighed. "You're strong enough to fight aren't you?" Reiner figured. "That's not the point." She replied. "Isn't this about protecting innocent lives you're so hung up on?" Elizabeth continued. "Someone else might become a message of war like that woman earlier." "But you are strong aren't you?" Reiner asked once more.

"Yeah, of course!" Elizabeth knew her strengths well, but diminished the fact that Crow wasn't quite. *Tsk.* She sucked her teeth. "What about you, you nerdy ass turtle, aren't you scared about your safety?" She tested his nerves. "I know my strengths, but learn from my weaknesses." He proudly said. "I have someone to protect, and wouldn't want to go into the unknown blindly just to prove that I'm the strongest and shit."

He got right to the point. "Strength is about enduring, and standing up for what you do to carry on despite the mistakes." "Then don't make any, and don't be reckless." Elizabeth rudely commented. "The reality is that we are fighting to regain power, whether it be your responsibility to protect others or not. This is the reality of the king's title and beyond for you and I."

The girl ended her statement there as she looked at the bigger picture. "To gain control over everyone's life, got it." His ideals still stood. "By the way, why did you want to talk to Reece so much?" This made her blush as it dropped the tension. "That's none of your business!" Elizabeth huffed.

"Then there's no point in letting you see him." He concluded. "I said it's none of your business, okay!" Her face turned tomato red.

"I…I have a *problem* with Reece and…" She felt embarrassed. "Do you like him?" Reiner asked. "Of course but…" She had to admit it, as it was half the story. "I wish I could be with him but he has a wife and unfortunately I can't interfere with that." Elizabeth was annoyed, yet jealous of that fact. "Fight me."

Reiner wanted to wage a deal. "If I win, you can't talk to me for twelve weeks and if you win, you get to see Reece." The young man declared. "That's a waste of time, just let me see him." She was annoyed. "Fine, just take me home." Once they reached Pruitte Dr. Reiner took the time to introduce his home. "There." He said. "The ram lives here with me. There's an upper level, and a lower level with five rooms." He figured she'd know where to go.

"Come inside and head upstairs two doors down to the right." The boy instructed. "Thanks." Elizabeth crept through the halls. She could feel the flustered sensations of warmth crowd around her head as she made her way to the door. Errk…"Who's there?" Reece said expecting it to be one of Reiner's friends. "Hi Mr. vice-president, sir!" Elizabeth took a bow. Her palms were so sweaty, and coupled along with her blushed out face you'd think she suffered from rosacea. "Oh, it's you…come in." Reece said, recognizing her face.

"What do you want?" Despite his tone of voice, and friendliness Reece didn't have time for chit-chats as he was in the middle of planning out a list of attacks and alliances. "Yes,

Reece…" The girl looked up to face him. "I received a word from executives Edward and Laura that a secret weaponry compartment has been sought after." She continued. "Many guilds are tampering with the condemned weaponry sir. Some are even using bio-chemical warfare for their gains."

"Well thank you my little messenger." Reece smiled. *I'll take note of that.* "I'll get out of your hair now." Though she didn't want to leave just yet. "Where is the boy?" Reece asked. "He was behind me, but I gave him advice on his new life." She said. "The title could be given over to anyone, and they can either flourish, or ruin everything as life is literally in their hands." "Our hands." He implied the guild.

"We will win on the day of kings, and our efforts will show." Reece was proud of himself and held faith in his team members. "Thank you Reece." Elizabeth said with gratitude. *That's why I like you.* Once the information was spread, the girl left the house and decided to investigate further for Crow's sake. "Yper pyli!" The girl created a planned portal into the other world; this would make it easier for her to teleport within universes.

"There, I'm in." The city of Meshenna was near dawn as the sunset was gleaming, brightening the entire town which was barely deserted, giving Elizabeth a way to make her way into the secret base with ease. "Alright." She said, giving encouragement to herself. Apparently, the compartment was underneath the floors of a ball venue; a massively elegant place to hide such a warhead. White marbled architecture, statues, and flowers were scattered all over the area.

Elizabeth found the centerfold of the floor and wedged her heel between the creases of tiles, lifting them up. *Perfect.* The tiles showcased a ladder hidden underneath them in which she climbed down from. "Steady now…" She made her way down inch by inch clutching on the bars tightly as possible as the height was at least twenty-seven feet high.

The underground room was glowing green as it was from the weapontry's bio-chemical substance infused with titanium, and radon. She stepped on the soil like ground. Cannons, ammo, and other weapons were stuffed into organized crates. "Wow…" The girl was beyond amazed, some of the weapons were clean, others were broken and tampered with.

Elizabeth picked up one of the objects to check them out; it would be extremely dangerous if left in the wrong hands judging by what they've done. "Hello!" She yelled testing the echoes within the massive cellar, moments later someone greeted her back. "Elizabeth!" A holographic man appeared out of a tiny flashing device. "Elizabeth, this is Xavier reporting." He continued. "I see you've found the base Edward was talking about." "Correct." She replied.

"The members from the other guilds are illegally tampering, and stealing evidence." He continued. "These weapons were used within the war of Heath two and a half decades ago. It was a civil war fought over the previous kings, and even challenged their treaties." "So you mean to tell me that these are ancient weapons sir?" Elizabeth asked out of interest. "Correct, along with having the guild leader's souls within them." The man confirmed.

"Amazing." Elizabeth said in awe as the thought of having ancestral leaders inside a weapon sent shivers down her spine. *What should I do to help this place?* Clack clack clack…Someone was nearby. "Who are—" The girl questioned before turning around to see a tall, docile looking woman with red unruly hair who was wearing a large black hooded cloak as if she was a home rebel. "Hmm…"

The lady gave Elizabeth a confused face before touching one of the weapons on the ground. "Hey, don't touch that!" She cautiously defended herself. "Why not? It's my business after all." The lady continued. "I'm able to revamp these weapons and find use from their components like warfare!"

The woman pointed a cannon onto Elizabeth. "Fire!" The cannon's blast was so loud, it made their little ears bleed a bloody nightmare. Luckily, the girl hid behind a far out crate. "My guild will flourish." The woman said as she slowly walked up to her, and violently grabbed her by the hair. "Ah!" She screamed. "You'll die here little girl." Suddenly the woman lifted Elizabeth's arm and burnt a quarter of her skin off causing second degree burns. "Haah!"

"You know, I'm using these weapons to enhance the human condition." She teased. With all her will power, Elizabeth tackled the woman and punched her face as hard as she could over, and over again. "I said don't touch!" She was irritated by this point. "You dumb bimbo, why must you do this on sacred grounds?" The girl was given a chance to investigate something great…

"Neo Kyma!" The strange woman yelled, turning the cellar into an acidic hurricane releasing the chemicals within the weapons. *Shit!* The girl made time to evacuate the room before taking a dagger herself. As Elizabeth climbed her way to the exit, she couldn't help but to breathe shallowly as the acidic fumes were masking the air. Luckily, she made it out on time. While laying on the ballroom floor, Elizabeth caught her breath once more and ran towards the emergency exit as fast as she could.

I can't let this woman catch up with me... She thought as she hid behind an alleyway between two buildings. *Did she even make it out alive? What guild was she from? I bet Siren...* Curiosity escaped the girl's mind as she wandered around town looking for a place to figure everything out.

CHAPTER XV

A Horde Of Crows

"Hello, welcome to Moonlight. How may I serve you today?" A bartender greeted Elizabeth up front. "Care for a seat?" He seemed polite and caring. "What can I get for you?" He asked. "Two chased rum please…" She anxiously said. "Woah, woah, woah…hold on there little girl." The man seemed surprised. "With rum like ours, and a size like yours you'd be hitting, and breaking everything by the end of the night. Are you sure? You might like something else." He suggested.

"Two chased rum please…" She said once more this time with a slightly pleased tone of voice. "Coming right up!" The man placed the alcohol beside the young girl. "Think you can chug all that in one go?" He asked. "She could." A voice of a man stood from the crowd as he got up to greet Elizabeth. "Hey Elizabeth, I see you took one of those weapons…"

"Xavier!…I mean president!" She exclaimed with honor. "What are you doing here?" "I should ask you the same." He smiled. "Wanna race?" "Woah, woah, woah sir." The bartender was concerned. "With any given chance she might pass out." He continued. "With alcohol like ours, and a structure like—" "I'll take twenty of your strongest gins sir…" Xavier said, handing over sack of two hundred thousand shekels. "Twenty gins coming right up!" "So Mr. president, Reece talked to me about employing generals around Crow's base, how would you feel about that?"

Xavier tucked a string of long blonde hair behind his ear. "I believe that we do need more armed factions to protect Crow, along with allies but some of our men act too recklessly." The bartender sat another drink down before having Xavier take a sip. "Some even go against strategies and rules by governing their own parties; setting up flawed ones instead of efficient ones." He told.

"Well, it's like teaching a dog new tricks." Elizabeth said. "What happened to your arm?" He assumed it was in regards to the mission. "A lady burnt my skin off, it still hurts…" She whined. "Here let me gauze it up." The president offered. "Thanks. Do you wanna race now?" She asked Xavier, pointing at the condensed row of glasses. "Fine by me." Her leader replied. "Hey, the winner takes all trophies from the back along with free bragging rights…" The man hinted towards his forthcoming enjoyment. "Ready, set…go!"

Drinks after drinks were being chugged one by one, left and right; the chilling sensation brought burns at the back of their throats. "Wow, I didn't think she would gulp the entire thing…" One spectator commented in which soon after, a crowd of onlookers were cheering her on. "Girly! Girly! Girly!"

"Ah~" Elizabeth was down to her seventh glass of gin, while Xavier was on his eleventh.

"Ugh…" The two were nearly wasted. "I qui—" Bang! The guild leader fell from his stool and collapsed onto the ground. "He-he-he, I win." Hazy dazed, Elizabeth closed her eyes and blacked out. "Great, now I have to clean this mess." The man said polishing his trophies. He moves the two outside of his pub. "Crow members, huh?" He said with a low foreknowing voice.

Elizabeth and Xavier were completely wasted, but luckily they managed to open their eyes. "Weer we at Xavier?" The poor girl struggled to talk as she slurred her words. *Damn…* Xavier felt as if his migraine would split in two. "Can you even stand?" He questioned. Surprisingly, he was coherent with his words and thought process. "Yeah, thanks."

It was a cool evening time, and Meshenna was as peaceful as she found it. Elizabeth opened a portal back to her home and decided to look upon the gigantic weapon. *The souls of the ancients reside in these weapons huh?…*

She thought to herself as she came to a conclusion. Two weeks have passed and Reiner hasn't been in school since then, he could be seen training with Reece outside an empty rec center.

"You gotta spare faster than that." The ram said. "Your opponent could see your openings, and vulnerabilities before you ever could." "I see now, thanks." The boy has gotten quite agile recently. "And what's with that bow? You know archery?" Reece asked with interest as if it were a level up in skills. "Yes." The young man said. "A little girl named Cammie taught me."

He continued. "Her parents died a few years back in which they would have seemed like good people."

"She was walking the trail I was at and wanted to talk to me for support." He was grateful to have met her. "Show me some moves then…" Reece said while placing multiple stickers upon a tree stump. "Very well then." Reiner picked up his longbow and arrows and began shooting as fast as he could. "Woah!" He made perfect shots around the tree timing himself with every range.

"Impressive…" Reece said, trying to pull the arrows that were stuck. "That girl could even do it when it's flamed." The boy stated. Speaking of flames…"Hey, did you know that Elizabeth liked you?" He continued. "And why didn't you tell me you were the vice-president of a guild?" "First," He responded. "I already knew that about her, I have a wife but she just won't quit."

"Secondly, I didn't let you know because I didn't want you to compare yourself to me, I'm your familiar and we're all in this battle together." Reece wanted Reiner to train and not use him for everything. "The day of kings is approaching ever so slightly." He said. "There's no time to fool around." *It gets serious.* The next morning felt cooler, and cloudier than normal. "Vitallin, could you please stand then slowly sit back down for me please."

The rehab specialist instructed. "Ouch!" She yelled in pain, it was still hard for her to move despite being bound for so long. "Hmm…" The woman thought about what could help. "Take this, it may make you drowsy; if so, sleep it off but it's supposed to numb your joints so you'll become stiff." The girl understood and let the medicine take its course. A few hours in and she was half asleep. *I hope I can walk again…* Vitallin thought to herself. Subtle, caring hands wrapped around her neck; the warmth seemed heartfelt as if the person knew her from somewhere.

"Vitallin." The voice of a mysterious woman called out to her. "Who are you?" She asks with slight curiosity. "My name is Racheal, your familiar please form a contract with me." Once Vitallin looked above her she saw a gorgeous woman with deep hazel eyes, and shiny long black hair looking back at her. *Contract… Why?* She thought. "Why would I need to form a contract?" The girl asked, unaware as to what was happening to her. "To make you apart of my guild as a sorceress." The woman stated. "We could rule all guilds, and even a chance for the king's title." The lady continued. "All of your dreams may come to fruition."

The woman tried explaining, and influencing her. *Isn't this like Reiner and that ram guy?…* Vitallin was quite on board with accepting everything at this point as she wanted to know what the other world was about. "I'll sign with you." She said, giving her approval. "Good, now go back to sleep." She said in a soft, elegant tone. What was going to be about this new sorceress? What would Reiner think?

"Breach, Breach!" A little messenger scrimmaged through the room. "Leader, leader! Someone violated our trust ma'am!" The boy yelled as loud as a blow horn. It was only five years away till the day of kings in which war will break for the king's title, wars and final goodbyes. "What are you talking about?" Their guild leader asks. "Whom, and what?" "An ally ma'am, there were four warriors of the Warfall guild who kidnapped a quarter of our general armies, and stole several confidential manuscripts."

"Really now…" *A guild strong enough to take my army men.* Gail was silent "Well let's surprise them shall we." She continued. "Maybe we should steal their army's general and skin them alive till they release our men, and return our books." But her nurturing instinct told her otherwise. "Or we could get them all back and showcase an even better army." The lady smiled with deceit.

"Once we get the title, I'll ensure you things will become safe again." Mrs. Gail was the president of Siren. She was cautious ever since she saw her granddad pass away before her eyes, due to this she was forced to treat her guild members like family and blood relatives, imposing strict combat upon them so none other would die. "But Mrs. president." Gail hugged the young messenger boy. "Don't worry, we'll become the strongest guild and avenge your family okay?" "Yes." The boy replied.

"Reece, what are we doing?" Reiner asked, panting enough to catch his breath. The two were zipping through the woods like wild monkeys. "I dunno, why do you think we're here?" He gave him a rhetorical question. *To find out where these monsters are coming from?…*He thought. "I…I don't know." "We're here to venture, and fight some lowlives." He seemed ready to go. They were upon the trails of Crow's headquarters near Vidalia town.

"So this is your homeland?" The boy asked. "Sort of." Reece explained. "My homeland is near the east where I'm treated like a god by some due to being the vice-president." Reece felt their constant gratitude from afar like a tsunami wave. "Aren't you lucky…" The young man commented. "Not quite." Reece said. "I may get targeted for something, or put through treason by some asshole. Least I know what these people are up to." He said. "Crow is getting stronger, aren't they?" Reiner wondered what his guild was like. "Possibly." His familiar replied.

"I hope my members were strategizing without me, they can do fine on their own. Wanna see my guild?" Reece asked. "Yeah!" Freckles said with a face of cheer. It wasn't everyday for him to say that though Reiner was wanting to see what his guild looked like from the very beginning. They head through Vidalia town before heading east. The town was beautiful; bloomed flower bulbs upon the gravel streets, the scent of a bakery releasing the most flavorful of cakes, luxurious buildings stacking high to the sky, and peace throughout the air.

"Amazing." The boy said in awe. "This is the section of Vidalia where royal and upper class families live." Reece said. "I used to live here before I became a vice—" Boom! Suddenly, a loud explosion was heard coming from one of the buildings causing a raging fire. "Ahh, don't kill me!" A woman screamed from the top of the building. "Ready to fight Reiner?" "Yeah!" He said as they rushed towards the flames.

"Help me!" The woman yelled louder and louder for everyone to hear as she was in excruciating pain from her stab wounds within the heat. "Ma'am, where are you?!" Reiner yelled frantically, finding his way through one of the village homes. "No, Stop!" A large bird-like creature lifts up the woman's leg and proceeds to stick its needle-like feathers through her thighs all the way towards her pelvic area. "Gahh, Help me!" Tears welled up within her eyes. "Polairma!" Reiner froze the flames and headed over to the unknown woman. "Baah!" The creature screeched. "Let go of her!" He yelled as he grabbed a t.v. from the living room and threw it at the monster.

"Ahh!" Sparks flew everywhere as the woman fell to the floor. "Thank…you sir." The lady struggled to speak. "Let me help you." Reiner said as he took the large needles out of her jeans. "Ouch, Please be gentle…" She whimpered. "Come on, we have to get out of here." Reiner wrapped the woman's thighs with his jacket and carried her outside the house.

"What's your name?" The lady gratefully asked. "It's Reiner…" Reece said, waiting patiently outside the building. "I should congratulate you on successfully saving that woman." He said, patting his partner on the back. "You're one of the head leaders of Crow aren't you?" The woman spoke though she knew she was right. "Correct…?" "Please win the title to make these abominable things go away!" She frantically cried.

Were they coming from another guild? "I'll make sure of that." Reece reassured. "For now, find a new place to live." "Thank you for saving me." She said once more. "No problem, the kid is skilled." Reece took pride in that fact. Once the situation was settled, the woman was taken to the hospital for reported injuries. "Where are those monsters coming from?" Reiner wondered. "I mean they attacked my school and sent messages, are they from another guild?"

Reiner figured he could solve this. "Well wherever they're coming from, they're wreaking havoc." He stated the obvious.

"You were nice saving that woman back there, you think on your feet." "You would've done the same if you were in my situation." The boy said. "Hmm, you're right but I would've been much faster than that. Stayed any longer and you both would have died a gruesome death."

"I know…" Reiner huffed. "Let's head east." Crow's headquarters were distanced beside the woods, away from Vidalia town. The area was calming; a black stoned building with many windows, and many rooms. "Impressive Reece…" The boy was amazed yet again. "Yeah, this is what Xavier chose, he loved the architecture. Do you want to meet the other members?" The ram offered up the idea. "Sure, if they're nice…" He was nervous. "Isn't everyone nice if you stay on their good side?" He has a point. "Ehehe…" "What's with all the tension, they won't kill you."

This was a perfect time to tease him. "Here, hold my hand if it helps." Reiner was so nervous it was as if his organs were gonna shut down any minute. "I…I don't know what they'd think of me." His inferiority complex was showing. "Ever since I've known you, you've been a pretty go getter kid, don't get yourself down." At least someone had faith in him. "Sorry, my anxieties are getting in the way, I just don't want to become a let down since it's our guild."

"Toughen up and come on!" Reece was being passive-aggressive, hopefully this meeting would be a breeze. The two walked inside. "Reece your back!" A woman yelled across a pub table. "Reece, how's it going?" A few guys chimed in on the commotion as they were pleasantly surprised to see as they haven't seen him in a while. "Long time no see vice-president,"

A tall, stoic, somber dark skinned man with an eye patch smiled at Reece. "What's up?" "Hey Nathan, I've been taking trips with my partner Reiner."

He pushed the boy forward to introduce himself. "Hi…" The boy looked at the ground. "So this is the fruit of Simmerton's law?" The man examined as he looked at Reiner. "He's so young, can he fight compared to you?" The man asked. "Not as good as me, but I can see his potential." Reece continued. "His combat is amazing and he's a fast learner who is faithful." "I see he could be of use." Nathan assumed. "This guild has more than enough people anyways."

"Aww, such a cutie~" A woman spoke up. "What's your name?" She delightfully asked. "Reiner, Reiner Strife." He was still nervous. "Reiner Strife, how cute the vice taught you everything you needed to know huh?" "Yeah, he's been great helping me along the way." He said. "Don't mind me asking, but are you a sorceress?" The boy asked. "Aren't you upfront, of course I am but I don't have a familiar I'm advanced."

"She has been fighting for twenty-six years ever since she joined this guild." Reece said, reassuring him. "Her nickname is hard ball, don't let her looks fool you." Rosie was tricky, she had long curly blonde hair, olive skin, and sported a white lace sundress. She was cute but her combat style spoke otherwise as she could strangle two rampant horses with her bare hands, punch through a punching bag, and sweet talk her way out of a warzone.

It was as if a teddy bear could protect a grown man. "He's right, roses have thorns you know." The woman added. "Where's the bathroom?" The boy asks. "Upstairs, three doors down to the left." As Reiner went upstairs to the bathroom, he couldn't help but feel nauseous and woozy as his stomach knotted and churned; the anxiety he felt was getting to him so much that he vomited near the toilet. *What's wrong with me? What's wrong with this place?* "Knock-knock!" Someone was at the door.

"Are you okay?" The voice of a woman was heard. "May I come in?" She was worried. "Ah, yes please." Reiner said, giving her permission to open the door. "Oh my god are you okay?!" The woman bent down on the site of seeing the boy suffer. "Here, wipe your mouth…" She hands over tissues knowing he was in distress. "Please, tell me what's wrong?" "It's my anxieties…" The boy said. "For some reason I don't feel comfortable here because the atmosphere felt strange; it's as if I couldn't live up to this sort of standard…" He was being honest.

"Aww, don't feel bad." She patted his back. "Most of the people here are nice, yeah some can act tough but they're just assholes." The woman continued. "My name is Ellis but you can call me Eli, I've been in this guild for about seven years." Ellis seemed interesting with her goggles, brown leather jacket, distressed jeans and big curly afro. "What's your relationship with Crow?" Ellis asked. "My familiar is the vice-president." "You mean Reece, really?" She was surprised. "He's quite powerful isn't he?" "Really." Reiner responded.

"So you should be quite powerful yourself, no?" This made the boy vomit some more. "That's the point, having Reece as my partner I can't live up to the guild's standards." "We all have insecurities but it's a good thing that you're realizing the severity of the coming war." She continued. "Everyone here is on guard for the day of kings. Now calm down, and come down stairs." Ellis comforted him.

CHAPTER XVI

Maturity

"Reiner!" The ram shouted. "The boy's fine Reece, it's just a stomach bug." She said walking him down the stairs. "I feel better now." Reiner said with a faint voice. "Great, we wanna show you around the guild." Despite all this Reece was enthusiastically excited. The guild had nine rooms and a spell room. "This is the frequency room." Rosie said. "It's where we meditate and enhance our hearing." She continued. "It can let us detect enemies miles away."

"That's cool…" The young man murmured. "Next we'll go to the spell room." The spell room was interesting to say the least. It was a glass room filled with many potions, and many black spell books that were dusty and nearly torn. Strangely enough there were three green and black scally unchained dragons guarding the area. "What's with this place?" Reiner asked. "The spell room is primarily for Xavier's sake." Rosie explained. "He would test experiments on his dragons so that he could use them for the day of kings."

"So it's also to protect the guild as well?" He asked. "Sort of." After their trip to the spell room, Reiner decided to go home; he talked to Reece about his situation. "Could we go, I enjoyed the time you've spent showing me around." He wasn't kidding, he genuinely enjoyed the tour after the fact. "Yeah sure." Reece replied. "Going already?" Rosie asked. "Yeah." "See you next time, Reiner." Ellis winked as she handed the boy a bag of potato chips.

It was past midnight and the facility was working. "Certus es, ut 'puella?" An unknown monster said in what was to be latin. The creature was petrifying, fat, and smelly as if it bathed in fermented urine and hot oil. "It is, she's a member of Warfall." The other said.

Vitallin was fast asleep next to Racheal in a peaceful content state when suddenly, "Ahhh!!" Boom! Boom! With such strength, the monsters rammed through the side of the wall. "Wha-what are you?" A nurse shrieked in terror. "Die!" The creature tore her limbs apart, blood was splattered near the sides of the halls in which a massacre of bodies began to take place.

"Get the girl!" The monster said in a low growl. "Ha—" Racheal gasped, peering behind the vertical window of the door looking upon the hall of dead bodies. "Vitallin wake up." She frantically shook. "Hmm?" The girl was confused as to what the fuss was about. "We have to leave now!" The woman exclaimed. "Gnostes pyles!" Racheal opened a portal to the other side.

"We must hurry!" She grabs Vitallin's hand and enters through. "You can rest on me for now." Racheal said as the two headed to their home guild Warfall. "Racheal, do come in." Their guild leader said. "Thank you Mr. President oh and by the way, I brought my companion here with me, Vitallin." Racheal continued her story. "We fled the rehab center because she was being targeted by monsters." "That's fine by me…" Victor said, stroking his black grayed out beard almost knowing they had an unchained on their backs.

"I knew you were gonna come here, this just means more training for us once those monsters show up." Victor had strong foresight abilities, he could anticipate the future and its possibilities. "This girl could be a useful hint towards the king's title, she's eligible to fight with power like hers." The two looked at the girl as she was fast asleep. "As long as you keep her safe." "Yes sir!" Racheal saluted. "Where…am I-Racheal!" Vitallin woke up before realizing where she was.

"Vitallin, I'm here." She soothes the girl's surprise. "This is your guild Warfall." *Is this the world Reiner was talking about?* She was delightfully surprised to be in such a world. They weren't ready to leave just yet. "Were you really that scared?" Reece wondered. "Yes, having such a responsibility on my shoulders is a lot to bear." He continued. "I'm not as strong as you, and I could let the guild down." Not this again.

"We're all in this together alright." "The king's title is the only thing I'm fighting for." Reece admits. "What about you?" "My father, and the title." Reiner admits. "Then cheer up, and don't let anyone stop you." "Whether it's your family, or team members, never give up on yourself." Reece was a good pep talker, and mentour. The next day Reiner heads off to school.

"Hey the wizard arrived!" People were wanting to talk to "The young wizard." left and right.

*Please no more of this…*The boy thought. It was a pretty mundane afternoon, people were chatting, focusing on their projects, and copying homework. Luckily there weren't any monsters around. "Hey Reiner, can you fly?" A boy asked. "Um, no…I can't." "So what kind of wizard are you?" A female questioned.

"I'm the kind with responsibilities and such I guess." Reiner announced. "Class, stop huddling around the poor boy's desk." Mrs. Brookes said. "Pick up your books and read chapter seventeen." Once literary class was over, Reiner decided to call his friend, or lover. "Hello?" She picks up the phone. "Hey Vitallin, long time no see." He says.

"Ah Reiner, what's up?" "The people at school found out I'm a sorcerer." He anticipated her response. "It seems as if magic does exist…I'm a witch!" This caught him off guard. "What?" *Really?* "And I now understand the world that you were talking about." She says. *She went inside the other world? Who did she form a contract with? When?* He wanted to disagree with the thought of her being a sorceress as she wasn't ready, and would be put in more danger.

"Where are you now?" He asked, rushing to his house. "I'm in the other world with my familiar Racheal, she's helping me walk again." *Her familiar…*"Hurry back, I want to talk to you." Reiner mentions. "She's a contract welder?" The ram seemed puzzled. "Yeah." Reiner responded. "What guild is she in then?" He asks. "I don't know, she didn't say."

"Well hopefully she trains well, her path is in her hands now." He said. *But it's still dangerous...*"Maybe her ideals towards the king's title are the same as ours." The boy assumed. "That depends on whether she's good or not, and her guild." Reece exclaimed as he had a point. "Everyone is different when it comes to ideals."

The air was shallow, yet crisp as the colors of the field was bright and had such calming undertones. "Could you stretch your legs?" Racheal asked the girl as she put some sort of light-blue gel on her knees away from her red striped dress. Vitallin tried stretching as far as she could. "My friend wants me to go back." She said. "Try walking then." The woman requested.

Vitallin got up from her wheelchair and made her way inch by inch to the otherside of the field. "Let me help." Her familiar politely obliged. The girl started walking smoothly back and forth across the field. "There you go!" It was like watching a baby take her first steps. *I'm...walking...*The girl shed tears of joy. "Ouch..." Despite being in pain, she could still walk again nevertheless.

"This is amazing!" She was happy, and grateful for any help given at that moment. It's been awhile since she last felt the ground beneath her feet. "Do you wanna go back now?" Racheal asked, already knowing the answer. "Mmhmm!" She was delighted. Foreshadowed questions were drawing suspense and tension within Reiner, with the way things are, would things tarnish their relationship?

"Hopefully the monsters aren't here." Racheal said. "Alright, let's head west." Once the two reach Reiner's house, Racheal rings the doorbell. Ding-dong! Ding-dong! "Hello..."

The young man said in awe upon looking at the woman before realizing Vitallin was there. "Vi, you're here." He hugged. "Where's your wheelchair?" He asked, assuming the obvious. "I can walk again, sort of…" Vitallin said. "So I abandoned it thanks to her."

She pointed towards Racheal. *Is that…? Could it really be?* "Who is she?" He asks. "My familiar." "Hello Reiner." The woman greeted. "May we come in?" "Uh…" He was stunned in thought. "Um, yes…yes." He said, now sounding stern. They walk inside and head up to Reiner's room. "Hello…" Reece says in a slow discerning voice, sniffing out anything wrong with Racheal.

"Hi Reece, this is my—" "I know." He said tossing his messy hair back in such a manner. "It's your familiar, when did this happen?" "When she was administered into the rehab center…" Racheal spoke. "I see…may I ask who's your leader?" Suspicions rose within the women as she cocked an eyebrow. "Victor, why?" She asks.

"I'm not finished." He said sternly. "What are your intentions on having the king's title?" "To give Vitallin all she ever needed." She replied exhaustedly annoyed. "Since you're Reiner's friend I can only tell you to trust him, I hope you know what you're getting yourself into." Reece told the girl. "Thanks." Though she knew better. Meanwhile, Reiner's head was at the door hearing through. *Is he interrogating them?* He thought. *Aren't they good?* "Since this is about the title, we are potential enemies." The ram declared. Racheal grew furiated.

"Let's go Vitallin!" She pulled the girl to the side and walked out the room just before having Reiner come in.

"What was that about?" He asks. "I dunno, I have a bad feeling about this." "Why did you interrogate them?" Reiner was disappointed. "Because we're enemies." He continued. "We're of two different guilds of different districts and as far as I know, that girl could be in trouble."

It was a stretch. "Vitallin's my friend." Reiner said. *But I guess it matters that she's in a different guild…* "You two need to have faith in each other. It's the only way to know she wont do any harm." Questions and doubts spiraled throughout the room. Is this the breaking point of their friendship? "Racheal, what's going on?!" Vitallin couldn't catch up as she only learned how to walk again. "Vitallin, the Warfall guild needs you ya know…" She huffed still annoyed after Reece's questioning.

"But why?" The girl felt nieve. "So you could become our legacy holder." The woman continued. "Victor sought you as important to protect because apparently you're one of his warriors. He thought of your victories through Simmerton's law" "So he's saying that I have a chance to win the title?"

"Yeah, with you on our side we can have a possibility of winning the title. I'll have my ways of training you." Her familiar told. For two months, Racheal and Vitallin trained within the wilderness; it was bleak, cold, and imminsfully wet. Any amount of strong men wouldn't want to bear what she went through.

"May I see your spell book?" Vitallin asks, trying to keep her content. "Sure, but why?" "So I can combine them." She handed her book over. "How about Skorpio and Orexi?" Vitallin went with the flow as she knew what she was trying to do. She then proceeds to prick her finger with a piece of bark, and smear it onto the words. "Enhance!" She yelled, causing an echo within the forest. "They're fusing." She smiled with amusement. "That's cool so you know how to alter spells?" The woman applauded as she questioned. "I guess so…I'm a gnostic who wants to obtain as much knowledge about mystic elements whether it's about this world or life in general." "You seem like an interesting person." Her familiar also noted her fighting style.

Winter break began and school was out for another three weeks, people were winding down saying their goodbyes as others were taking trips with their friends to relish in the memories. *Reiner…* Erika looked on at her previous amusement park, and yearbook photos reminiscing on the time she and Reiner spent together. "Ah, Reiner!" She caught him in the nick of time as he was about to pack his bags and leave.

"Erika, long time no see." He was delighted to see her again. "Uh, you too boy wizard." "So you know." He expected she would. "Yeah, and all the monsters flying around who wouldn't?" She wanted to get to the point. "Do you want to go on a date?" She asks. "Or at least a trip till next semester?"

Erika hasn't felt her heart flutter this much since they first met. Maybe that's why she wants to rekindle those feelings. "Yeah, where did you want to go?" He asked. "To the beach! We could even rent a hotel and see the sights." "They have beach suites in Seattle?" Reiner wondered. "Yeah, near Alki beach…" Her advances were working. "Alright, that sounds like fun." Excited with the plan, Reiner hugs her softly.

"Your hair has gotten longer." He was in slight awe as it was touching her back. "Mmhmm, I've been wanting to grow it out for a while." "Well it seems like whatever you're doing, it's working…" He joked. "I'll catch you later—" "We're leaving tomorrow by the way." Erika excitedly announced. "Will be there!" Reiner threw on his jacket, grabbed his things, and left the school building.

*Erika seemed quite beautiful today, and smelled nice too. Vanilla…*He thought to himself as the scent lingered onto his uniform. "Reece, what are you doing?" The boy said, stumbling through the front door. "I'm wanting to mix my regenerating candies with one of my other potions for bodily enhancements." Reece smiles as if he accomplished a grand scheme of things. "It's for the day of kings." He continued.

"The other guilds have different skills, and tactics. I'm wanting to improvise my own." "That's interesting." Reiner said. "By the way, I won't be able to travel with you for a while. I'm taking a trip with a friend." Saying that made him relieved as he needed a trip from all this. "I don't care, take your time." He was snubbed about the entire thing.

The young man was stoked for his day trip to the beach. "Ready my boy?" Erika drove over to Reiner's house in a new black jaguar xe. "Hey Erika!" The boy hulled his blue luggage down the driveway. "Nice car." "Thanks, nice luggage you can put it in the back, there's room." She said with excitement in her voice. The back was filled with designer handbags, jewelry, and her red and black luggage.

"Come, sit." She opened the passenger side to reveal its butterfly doors. *Damn.* He thought. *What's your salary?* He was beyond impressed. "You like?" "Yeah, ready to go?" He asked. "I should be asking you that." The two made their way to the

Four Seasons hotel where they decided to settle down before having their fun.

"This place is nice." The boy said. "What's the budget?" "Hundred and ten every two nights." She replied. It was a two bedroom room with knitted tan blankets, oversized throw pillows, a large flat screen t.v., breathtaking scenery of the city, push-in closets, and a fruit bowl and champagne for refreshments. "Ugh, I needed this." Reiner plopped on the bed as if he fell from the sky. "Hehehe." The girl giggles. "I wonder what you've been up to, It's been awhile since we last spoke."

Yeah, lots has happened. "Uhh…" He had to think of something. "I had to help Vitallin with her studies, along with moving around and all…" He was telling the truth, sort of. "I see so you've been busy." "Last time I remembered you were with a guy named Reece." She continued. "He's the guy whom my sister was crazy over, though I don't remember seeing them together." Erika took a sip of champagne. *Does she know that her sister's a mage?* "What is he to you?" She asked suspiciously interested to know. *Reece…?* "He's my mentor." The young man fabricated an interesting image.

"My mom hired him for resources, and educational purposes." "Fair enough." She bought that. "Rinfer have me working my ass off," Erika twirled her drink around. "So isnt being a spy pretty risky? Aren't you afraid of getting executed?" Reiner put his two cents in. "I work *along with* spies. Whether they get caught or not pertains to them, not the company. I'm just one of their computer scientists who overlooks their country's governmental traffic so execution…isn't quite on my list." The girl paused then smiled at Reiner with a weak expression as if she was trying to hide something, something devestading. *I see…* The young man thought. "Wanna hit the beach now?" The girl asks lifting up her black, ruffled bikini in which Reiner smiled. The sun was up and glistening; people rushed to swim like there was no tomorrow. "Wow you workout…" Erika was shocked to see such a sculpted body underneath his uniform all that time. "You too." He complimented back.

The two were enjoying themselves quite nicely. The water was fresh, clear and fun. "I bet I could race you on sand." He challenged. "Whoever loses has to buy the other dinner." "You're on!" She was pumped. "Ready…set…go!" The hot sand sunk between their toes, it was nearly ignored as the thought of winning shrouded their minds. They were zipping through the beach bypassing objects, families, and other people around.

"Ah!" Erika tripped and scraped her ankle on a large rock. "Erika!" Reiner ran back to check up on her. Blood was oozing out ever so slightly, it wasn't that severe though Reiner still paid close attention to it. "Hold still." He lifted her leg onto his knees. "Ouch, that hurts!" "Kryopagima." Reiner concentrated on the wound covering it in a ray of ice crystals. "Ow…" Relax, they're only crystals.

"There, it should heal within three days." "What was that just now? How did you do that?" The girl was amazed to know. *Amazing.* Erika thought. "I used ice magic to stop the bleeding for some time, there should be some regeneration candy in my bag at the hotel." Reiner then carried the young girl back to get some. "When did you learn magic?" Erika said while laying on the boy's bed expecting some bizarre yet nonchalant answer.

"Reece taught me…" "Your mentor?" "Correct." He said. "Well he's not really my mentor per say." He knew where he was taking this. "He's my familiar." *So you really are a sorcerer.* She thought nonetheless. Should he have revealed more? "There's another universe out there that's greater than our own, I've been chosen to take part in winning what's known as the king's title." Reiner continued. "I would be able to control everything, make laws, and other things." *A title of a god huh?* Erika understood parts of it. "If my brother in law is a familiar, then my sister might be apart of this too!" Bingo for you. "Hah!" She gasps. *Could she be alive? Is that another heaven?*

"I hope you win the title Reiner, you'd be a great leader someday." She wanted to exalt him. "Thank you—" Before he could say anything else he found himself locked into a heated kiss with Erika; tongues shifting around each other as she tasted the spark of nectar within his mouth soon trailing down to his neck. "Ah…!" The boy flinched back for a second before noticing she was stroking the genital area of his trunks. "Erika, let's stop." "Mmm, how come?" Erika says, biting her lip in a sex dazed haze. "Because we should take things slow like going out, are you ready for dinner?"

He awkwardly asks, fogging his memory from what just happened. "Sure." The two went to a local bistro called Hobb's. "Hello, welcome to Hobb's what can I get for you today?" A waiter says introducing himself. "Um I'll take the Bouillabaisse and prawns." Erika spoke up with a delight than normal tone. "And you sir?"

The young man lost his train of thought. "Miso-glazed black cod, summer vegetable soup, and two waters." The waiter soon took the menu boards leaving a sense of awkwardness between the two. "Are you enjoying the trip so far?" The girl mentions, noticing Reiner quiet and slumping his head on the table. "Yeah." He says in a low, slightly annoyed grumble. "Cheer up Reiner, I have more places I wanna go, and things I wanna do with you…" What things were she implying?

"Why did you kiss me?" Despite knowing, Reiner still wanted answers out of her mouth. "I like you," She calmly says. "Don't act as if you didn't like it." "I…" Did he? "I love you Reiner, and I don't want anyone or thing getting in between us." *Even if it's that blonde bimbo…*"Erika I love you too, but only as a friend nothing more or less." He was honest with his decision.

"Why?…" Her voice lowered with a face of concern. "Why can't I have you?" She whined with sadness. "Your kindness, happiness, everything…ever since I met you I wanted all of it; you've made me feel happiness once more." "Erika…" Reiner wipes her tears with his hands. "I could've died before meeting you." She continues. "Ever since my sister died I've felt nothing but doom, a piece of me was shattered." She continued. "You were the one who filled in that aching gap within my heart…I wanted to commit suicide."

It was hard for her to admit but suddenly, Reiner hugged the girl tightly around the waist. "I hope you find someone special, someone who loves and listens to you." Reiner continued. "You are valuable, and I don't want to see you hurt again." He planted a sweet kiss on the forehead. "That's why I love you." She snuffles. "I already have someone I love." He needed her to understand.

"Why Vitallin?" Reiner didn't want to say, they've been through so much together. "Can you at least hold me a bit longer?" She requested. "Sure."

CHAPTER XVII

Ancients

"You've trained well Vitallin." The two were taking in the scenery of the hills before catching their breath. "So the king's title, what would happen to everyone and the rest of the guilds?" She minded to become insightful. "Until the battle is over, the victors would come together to make laws, create new life, imply a new ruling/structure of life and bear the truth as a new creator." Racheal said solemnly. *This is bad…* Vitallin thought. *So anyone could become a god…*

"So until that day, fight with your head and fists!" Her familiar said. "You'll fight too right?" She assumed. "Of course." They were five years away from the fight of their lives. Meanwhile…*Ancient leaders huh?* Elizabeth thought to herself while aiming the weapon at her bedroom walls. "I wonder why Xavier gave me this assignment." *O' Galihade knows what catastrophe might come about.*

Beep, beep, beeep! Suddenly, the dagger began beeping over and over changing frequency with every sound. *What's going on?* Elizabeth covered her ears as the sound was unbearable. BEEP! BEEP! BEEP! BEEEP!" Then it stops. "Is it over?" Curiosity sinks in as the girl leans over to touch the alarming object. "Borox!, Rexi!, Ultz!, Jörg!…"

Startled, Elizabeth backs back into a corner. The voice of the ancient shouted out names here and there, were these the fallen ones of the previous kings war? "What the hell?!" Elizabeth had to toughen up so she pointed her wand, preparing for anything to jump out at her. The voices soon manifested into a dark, gigantic, hideous-looking, somber old man scaling the height of her room and looked as if he was ready to attack.

"THIS IS WAR!" The gigantic old man let out a growling scream with the deepest voice possible. "Thermiko Simeio!" The girl casted a fire spell.

As sparks rang out, her wand grew as hot as a flamethrower. "Get away from me!" Her entire room caught on fire when suddenly, the old man grabbed Elizabeth by the throat and began choking her.

"No…stop…" Was this it? Elizabeth knew the ancients were powerful enough to break through any magic sequence. "Let go of that child!" Suddenly, the old man slowly released his grip, ran towards the other side of the room, and began bashing his head against the wall whilst foaming from the mouth.

"Ahh!" Elizabeth caught her breath before realizing what was happening. "My house!" She wanted to run away as far as she could. "This guild must die!" The elderly man yelled, giving Elizabeth the idea to use an enchantment spell. *Hopefully it's strong enough!* "Kathari Alysida!" She yells with every strength in her lungs.

The room froze in place as chains rained from the ceiling; grasping onto anything it could. This gave the girl time to run away. *Alright!…*Elizabeth wandered through the town at midnight trying to reach out to Xavier. "Hello?" He picks up. "President, I've lost my home." She continues. "The ancient guild leaders came out and nearly killed me, I used a prison spell to bind them and now they're trapped inside my house…" She thought about where she would live now. "It's impressive you've managed a fight, where are you now?" Xavier asked. "I'm at the gift shop." The girl felt apprehensive about the old man, and herself.

"There was a war going on within that old man." "War… within himself?" Xavier couldn't understand. "The generational war…" She continued. "Once the man released me I knew he was fighting other guild leaders; a voice told him to *unhand that child*." "Really?…" Xavier tried understanding.

"Yeah, maybe one of them realized I was a crow member." They could be of use for something. "So where do you plan on living now?" The man questioned. "I was wondering if I could stay at the guild…?" It was her last resort. "Yeah sure, I'll see what I can do about the ancients." The president offered to help anyway he could. "Thanks."

After dinner, Reiner and Erika head back to the hotel. There are two days left before their vacation ends. "Should we go to a gift shop for souvenirs?" Erika was still downhearted by his confession, but carried on nonetheless. "Yeah." But he wanted to talk first. "Erika, I hope you find someone better than me in the future but I meant what I meant, I love Vitallin, she's the only one who knows me best." He squeezes her hand. "Yeah, I know." Her expression softens. "You and Vitallin must've been friends for so long, I couldn't possibly get in the way…" She continued.

"At least you've given me a new hope after my sister." Erika pecks a kiss onto the boy's neck. "I'm glad you loved me." Meanwhile, the siren guild was on high alert as outsiders were not allowed in, and armies were coming out. "Find the Warfall members and bring me their heads!" Mrs. Gail commenced her now powerful group of soldiers. "Since they stole our books, we'll steal their pride by taking their lives." "Yeah that'll teach them not to mess with Siren!" The squad shouted. "Everyone, scatter!"

Vitallin and Racheal were walking upon the outskirts of Viewmann town near their home guild. "So how's Warfall like?" The girl asks. "Good, Warfall is a guild of home trained assassins whom were all picked by Simmerton's law." "So they're extremely powerful, correct?" Vitallin wondered. "More so…" She was honest. "You'll become quite strong yourself some day." The woman remarks. "Thanks."

The two stopped by a vendor before suddenly being approached by an elderly old man. "Hello young ladies." He said. "May I interest you in today's daily artifact?" The old man was tall, and sickly-looking as he wore baggy clothes that insinuated his slightly frail physique. His beard was unkempt and greasy, and his skin had scabs all over. "Well ladies…?"

The man revealed what was a gold statuette of a monk taming a tiger with the words "atoned for the fallen" embedded on it. *What? It can't be…!* Racheal was stunned. *How could he be…* "You, how did you get that?" Racheal wanted her question met directly. "I am one of the top prestiged fighters within this district, Vitrolf Neisim!" The man exclaimed with great seriousness in his voice. "What's going on?" The girl was confused as to what was going on.

"The statuette of Enoch was handed out to fighters of the previous generational war as a commemorate." She made a point. "He's an ancient!" *And…* Vitallin wasn't impressed. "I've mastered flaming wind spells, soul binding techniques, and nebula binding techniques." He *was* an ancient… "He's able to train us." Racheal whispered into Vitallin's ear with child-like excitement. "Let's see what he's about then…" She took on that challenge as things were looking up for her. "Teach me!" The girl yelled, taking an interest in the old man.

"Very well then, meet me at the mountain tops by dawn, I'd be happy to teach you all you need to know about the ancient arts young lady." The old man gave out a grin of mystery as if he knew what was to come. "Will be there." Racheal said determined to help Vitallin anyway she could. *The power of the ancients…training me?* She knew it wouldn't be easy given her first sparring with Racheal.

"Let's visit him tomorrow shall we?" "Where's the mountain top?" The girl asks. "The east of Viewmann." "It's dusk hour, we should get some rest." Her familiar suggested. "You're always right about some things…" The two slept peacefully within a nearby inn where there were no creatures, or monsters in sight. Speaking of which..."So this is her house huh?"

Elizabeth gave directions to her home in exchange for sleeping within the guild. *So the ancient leaders were trapped within her room...*The man decided what his next move would be. Xavier took a pin from his hair and unlocked the door. The rooms were completely furnished and intact, but the aura was unusually heavy. He didn't know what he was getting himself into.

The hallway's ivory carpet was now charred and completely ripped apart. "Grraahh!!" The gigantic old man let out a loud groan of pain. "Whoa, this must be her room." Xavier said to himself while signaling the area. *The flames are still...was this an enchantment spell?* "Must...beat...guild!" The man looked up upon seeing the gigantic elderly ancient, whoms aura was strong enough to cause many brave warriors to crave death. *What the hell!*

The man held his breath as the atmosphere grew toxic, nevertheless he sucked up and fulfilled his plan. "Who are you?" One of the voices of the old man spoke, the same voice that saved Elizabeth. "I'm a Crow leader sir!" Xavier explained himself. "What shall you seek, successor?" The omnipotent voice asked. "I'd like to use you for another war sir." "MY GUILD BIRTH YOUR DISTRICT AND YOUR LIVES!" The voice stated. "My thankfulness is beyond measure sir, but the day of kings is upon us..." He tried reasoning, but that favor wasn't gonna come without a cost.

"Try proving your worthiness as a leader." "Deal." Xavier had to take on that battle. "Berserker!" The man caved upon using this forbidden spell as his muscles fatigue yet gave out all his strength. "GAAHH-!!" The ancient's mind went haywire as it crashed into everything; banging its head against the walls over and over.

Amazing, it worked…"You think this is over?!" The old man struggled to speak as he challenged Xavier. "Indeed." He smirked. "Xiropago Koilo!" The man concave the ancients within a crystal then contracted their blood into three large potion bottles, each being marked with the letter x. "Thank you for your sacrifice…" Xavier calmly said as he flipped his hair to the side; he left the house as good as new before heading his way.

"No birdie, don't fly away~" Vitallin and Racheal were fast asleep inside the Meadowview inn. They would have a lot to go through since they were training with an ancient. It was morning time and the glistening sun peered through the windows, and overhead waking them up with such warm undertones.

"How was your sleep?" Racheal asked as she stretched for the sky. "No birdie don't fly away~" Vitallin mocks to the woman's embarrassment. "Ready to give it all you got?" "Maybye, only if he goes easy on me." Vitallin has indeed gotten stronger by now. "No worries my dear, I'm sure he will." The two took their trip to the east of Viewmann town where they saw the view of the mountains.

"So which one is it?" The girl asks, pointing afar. "The one near the left…?" Her familiar wasn't sure either. "It's the tallest one in the middle if you're wanting to get to Vitrolf's home."

An elderly woman pointed. "Race ya!" "Akrida!" Suddenly the woman jumped high into the sky surfacing near the trees.

"Wow…" Vitallin looked on with amusement. "I guess we gotta go the hard way, hang tight!" Racheal carried the girl tightly within her arms. "Tachytita toufotos." With a jolt of lightning, Racheal sprinted through the forest as fast as she could. "Follow the lady!" Vitallin shouted. They have to try really hard to reach the top, that's for sure!

Hmm…I wonder what they're here for anyways? The old woman thought to herself as she stood on top of the mountain. "She's gone…" The girl was in disarray. "We have to get to the top somehow." *That woman must be an ancient.* "Ready to climb?" "What?" She wasn't having any of that.

"Calm down, it's only a joke." She *was* kidding right? "It's so high." She was concerned. "Here give me your feet." Her familiar conducted an anatomy spell upon the girl so there wouldn't be any freight. "Try jumping." Racheal instructed. Vitallin did as told and yielded gravity defying results.

"I'm floating." "That's because the atoms underneath you are slow." She continued. "In this case if you fall, you'd have more time to grab hold of the rocks." "So I wont die?" The girl asks. "Correct." The two made their way onto the base of the mountain. "Let's get climbing!" While the two struggled with their rocky endeavor, Erika wanted to part ways with her semester trip by going to the bookstore and gift shop.

"Here, isn't it cute." She hands Reiner an adorable tan bowed teddy bear as a reminder of their friendship. "What's this about?" The young man was curious to know. "It's a symbol of love and respect." She respects his confession, and accepts it.

"Thanks but what's with the other stuff?" She carried a whole load of books, tee-shirts, soaps, lotions, and an adorable ram plushie. "It's a gift shop silly." Erika smiled sweetly. They seemed so close to be pulled apart so suddenly.

"Let's head home." Reiner suggested as he was curious to know what the ram was up to. "What are you up to?" Erika asked as she was wanting to stay a bit longer. "I'm just wanting to know what Reece is up to that's all." "My brother in law?" "Yeah…" Come to think of it, does she really know Reece? "Fine." Unfortunately she couldn't have it her way.

Afterwards the two hopped into the car and drove downtown to Pruitte drive. *Finally…* They had such a fun and successful trip, hopefully a successful semester as well. "Liz… liz wake up." A girl said while nudging the poor girl with her elbow. Elizabeth was knocked out cold on the side of the guild couch drooling and all.

This gave the woman an idea to pinch the child's ear and yell. "Whisper, whisper! Whisper in the dark!" "Holy shit Max!" The poor girl nearly had a heart attack as she flinched back. "Wake up bed head, you're embarrassing yourself in the middle of the lobby." The lady mentions as people were going in and out of the guild house snickering and laughing.

"What…time is it?" Elizabeth was drowsy, confused, and annoyed. "Haven't you gotten enough sleep at home?" Maxine questioned. *That's right…* "I lost my home to an ancient leader, and now Xavier is…" "Ancient leaders?!" She was shocked. "How are you still alive?" "Xavier told us about this in one of our meetings, I'm just shocked you survived." Maxine was impressed.

"Yeah but what about the president?" She knew he wouldn't stand a chance. "He uses forbidden magic all the time, it's fine…" After what the girl witnessed, she could only worry. Maxine tied her short blonde hair into a messy bun, revealing her numerous ear piercings. "Come, we're having a meeting at twelve in the library." "Will do." Elizabeth choked as she spoke.

"Almost there Vitallin, keep climbing!" "I know…!" The girl panted heavily as she was exhausted. "Don't look down! Keep pushing!" They would have won a medal by how far they've climbed. "Racheal look, the lodge!" *Vitrolf…!* With a mixture of success and annoyance, Racheal was ready for payback. Upon the surface of the mountain was a large wooden lodge house.

"I see you've made it, nice progress." It was the elderly woman from before, "Where's Vitrolf?" Vitallin asked. "My husband is in the house cooking." The woman politely says. "He told us to meet him here by dawn…" Racheal spoke. "Oh, you guys must be one of Vitrolf's trainees." "He has trained many witches and wizards alike. He's an ancient magic user who fought in the generational war and survived to tell."

She continued. "Many people who come here leave with strength, and insight towards the war ahead so please, do come in." The lodge was clean, and comfortable which had many rooms to spare as if it were a family house. "Vitrolf, your visitors have arrived." "Yes, it seems that you've made it past the mountain." Vitrolf laughed as he was sitting in his recliner playing chess while hissing noises came from the kitchen.

"Care for a game?" He asked. "Enough bullshit Vitrolf, we're here to train." Racheal lost her cool as she was annoyed. "Calm down, a beautiful woman like yourself shouldn't lose her way." The mountain climbing was a test. "Now care for a game?" The old man said once more. "Sure."

Vitallin took up that offer. "Very well then…" Vitrolf moved a pawn two spaces forward, while Vitallin moved once. "Let the game commence!" A voice monitor yelled out of nowhere. "Wha—?" Suddenly the floor turned into gravel, the sky into blood, and strangely enough there were castles nearby. "What's going on?" Racheal was getting concerned.

"Where's Vitallin!" "Relax lady." The elderly woman calmly said. "She's interacting with Vitrolf in a game of chess." But what kind of chess were they playing? "What is this?…" Vitallin was amazed as the lodge was gone, castles and churches were everywhere, dragons were flying high above the skies, and human pawns were standing around.

"This is literal chess milady." Vitrolf said. *Impressive…* An enchantment spell nonetheless. Once Neisim captured the girl's pawn, it slashed him to shreds with a huge swing. "What the—?" Vitallin laughed at the whole thing. "Chess is war Vitallin." The old man said. Midway into the game, strategies were being implemented as people were getting captured and destroyed. "Please don't let them get me!" Vitallin's queen yelled.

"Don't worry ma'am, I'll try my best!" So far Vitrolf had five of Vitallin's pieces; three pawns, one knight, and one bishop. The girl only had two of his pawns. The outside board on the other hand was a true to life battlefield. "Who's winning?" Racheal said, trying to peer through anything she could. "Vitrolf is…" His wife replied. "And don't worry, everything will come back to normal once either of them win."

The two were trapped in a glass room where no light was visible. *Let's hope so…*

CHAPTER XVIII

Stronger

"Welcome home." Erika said driving up to the boy's driveway "Thanks." Reiner got out of the car and stretched for a while. "Hmm?" Reece opened the front door to get some fresh air. "Brother!" This caught Erika's eye as she hopped out of the car and ran to give him a big hug. "Hey Reece!" Her day was brighter. "Hey sis how's it going?" Reece seemed happy as well. "Reiner and I just got back from vacation, I didn't know you were a wizard."

She continued. "And about my sister, where is she?" The girl released her embrace. "Come inside I'd like to talk to you about that." The ram offered to walk the girl into the living room to sit down. "Anri is alive and she remembers you dearly." He continued. "She's apart of a world that encrypts magic for the sake of fighting, she's a sorceress whom is fighting for a greater cause to protect you and I."

So Reiner was right, she is a witch. Erika understood as she cocked an eyebrow. "So she's a witch huh? Would that explain why you're a ram man?" "Correct. Your sister did a slip up spell on me and hasn't found a way to undo it all this time." He confirmed. "So she's alive? For real?" "Yeah." This gave Erika the thought of a revenant. She then got up from the couch and hugged Reece once more; no more doubts, or shattered memories behold, all things were made anew.

"I'm happy now." The girl said it with her heart as she shed a tear of relief. Meanwhile the other girl wasn't so happy. "I've got the blood binding potions right here with me Liz, no worries." Xavier managed to tear down an ancient…wow. "I'm at a meeting with the executives…" Elizabeth calmly whispered into her cell phone trying not to go into hysteria because of her demolished valuables.

"It must be hella fun since I'm not there, what are you guys discussing?" "The hidden unchained: Their methods of mutated magic." Elizabeth told. "I see I'll be there shortly." Xavier said. *This will help us win the new gen war for good.* The man examined the dark, molten liquid. That had to be his most valuable fight for sure.

"Hey Elizabeth, come check this book out!" Maxine shouted across the room showcasing a book called Herold. "It's about a man living half-brained and overcoming homelessness turns out he became filthy rich, haha!" "It's not a joke." The girl silenced her coarse laughter. "You'll become successful yourself someday too." The woman reassured as her chuckling died down.

"Maxine! Elizabeth! The meeting…" One of the male executives subtly took a seat out signaling them to sit down. The man was handsome and well dressed; light green eyes, brown hair, and strong cheekbones coupled with a black brand suit, and brown leather dress shoes. "Now, unchained familiars may pose a threat to civilians within both worlds. They are monsters fabricating your reality to take your lives for power; kill, steal, and destroy."

The man continued while pointing his pointer onto the projector screen. "The only way to take them down is to use forbidden magic, but they may use mind control and external forces to bring you down. Any questions?" The man asked, anticipating any show of hands. "I have one!" A cheery female voice shouted amongst the crowd. "Ah yes Ellis, what's your question?"

"How did they come about, and whoever's causing it can we beat their asses…?" Ellis genuinely wanted to know how strong they were. "These are monsters of the unchained depths of Vülenberg; another piece of Novo Incipere's past. They are vicious in which they were bred to deceive, and kill all life from past to present." The instructor continued. "They are all extremely dangerous to come by; only experienced forbidden, or ancient magic wielders can take them on." "So that's a no?" Ellis was ready to kick some ass. "Not unless you learn the arts perhaps, other than that it's not possible."

"Ancient magic is a privilege to have indeed." Vitrolf said. The two were on their twenty-eighth move. "I'm winning my dear!" The scene was bloody. So far Vitrolf captured most of the girl's pieces, leaving her with only nine of his. "No!!" He captured her queen and king. "Scene!" The voice monitor shouted. "Game over, Neisim wins!" Suddenly the ground shook with a vicious roar. *It's reconstructing itself…* Vitallin was right. The house went back to normal as Racheal and Vitrolf's wife were able to see them again.

"Vitallin!" Her familiar ran to check any injuries. "I'm fine, thanks mom." She mocked. "You were great young lady." The old man applauded. "That was an ancient enchantment spell. I'll get to the fighting soon enough." Vitrolf took the spaghetti out of the pot. "The generation prior to yours was much tougher; laws and treaties were strict, and guilds were not allowed to mingle." He continued.

"My leader Rexi wanted to do what it took to stop the wars and live as a democrat, but greed and personal loathing pushed the idea of a king's war forward." "So Rexi was a good guy?" Vitallin and Racheal wondered. "Correct, but unfortunately he had to fight for his ideals and sanity; not wanting anyone who would do harm in power." Vitrolf, being one of the few who survived the previous king's war grew to establish his own version of peace by living away from all guild relations, knowing the damage and harm they cause to the person's mind and soul.

It was as if it were a deadly game of chess at every generation's end. "Come, follow me to the backyard." "Backyard?!" The two thought he was joking. *But we're on the freezing peaks of the mountains. How could there be a—* Errk. He opened the back double doors to reveal a beautiful meadowview of a park with multiple areas.

"Welcome to my backyard." Vitrolf laughed. The grass was greener than green as the sky was that of heaven…a peaceful paradise. "Amazing, truly amazing." Racheal said in awe as the crisp pure air filled her lungs. *Liking this place now huh?* The girl thought, scolding the woman from before. "Pick any area you'd like child." The yard had multiple circular style trimmings upon it.

"I'd like the one far out to the right sir." Vitallin commanded. "Very well then, come!" Things were about to get serious as Vitrolf's voice was authoritative and significant. Unfortunately this made Racheal tap into her nurturing instincts. "Vitallin!" "Stay back!" The elderly woman yelled. "It's too dangerous for you to get caught in the crossfires." Their battle was starting.

"Flaming winds are one of the techniques my members taught me." Neisim explained. "Air has a core temperature of twenty-four degrees celsius, if given much strength it will rise thus making it hotter and if so, I'm able to control the air within a person's lungs as well." The old man slowly moved his arms in a circular motion.

The once crisp, humid air became dried within seconds. "Mikos Kymatos!" With one swift move Vitrolf sent a gust of heat towards the young girl. "Shit!" Vitallin yelled as the air was scorching hot. "Pagoma myalou…" The girl kept the air within her brain and lungs cool. *Use the core of the air huh?*

She thought of copying him. "Strike!" Vitrolf yelled. "Mikos kym-ah!" She was too slow as the old man grabbed her by the arm and swung her across the field. "Constrict your muscles and force a temperature within your core child!" *Shit!* The task was too strenuous, and exhausting for her. "Don't die on me!" The elderly man said, coming around the fields. "Mikos Kymatos!!" Vitallin yelled in the heat of the moment as she was scared, scared to die, even worse scared to fail everyone.

Fwwshh! Suddenly a gust of roaring wind exploded onto Vitrolf's face causing severe burns. "Gaahh!" She got him good. "You see, that's the progress I need you in." He applauded. "I'm not going to die here!" She was willing to fight. "Then learn! Chersaia!" The man yelled. "What's going on?!" The poor girl couldn't move to save her life. "You're bound onto the ground." Vitrolf explained. "Soul binding magic, it's an advanced level spell even familiars can do."

As Vitallin's body weighed upon itself, she began feeling as if the ground was whispering to her; better yet merging with her. While the thick, sweetly pointed grass laid beneath her feet, the apple tree's roots became mobilized and clenched onto her; she was able to move nonetheless. "You can move girl." Vitrolf sternly said. Vitallin managed to grab an apple by the stem and throw it at the man in which he smiles. "Vitallin if you don't move I'll kill you."

His voice was tarse yet his eyes were full of compassion. *Fuck!…* The girl got up and ran behind an apple tree. "I moved! I moved!" It was a stretch. "Good child, now focus all the air within your lungs and blow. You'd be using the flame technique." Vitallin did as told as flames and ashes were coming out of her mouth like a fireplace.

"She's doing slightly well." The old woman said. "Yeah… may I ask, what's your name?" Racheal wondered. "Helena." She spoke. "Helena Neisim." "Nice to meet you." They said as they looked the training before them, when suddenly… "Prepare to die girl!" A female voice shouted on top of the mountain. Within a flash numerous men jumped down from a ginormous white bird ready to fight. "Elafry daikopti" One of the men caused the girl's sight to go out.

"Vitallin!" Racheal ran to help. "Stay back!" Helena yelled. "You don't know if they are forbidden magic users!" "What's going on?! Help!" There was only one thing she could do. "Mikos kymatos!" Vitallin swung her arms around trying to cause damage to anyone nearby as she couldn't see who or what anymore.

"Mati tavron." Another hooligan shot darts at the young girl in which it was a direct hit. "I won't let you get away!" Vitrolf blazingly shouted. "Kolasi angelos!" "Fuck!" A pack of guard dogs appeared and sunk its teeth into the man's calves as he quickly tied the girl's wrists with wire rope then put a sack over her head. *How could this happen…*Racheal was forced to watch the whole thing unfold as her friend slipped away.

"They're Siren members." Helena said. "Of course…" Racheal's voice grew low as she sounded ready to fight. This was a situation that needed to be solved. "I'm glad you get to see your family again." Reiner said, sitting on the floor flipping through Reece's notes. He gives the boy a daunting gaze. "These are family matters, kid."

"Give him a break Reece, he's a friend." Erika chastised him similar to Anri. "So this magic world, what's it called?" "Novo Incipere…" *Novo Incipere, he never told me that…* Reiner thought. "The enchanted world filled with familiars to investigators and such unchained monsters." This piqued the girl's curiosity. "I want to see…" She said. "Na, it'll ruin the surprise." Reece knew what he was up to.

"Besides it's too dangerous, you might get killed." *So that's a no then?* Erika thought. "No." The ram knew her mind. "Stay out of trouble by staying here okay?" "Fine, love you brother." Erika submissively obeyed. Once they finished chatting, the girl decided to leave the boy's home; they said their goodbyes and committed to a brighter future.

"She was really happy to see you again." Reiner said. "Likewise." Reece felt sentimental when it came to his family. "It's been a long time since I've seen that girl." "Your bandage gauze is gone, are you fully healed?" Reiner looked at the faun's pale arms. "Yeah, I'm gonna show that old cock sucking fart a bloody nightmare during the day of kings." Reece kept that fight in mind. "I'm back!" Meanwhile, Xavier yelled and placed three red plastic bags onto the guild's library table. "Did you see that thing?" Elizabeth spoke. "Yeah and I got its blood as well…" He lifted up the tube of red molten blood. "First, I'm gonna need one of you guys to test this…Amanda how bout it?" "Um, I'll try…"

She was hesitant to bother. Amanda was a five-foot, five inch woman with blonde frizzy hair and wore thick framed glasses over her honey light eyes. The lady wasn't too exciting as she was the most humbled and reserved person out of the group, and a bookworm at best. "Drink this." The president instructed. "Sure…" She shot the tube of blood down her throat; it tasted like licorice, dark bitter licorice.

"What's this supposed to make me— OH MY GOD!" The woman was frightened as she saw two gigantic lions pacing around the flaming library sniffing nearly everyone in the room. "Take me back! Take me back!" Soon one of the lions encountered Amanda, sniffed her palm, and bowed submissively as if it were obeying.

"No!" The other lion attacked the Crow members sinking their bloody teeth into their necks and skulls as if they were hippos, and antelopes. "No! My family!" With ever loving care in the world she wanted it to stop. *Johnson, Maxine, Ellis… the others…* "Amanda wake up!" At that moment she snapped out of it. "Oh my goodness, you're all alive…" Tears were drastically welling up within her eyes.

"What did you see?" Xavier asked as he and the rest questioned her psyche. The woman quickly fell to her feet. "There were lions attacking everyone!" The scene was too scary for her to retell. "Lions?" Their president was interested. "You have to believe me!" The poor lady yelled. "That potion is too dangerous for the human soul." She sobs as she continues her story.

"Miraculously, one of the lions kneeled down to me once it sniffed me…" "So you can control animals?" He figured. "I don't know but it was as if I was one of them." *It felt powerful.* "So you became an ancient." The man was right. "I gave you ancient blood *so* you'd become stronger in the path of your destiny, and for the sake of the guild." Did he know about this all along?

"Everyone head home, we have much to do this following weekend." The president said. "Think you'll be able to sleep tonight?" He cared for her safety. "I guess so." Family is a tightknit bond that is inseparable, as an iron link that is imperishable. "Get the fuck up girl!" A young girl shouted. She was the one from the gigantic bird earlier. She was dark-skinned, had thick layered hair, and wore a blue military dress as she was the chief of Siren.

"I'm sorry…" Vitallin whimpered. Tortured and bruised, she struggled to stand while regaining her sight ever so slowly. "This is punishment for stealing our manuscripts!" The girl yelled. "Don't ever cross paths with Siren ever again, got that!" The young lady threw a knife through the cell bars missing the girl by an inch. *I'm not gonna die here!*

Vitallin prayed for salvation, but would it ever be? "Abigail, please stop." The voice of a woman commanded. "But Mrs. Gail—" "I said stop!" She yelled with intent as she opened the jail cell. "Who are you?" Vitallin frantically asked. The woman untied the sack from the girl's head. *Woah…* She saw a tall, fairly old woman with light rose gold hair and honey eyes discerningly staring back at her.

With a smile that literally kills, God only knew what was going through that mind. "How did a girl like you get into my base?" "Sh…Shit!" Mrs. Gail choked the girl with her nails so forcefully she was bleeding and panicking. *She's really gonna kill me…* "Erotiki apogoitefsi." At that moment Vitallin dropped down to the ground and held her chest as it began contracting. *Someone help! Reiner, Reiner I need you!* The girl was in excruciating pain so much that she craved death at that moment.

The afternoon sun was dimmed hiding beneath the clouds as the seemingly endless rain poured down harder and harder. Racheal was sitting on her bed at the Meadowview Inn upset. Regretful was an understatement once she failed as a guardian/familiar. "I could have stopped them." *I have to find help.* The woman knew what she had to do so she opened a planned portal to the other side.

CHAPTER XIX

Friends

"Welcome back class!" Said Mrs. Brookes with a hoarse voice trying to sound cheerful than ever. "When I call roll please say here." *Strange…* As the teacher called attendance Reiner had a nagging feeling that something was up. "Vitallin Dubarse…" She called. Not present. *What's going on?* He thought to himself. *To miss five straight weeks near the final exams?* The boy checked his phone for any recent and incoming messages. Nothing.

"So how are you doing in this class so far?" A male student asks the freckled brunette who was slouching on the side of his desk trying not to get caught. "Can't you just turn your phone invisible or something?" The kid suggested. "No, it doesn't work that way." Reiner said. "It's still audible."

"Then let me help," The boy got up from his seat and got into Reiner's space. "You'll never see your friend again." The young man gave out an ominous tone with a chilling, arrogant smirk. "What did you do?" Reiner exclaimed as he seemed slightly anxious. "It's not what I did to her, but what she did to us." Once school was over Reiner ran over to the girl's house and knocked but no one answered. He had no other choice but to barge through. "Whoa!" Little did he know, Mrs. Dubarse got smacked on the receiving end. "Rei…Reiner is that you?" She asked, feeling her face. "Mrs. Dubarse sorry to barge in but is Vitallin home?"

"No," She continued. "She's back in rehab due to be released in February." It was hopeless as the young man had to confess what was happening to her daughter, or thoroughly search some more. "Nevermind ma'am." "No please, tell me what's going on." Mrs. Dubarse wanted answers as well though it is too bizarre for her as it would be hard to get her to believe. "Ah…" But he had to say it.

"Your daughter's a witch Mrs. Dubarse, and she's most likely in danger." A concerned expression marked the woman's face. "Pfft..hahaha!" She laughs. *This isn't a joke, your daughter really is in danger.* "Have you been reading too many comics, Reiner?" Just as he figured she wouldn't believe him. The boy left the house determined to find his best friend.

"Hey Reece!" He stumbled through the door in a complete mess. "What is it?" The ram asks while sipping tea and reading on the young man's computer. "I need your help to find Vitallin." "She wasn't with you?" He asks. "No." "At home?" "Neither." The boy replied, but he wasn't out of clues. "Maybe she's still with Racheal." Reece figured.

"Probably…" *You'll never see your friend again.* The kid's words resonated within the young man. He couldn't help but feel as though something fishy was going on. *He might have something to do with it, that bastard.* "Wanna search elsewhere?" The ram said, opening a portal to the other side before suddenly having Racheal come through. "Young boy please help," The woman was panting in exhaustion. "Racheal why are you—" "There's no time to explain your friend has been taken by Siren forces."

So a guild took her… He knew he had to fight with all his might. The two followed Racheal west out towards the sea of Nivera as they crossed through the city of Rochester and around the forest near a harbor. *So this is where Siren's guild is located.* The boy thought as he saw ships filled with cargo transporting in and out of the docks, along with people working. "There's the castle" "I see…" The large cut stone castle was off the shore near a body of water. "Why so secluded?" The boy had to ask. "Secrets." In which his familiar had answers.

"Now's not the time for questions," Racheal interrupted. "we have to find a way to devise a strategy and get rid of the guards." Agreed. "Who knows how many members are in there." Reece noted.

"I say you and Racheal go before me and blend in while I take out the guards and the ones in the lobby." He explained. "Try to find the girl before anyone gets onto you guys." Reece suggested. "Yeah, but first…" Racheal grabbed some sort of blue rose shaped plant and peeled its thick stem off. "What's this?" The young man asked. "It's a Dacci plant." The woman explained. "It only grows out west during winter." She continued. "Its secretions act as a dye, we can cover up our guild tattoos using this." It was slimy and transparent yet had a citrus aroma. "Alright."

As the two went ahead and snuck their way around the guards, the ram wanted to be a show off. "Moira!" The guards suddenly attacked each other mercilessly without thought. "Nice." The castle's interior had a light blue, cold feeling to it as if it were made out of crystals. "Well now…" Said Reiner, skimming the area. *Too many rooms, so many people. Where could she be?*

"May I help you two?" A soothing and handsome voice rang through their ears. "No, we are fine." Racheal quickly replied, once she turned around she saw a tall dark skinned man with hazel eyes and a loosely curled afro.

*Wow…*Racheal blushed as she quickly darted her eyes to the floor. "I forgot where the restroom was." Reiner spoke of an excuse for them to go away. "Yeah you take a left from here and it's two doors down." "Thank you." The man glanced at the boy's forearm. *Hmm…suspicious.* He thought. "What business does a beautiful woman like you have with Siren?" The man smirked as he tried smooth talking.

"Well I came here upon hearing Mrs. Gail's tier proposal, I'm a Rochester citizen who wants to object to it." She told a story. "I see, so you don't like the idea of having your combat determine class?" "Certainly not." She said as the man stepped in closer. "The name's Luther, what's yours?" "Martha." The woman lied. "Martha Allistor." "Well Martha I have something you can't object to." As the man leaned in for a kiss, Racheal kicked him in the groin and punched him by the side of the head. "Despite looking attractive you don't have much manners do you?"

So many rooms. Reiner peered through most of the rooms down the hallway though he couldn't find her. *Must be upstairs.* The boy maneuvered his way past some of the people and ran up the stairs. "Ha, Vitallin!" He ran towards her before seeing the state she was in. *Dammit, how could they—* "Reiner, please leave before she finds you." Vitallin spoke in a low whisper as tears ran down her cheeks. "I'm not leaving without you no matter what the circumstances are, Vi."

He knew that for a fact. "You're gonna die because of me, she's too strong." *Trust in me.* "She's right, you know." Mrs. Gail said from behind. "Abigail, go see if there are any more unfamiliar faces." "Roger ma'am!" The young girl saluted as she left the scene. "So this is the Siren headquarters, how snobbish." The ram scoped the area.

I wonder how many members they have…"Hold it right there you goat!" Abigail yelled running downstairs. "Don't expect me to go lightly on you just because you're an annoying pipsqueak." Said Reece pricking his thumb with his fingernail. "Omichli aimatos." *Shit!* The little girl stumbled upon other people feeling light headed. "Abigail, seems like you need help with that beast." A woman noted the fight and pitched in.

"Let's see what you guys are made of!" Full of enthusiasm, Reece pinned the woman onto the ground and began punching her with full force. "To think you guys were inspirational." The ram complemented their strengths. "Mastigoma!" The woman yelled, causing the faun's muscles to jerk violently. *Shit!* The pain was frightening but he sucked it up. *Was that a forbidden spell?* "Die you ugly goat!" Abigail swung her wand near the ram's torso before having her body pulled towards him. "Antigrafo ekrixi…" A mini blast ray shot out of Reece's mouth.

"Abigail, duck!" The woman hollered while holding up a mirror behind the young girl. The mirror sucked up the blast as the ram saw his reflection, "What the hell?" Suddenly cuts and a gash wound opened up his skin. *It's…hot…*Abruptly, Reece fell to the floor unconscious.

"To think that that girl had help along the way, I should've killed her to warn that *no crime gets over Siren.*" Mrs. Gail exclaimed. *You old hag!* The boy charged and struck the woman's side before getting knocked to the ground. "Your attempts to strike are pathetic." The lady commented with an annoyed expression across her face.

"Erotiki apogoitefsi." *Ah!* Reiner had to hold his chest as it was contracting. "Pyro…vo…litis." Struggling to speak, the boy sent out radioactive blasts from the walls but Mrs. Gail quickly dodged. "Nice magic young man, you're certainly stronger than that girl." She noted. *Such power…*Vitallin smiled knowing her friend was this strong, but not strong enough. The woman dashed towards Reiner and locked onto his eyes.

"Diakoptis eikonas." The room became distorted and warped as the boy started hallucinating, he didn't quite know what was what. *Huh, illusions?* "Try to find me, boy." Mrs. Gail was auditory yet nowhere in sight. "Ah!" Blunt stabbing sensations were all around himself.

"Dammit, where are you?" There was only one thing he could do so he cast himself within a bubble so that she couldn't touch him. *I need to concentrate, at least for now.* Reiner looked at his wounds. *She's much stronger than Mrs. Moon, and could kill me like Maria…I have to be careful. I'm gonna save you no matter what Vitallin, yeah I'm not gonna lose you again.* "I need to find her." The boy then decided to move into another room of the castle.

"Reece, wake up!" Racheal kneeled near the faun's body while shaking him. "Not so tough after all huh?" Abigail commented. *How did you?* She figured Reece was stronger than this. *I see…* The woman stood up and glanced at the little girl. "I see Siren's pretty strong." She said a slight compliment. "All the guilds need to be more self aware and wake the hell up, you're all no match for us!" Abigail exclaimed. *But I might be.* Vexed and annoyed the girl swung at the woman's head before having her block the wand with her hand.

"Unfortunately for you, I use forbidden anatomy magic." "And?" The little girl mocked. "Atychies." Racheal ran her finger across Abigail's forehead. "Ahhh!!" She screams. *Wha… What's happening? Damn you!* Her brain felt like it was going to explode so much that she lost some of her speech and functionality.

"Can't attack now can you?" The woman taunts. *A… ah…ugh…* "Sh…shi…shaa…" Feeling defeated, Abigail fell to the floor as her despair crept in silence, unable to cast a spell or even function properly. *Seems as though this fight is over.* Racheal's magic was immeasurable beyond belief. *I must find that girl…*

"Where could you be old wench?" With sight slightly distorted, Reiner still searched the area as best as he could. "Sympiezo." His protection diminished. "Ah!" Mrs. Gail kicked Reiner onto the ground. "Try fighting back." She noted. The young man grabbed a spear from the wall and hurled it at the woman as fast as possible. Straight hit.

"I'll let you have that." She casually smiled as she slowly took the weapon out of her side, splotches of blood were pouring onto the ground. "You have a long way to go if you're fighting for a certain title as well boy." Mrs. Gail remarks. "Even so, there's no way you'll have it." Suddenly the boy got up and charged at the lady, attempting to grab onto her red cloak. "Flegomeno revma!" He yelled as the piece of clothing burst into flames. *How nice…*

Mrs. Gail smirks as she quickly takes off the cloak and throws it at Reiner as it suddenly explodes. *Dammit, where are you guys?* Meanwhile within the lobby, Reece finally regained consciousness. "Shit, those bastards…ow!" "Don't try to get up just yet, your abdomen got split pretty deep." Said Racheal feeling on the ram's muscles with care.

"Don't touch me I'm fine, you better go ahead and help Reiner I'll meet you—" "I'm not leaving you behind." The woman exclaimed. "I'm not gonna want a dead body on my hands." "You're calling me a burden?" Reece questioned with a challenged expression. "I'm saying you couldn't even take on those two, how would you expect to fight more?" "Strength and power varies from person to person lady; if I wanted to I could beat the living shit out of you right now." He tested. *Such irritation…*

"Calm down," Racheal huffed. "Prove to yourself that you're able to fight until we get Vitallin back." "Whatever…" As the two quickly made their way upstairs they noticed they were being followed by a group of men now. "You won't get away!" One of the men threw a dagger straight shot at Racheal. *We don't have time for this…* She thought as she took the weapon out of her arm and sliced through the man's chest.

"Mesanychta." Half of the other guy's body turned pitch black as mini stars began to form. "Hold still," Reece sliced his fingers and smeared the blood in Racheal's ears. "Now cover your ears, Mavro thoryvo!" The ram yelled when suddenly loud music played in the background. "Dammit!" The man tried covering his ears but it wasn't enough, the sound was nearly a hundred and ninety-seven decibels loud; too deadly for the human body.

"That takes care of that." He said. "Come on, let's split up and find those two." "You search through this side of the floor while I search the right okay?" Racheal pointed. "On it." Reece agreed as he saw Racheal dash towards the other side of the lobby, looking and searching through the doors of the hallway. "Wow, she's faster than I thought." He said to himself.

I wonder what plans they're hiding… "Racheal!" Vitallin yelled as she saw her pass by. "Vitallin, we're here to get you out." "It may be difficult," She said. "Mrs. Gail has the keys and I even tried certain spells." "I see so spells won't do." Racheal thought of something as she placed her hand on the cold bars of the cell. "But hopefully Reiner's winning." The girl hoped as she crouched to the ground. "Yeah and Reece is helping too."

With as much strength and hope Reiner charged at the woman pinning her to the balcony railing with hands clasped around her neck. "That a boy Reiner!" The ram smirked. "Evdomos kyklos." Reece casted a wide flame ring upon the ceiling causing various unchained demons to come through. "Attack the old wench!" They did his bidding.

"Foolish faun—" Mrs. Gail shut up as one of the demons struck her mouth with its tail while others began clawing and gnawing at her clothes and flesh. *Keys…*Reiner saw a set of keys around the woman's waist in which he attempted to grab. "Cross over old hag!" Reece placed his hand on the railing causing the entire thing to disappear. *What?* "Step back kid!" The ram then grabbed the young man in the nic of time as they watched Mrs. Gail fall with a sinister smile having the demons follow suit.

You thought you've won, boy? Siren isn't defeated, and that girl will die! "We have to leave." Said Reiner looking at the set of gold keys. "Thanks Reece." "No problem, gotta admit these people were annoying." The duo ran to the cell room and met up with Racheal. "I'm so glad…" Vitallin was wide eyed with relief.

"You were strong out there." She smiled with relief. "You should be too, don't ever let go of your life like that." The boy unlocked the cell and hugged her tightly. "I see you've made it out alive Reece, good for you." Racheal was impressed. "Of course." Once outside the castle, the group sat down to think a bit while the cool breeze aided them from the nice afternoon sun. "Here, eat this." Reiner handed her hard pieces of candy.

"Why candy?" The girl squinted her brows. "It regenerates the cells and tissues within." He explained. "That's so cool, you could have immortality with this plus it tastes great." "I've tried mixing it in with potions so it helps a little." Said Reece. "By the way, why were you taken prisoner?" "Their leader thought

I took some special book and secret document; either way it wasn't worth my life." She spoke the truth in her defense.

"Let's get going." Once home, Vitallin pestered Reiner to talk about life. "So…" "So?" He seemed confused. "How's your life going? Did you do anything exciting?" *Um…* He had to be honest. "I went to the beach with Erika and—" "Did you have fun?" Vitallin cocked a brow with a playful smirk. "Yeah for the most part." "Did *she* have fun?" Reiner knew where she was getting at. "It's not like that," He explained. "All we did was kiss and yet she wanted to take it further."

*That irritating slut…*She thought. "She confessed but I rejected her feelings." The young man went on to explain even further. "She told me about her past and feelings as to why. I only love her as a close friend, nothing more or less in that matter." Reiner felt a sentimental feeling of warmth in the pit of his stomach. "But as long as you guys can keep moving with hope in mind the outcomes of your lives might change for the better."

"So survive…" Reece said butting in between the two. "You two are both fighting for a title that would possibly impact everyone's future. Your loved ones or even everyone just might get the life and happiness they deserve in the right hands at least." "Thanks, that makes me happy." The boy smiled. "Interesting how far teamwork goes…how about it?" The ram extends his hand towards Racheal. "Weren't you suspicious of me when we first met?" The woman had a point. "See it as a change of heart." Reece said under his breath. "No." She didn't want to form an alliance.

"Come on we got your partner back at least, we scratch your back you scratch ours." "Yeah until blood shows? No." The woman left her decision there.

CHAPTER XX

Futures

The next morning was brutal as a snowstorm stuck to the subcity streets of Highliner and the school yard. "Yo, turtle!" It was Elizabeth Valentine in her black and gold puffer jacket. "Here, take it." She gave Reiner some sort of present wearing a velvet bow tie. "A stuffed rabbit?" He questioned as to why. "Not just any stuffed bunny." She smiled. "It's name is Nero, he can take away mana as well as corrupt it, he can also be your companion since you don't have any friends and all." She snickered with a joke.

"Why would you give me this?" He asks even further. "Because I'd figure you and Reece might make good use of it, it not only interferes with mana production but also allows the owner to alter another's past and future." Elizabeth continued. "My cousin made it a long time ago when I was in elementary school." "That's nice." The young man casually smiled.

"So you think this could help out Crow?" He thought this was it. "To a certain degree but mainly your case." The two parted ways once they reached the second floor of the building where they saw Vitallin. Class was in session as kids were chatting, copying homework, and studying for upcoming tests but there was one particular kid who was writing something strange upon his desk.

Magevo, Taro, Anastasi, Archaios, Gemisi…there, all done. As Reiner walked pass the blonde boy he realized something was up. *It's that guy from before…*He thought. "I see your girlfriend's alive huh," The boy spoke. "You must've done a number on president Gail though she wouldn't die that easily." He smirks ominously. *President Gail…so he's…*"A Siren member." The boy spoke up once more. "I know all about the documents that wench took, they were solicited information for our district!"

"I didn't steal jack shit!" Vitallin yelled so loud that she caused a scene. "All that torture was fucking pointless, that old hag is ruthless and deserves to burn in hell!" "Don't you dare say that about my leader you piece of shit!" Suddenly the young man got up from his seat and lunged at Vitallin, grasping her neck in the process. "Lance, stop!" The crowd of onlookers were surprised while most wanted a good fight.

"You'll pay for stealing!" The boy took out a suspicious needle from his back pocket and stuck the poor girl in the arm. "Vitallin!" Reiner kicked the boy's side and stomped him onto the ground. "Noitiki mimisi." Lance grabbed his wand and shot at Reiner with the strength of twenty horsemen. "Dammit!" The girl was furiated. "Kafsi tou—" Before she could finish her spell Reiner grabbed her by the hair and bashed her head against the chalkboard.

Ow! "It's out of my control!" He said. *He-he-he!* "Perifronimenos/Flegomenes floges!" "Ahhhh!!" The students were panicking as fire blasted out of the ceiling engulfing the entire classroom, parts of the hall and combusting the windows. The class scrambled out to get a nearby fire extinguisher; luckily there were two.

"Squeeze, squeeze!" By the time the students put out the fire, the classroom was nearly charred and destroyed. Fortunately there were only injuries and no deaths but unfortunately, Lance disappeared. "What the hell was all this shit for huh?!" A female student walks up and smacks both Vitallin and Reiner with the fire extinguisher, thus breaking his spell.

"Damn that hurts you know!" "You demons better get out of this school or else! It has been nothing but chaos ever since you guys showed up!" The girl continues her statement. "Whatever you guys are, it's not worth putting our lives at risk!" "We can explain, just don't scrutinize us!" Reiner yelled, shushing her up.

"Vitallin, and I aren't here to harm your lives..." He explained further. "We're fighting for a title that dictates the fate and future of your lives and humanity entirely." "Our guilds are fighting for **everything**, all in all we're here to protect you guys from *this* becoming your future." They all scoped the scene of what was left of the classroom as the smoke filled their lungs.

Melted textbooks, charred walls to third degree burns and perished valuables; all is what would be their *future* if they were put in the wrong hands. "Just trust in us." Vitallin spoke up.

"It would be a tragedy if you guys were in the wrong hands." "Believe in everything they're saying, alright?"

A female voice cracked through the massive crowd of onlookers. It was Erika Marvel with her red ribbon hair tie and bodacious tone of voice. "Please believe in what they're saying, they mean no harm." *Erika…* Reiner was proud of her. "I also have faith in them." Elizabeth spoke out of the blue. "In the end they are loving people who care so much for our lives." The girl winked at the two.

"What's happening?" Some of the teachers came out of the other classrooms upon hearing the commotion. "There was a fire going on and Lance and Reiner were fighting." A student told. "Is anyone hurt or killed?" Mrs. Veiter asks. "Only three people were injured and needed to visit a hospital." Said Vitallin.

"Alright students, leave the building at once school will be canceled for two weeks and I'll give those in my class online homework so please go home!" They all heard the woman. The kids went home as some waited for the bus. As Vitallin and the boy walked home Elizabeth wanted to go with them, she was curious as to what happened between Reiner and Lance.

"So there was a fight between you and Lance I heard." "I don't want to talk about it." Reiner was annoyed. "Lance is a Siren member and I was held prisoner by their president." Vitallin explained. "I see…by the way, you're a witch?" "Yeah It's a long story." She knew she'd know.

"That explains why you can walk, right?" "Yeah, my familiar helped." She said. "I see, I see…" Slight silence came between the two as she looked straight forward at Reiner then back at Vitallin. "Just to let you know Vitallin, promise Reiner whether your guild or Crow wins that you try to change the world for good, okay? Imagine a world without misfortunes." Her voice was low yet reasonably serious.

It was similar to what Reece told Reiner, almost as if it was about a sense of trust and reliance. "Of course, I'll also try to keep him in mind as he's done so much for me over the years." They both kept their word on it and before they knew it they were near Pruitte drive. "By the way Elizabeth, where's your house?" The girl wondered. "I sleep in a guild now," She said.

"But don't worry about me, I'm emancipated anyways so I can take care of myself," She explained. "An ancient destroyed my home when it was *supposed* to be trapped within a weapon." "That's funny," Vitallin said. "I was training with one a while ago." She continued. "His name was Vitrolf and he taught me a flaming wind technique where you manipulate the air in your lungs to breath out fire." "That's cool, hopefully you'd get even stronger and master other ancient and concentrated magic along the way." Elizabeth gave off a cool smile.

"Within the time of the day of kings, many guild members will go all out and make an impression even towards the next generations." "Hmm, I see so when—" At that moment Elizabeth disappeared into thin air. *Wha...what the...what was that just now?!* She was impressed. *That was awesome.* "Hey Reiner did you see that?" The boy was silent yet looked concerned.

The possibility of having everyone's fate be a part of our hands seems so dire, what if something doesn't go right? Would there really be a perfect world? What about my dad, along with Hide and their plans?…Reiner started to think about his position within Novo Incipere and what he stood for. He felt the pressure.

"Hey Reiner, snap out of it." Vitallin said from behind as she slapped the boy on the shoulders. "If something's bothering you, say it." The young man looked at her then smiled. "No matter what Vi, I'll always be there for you and we're gonna see life beyond the day of kings, that's a promise." "Yeah, we *will* change the world."

Once Reiner got home he thought of the stuffed bunny and its powers. He sat down on the living room couch and began playing with the thing. "Nero huh, can you even talk?" He wondered as he ripped a sheet of paper from his notebook and began writing down his name and a greeting. *Would this even work?* The bunny bowed in a respective manner.

*So it does understand…*Reiner then wrote something else. *Could you show me the past of Jeffery Strife?* He wanted to see his life out of curiosity and a sense of wonder. Suddenly, the stuffed bunny started clapping its hands in and out faster and faster. "Wha-What's happening?" It was the sound of an earthquake as the walls within the house started cracking, exposing the outside of what seems to be a location other than the suburbs of Highliner. The sun was shining as the boy felt his temperature rise up. "The house is gone!"

Reiner yelled with concern as he looked over his surroundings. He was on a street called Dire St. where he realized he was in a town of some sort. "Dad!" The young man saw Jeffery walking into a bar nearby in which he decided to follow behind. It was late afternoon and the bar was packed and completely furnished with red couches, a pool table, and dart boards.

People were eating, chatting and enjoying themselves as the atmosphere wasn't moody. Reiner sat at the end of the bar counter, a seat away from Jeffery. *Could he see me?* He thought whether or not this could alter his future self. "That's three times in a row Mr. Strife, did you and Kareen get into a fight recently?" The bartender said, wiping away glasses.

"You're becoming a regular, I like that." "Yeah well, I'm feeling peachy." The man sarcastically smiled as he glanced up seeing the bartender tie up her chestnut hair into a messy bun. "But not exactly," Said Jeffery, taking a sip of Gin. "Some of my closest friends and family were murdered back to back." He explained. "I'm afraid they're trying to send a message to me." "Seems like you're acting paranoid about that."

Who wouldn't be? Jeffery thought. "Look, I know what happened to your friends and family was sudden but take it like this: life and death comes and goes so you could view life like a legacy and live positively with every day being a journey." She gave him reassurance.

"You're still living and could live proudly like everyone else." "Is that really a life I'd like to live? To live like everyone else? I don't like normality. I have dreams, you know." Jeffery proclaimed as he wiped his hair away from his face. "And what dreams might that be?" The woman asks. It was a forthcoming wish that led to an adventure for him.

"To leave my past behind and go beyond life itself and find another world greater than our own." He smiled. *I also wonder if those deaths are connected somehow.* "Ahahaha…" The lady laughed. "You sound like a child but you have great faith in yourself." "I'm serious Sydney Sanderson," Jeffery said in a singing tone of voice. "I'd be happy to see if there were phenomenal places out there, a world filled with peace and happiness."

"Hmm…" Sydney thought of something. "There's a psychic a couple miles from here, maybe she could help you out." "You mean Miss Marge right?" The man glanced up, sounding quite attentive. "The busty blonde woman with glasses, yeah her." A grin planted Jeffery's lips. "You think she could help me with my dreams?" "Well yeah," Sydney said. "along with being a powerful psychic, she's also a witch." The bartender crossed her arms in a standish manner.

"She's a witch?" The man was in disbelief. "Of course, have you seen the potions and torn spell books in that woman's house? There's a ton, she must've been putting them to good use." Jeffery thought about Marge's abilities. *She's a great fortune teller and is able to read my past, and she's a witch…she may help me break out of this god forsaken world.* "Thanks Sydney, I'm gonna head over there now."

Jeffery got up from his stool and headed down the street to Marge's house. Reiner noticed him and followed behind questioning his dad. *So who's Marge, and how does he know her? Does this have anything to do with Hide? Or the other world? Maybe…*Curiosity ran through the young man's mind as he hasn't *known* the man since his disappearance. Reiner looked straight at Jeffery.

"Such an intriguing person." *What other secrets are you hiding?* The man stopped at a small gable front house with black sidings and white window trimmings which looked aesthetically pleasing. The man rang the doorbell. Ding-dong!

Ding-dong! "Why hello Jeffery, nice of you to stop by." A woman came out in a black lace sundress; her makeup was dazzling as well with the red eyeshadow complementing her light blonde hair and plush pink lips.

"Yeah, nice seeing you too miss Marge." Jeffery let out a rough cough before saying anything else. "Are you wanting to know about your lifetime now? Or perhaps a fortune reading?" She asked, sending off a little smile towards him. "Ah yes actually…I'm wanting my future and past shown and ways I can alter it." He explained.

"I'm wanting to leave this place behind and wake up in a better world, some place where I become somebody with a purpose and somewhere where there is no suffering like a paradise, tell me Marge is there really a place like that?" Jeffery insisted that she would tell him since he's been through so much in his life. "Yeah well, come inside. It's pretty hot out here." Reiner snuck through the door while Jeffery stepped inside a fully furnished home with broken beakers, test tubes, and torn grimoires scattered on the floor and living room counter.

"I see you've renovated since I've last came over." "Yeah, I've got new marble floorings, curtains, sculptures and even picked up painting so yeah I'm happy with the new look." They looked around the living room before sitting down on the couch. Miss Marge grabbed a crystal ball from the side table. While holding it in her hand she placed Jeffery's left palm on top and tightly grabbed hold of his right hand.

"Multre, multre na gate of time dura nepe shake torou…" *What is she saying?* The boy wondered to himself. Marge said a sequence of words which made the ball warm. "Whoa." Suddenly sequences of the man's life appeared onto the crystal ball. His decent memories along with the painful and bad ones. "Jeffery, you may get over your friends and family but one may not get over you, I can feel how bad your son wanted to be with you and how he felt when you left him."

Yeah, how could you? The young man darted his eyes towards Jeffery. A sequence of Reiner's young life appeared on the ball. *Reiner…you'll know soon enough I've tried but am sorry.* The man kept his thoughts to himself. "You'll come to know that what you wish for comes with consequences." "So you mean that other world is real?" Jeffery caught onto what she meant. "Yes but it's far from a paradise for you." Marge elaborated.

"You'd question a man you work for and kill others for those causes you so wish to meet." "There is a world filled with magic, magic that encompasses miracles and life itself within people of that world; you'd even have to consider blood for blood in your case." *She must be talking about Novo Incipere? And the fact that he has to fight us…*Reiner felt a slight warmth in his body. He was concerned with the man's affiliation with Hide, their goals, and whether he would ever have a proper relationship with Jeffery again.

"Blood for blood? What does that mean?" Jeffery waited a moment for Marge to speak. "Your son hosts various types of magic and would soon be looking for you, he's a sorcerer who loves you which would be a problem." The woman told. "So Reiner's a sorcerer huh? If that's the case he'd have a new wonderous situation in his hands, I didn't know we were from a line of wizards and witches." "Yeah…" Marge took this opportunity to act upon a similar topic so she sat the ball back onto the table.

"Let me see your palm." "Why?" Jeffery wanted her to talk more about his life and about the other world but then figured something else. "Here." The man extended his hand out to Marge. The woman soon licked her finger then traced it on the creases of his hand. "Ah shit! What are you doing?" Blood began to profuse as Marge's finger cut through the creases of his hand.

"Fuck Marge! Please stop!" The woman smiled then kissed Jeffery. Their tongues shifted around each other as the bitter taste of medicine trickled down his throat. Soon Jeffery's body relaxed as the pain subsided. "What kind of magic is that?" The boy mumbled to himself as it piqued his interest. Marge balled his hand into a fist then unraveled it back open to reveal some sort of yellow paper. A note of some sort.

"What's this?" The man wondered. "Take it as an opening to the other world, and a message from Shuttman." "Shuttman? Who's he?" "The one working on the same path to a utopia like you. He's the leader of Hide, a parent organization co-functioning with others like Rinfer and Peradine inc."

Rinfer…so Hide has something to do with that organization? Reiner couldn't find a way to put the two together. Before talking any further, Marge squirmed on the couch and smirked as she felt a warm, tingling sensation within her chest and between her thighs.

She bit her plush lips before looking down at the thick crotch of Jeffery's jeans. "How about we finish that kiss with something more…" The man blushed, giving his slightly freckled face a sort of young flushed look as if he ate something hot. "Well how about we—" Unfortunately the man couldn't get out any words as they locked lips together finishing the kiss from last time before having Marge strip off her black sundress.

She toppled over Jeffery zipping down his jeans while pulling out his thick, wet penis laced with semen. *Oh shit!* Holding the stuffed bunny Reiner jetted out the door faster than you can say the word *Go!*

So he's having an affair with a psychic behind Mom's back… such a sleazeball. As Reiner tried getting rid of the illusive thoughts in his head, he also appreciated gaining insight on his father. Now all there is was to go home. The young man placed Nero on the ground to grab a piece of cardboard from the other side of the street and an ink pen from his pocket.

Nero, take me home now. He wrote. The bunny shook its head and grabbed the boy's pen with both hands. *Just walk over to Pruitte drive, it's forty-seven minutes away, I'll wave my hands later once you get there.* It wrote back. "So you can write back huh," The young man was surprised as he continued writing back and forth with Nero as he walked home with him.

CHAPTER XXI

Keeping Hope

Raise and shine. Reiner reached for the skies, yawning enough to the point of waking up Reece. "Are you planning on making a mixtape with all that yawning?" The ram said, chuckling at his own joke. "I bet you would listen to that." Reiner laughed. Reece geared his attention to the brown stuffed bunny rabbit sitting on the headboard of the bed. "Such a cute bunny Reiner, got any other playpen toys?" He snarled in a playful manner while examining the plush rabbit all around, even taking in a whiff.

*Strange…*The pungent odor of ammonia mixed with peaches shot up the faun's nostrils, it was an odor so vivid it almost gave out a weird taste in his mouth. *It must be enchanted, powerful perhaps.* "Who gave you this?" The youngman looked at the boy interested as to why. "Elizabeth did," Reiner explained.

"She figured we might make use of it. Its name is Nero, it has the ability to look through and alter a person's past and future along with constricting and corrupting another person's magic." "That's good…" Reece was intrigued as he thought about its capabilities in regards to fighting the other guilds as well as the day of kings.

Maybe I could get rid of those annoying ass guilds like Magnum and Siren. Getting stronger isn't only about broads of muscle it's about brains as well, yeah think about all of the intellectual people who transformed this world. The ram remembered his conversation with Merium and wanted to prove his point.

"Got any other powers I'm unaware of?" "Not that I know of." Reiner rest his case as he hopped out of bed, grabbed his uniform and headed to the bathroom. It was a cold yet calming day outside as the sky was grayed out from the previous snow storm. The air was so cold and dry that with one deep inhale it would tingle a slight burn within the back of your throat and having that coupled with a thick foggy mist stretching miles away only made it colder.

"Yo turtle, look up!" A voice hollered above as loud as they could. *What the hell?!* Reiner looked up above and saw Elizabeth falling from the sky. "Brace for impact!" Reiner said, preparing to catch her fall as he threw his backpack to the ground. "Shit!" The girl laughed as she not-so-gracefully fell into his arms.

"That's one way to start your day." Reiner was amazed and laughed from the scene of it all. "What were you doing?" He asks. "I was eating breakfast and talking with Xavier about Novo Incipere's history and the guilds within the other regions." Reiner cocked a brow ready to say some questions. "So there are more guilds I don't know about?" "Yeah, they're all across

Novo Incipere spanning amongst many regions. There are at least three hundred guilds in total."

Reiner's mouth went agape. "Three hundred! That's crazy." "Well duh," The girl playfully flicked the boy's forehead. "It's within an entire world you dope, just culturally different from ours." She continued. "Anyways, what did you do yesterday? Did you use precious Nero?" "Yeah to my advantage," Reiner said.

"I've got at least some information on my dad." "Your dad? Why?" Elizabeth squinted with a confused expression. "He disappeared from my life and it tore me up. It turns out he's a Hide affiliate who wants to find a utopia that would end his suffering." The kid was just unsure with one question. "Your father's a Hide member huh? Well that must suck the biggest balls." The girl tilted her head with difficulty.

"Yeah that leads me to my next thought. Do you think Hide is good?" It was a question that's been nagging him for a while. "Well if you want my opinion, no." She said sternly as she shook her head. "Hide would slaughter anyone who produces magic whether they are a familiar, or sorcerer and witch as they would kill to see their goals fruition."

"What are their goals?" Reiner asked a convoluted question with no clear answer. "I don't quite know exactly," She replied. "They test and study the magic coursing through our blood and do whatever with it." Elizabeth rested her head on the young man's chest.

"Do you think my father would have the guts to kill me?" Reiner thought of a rather bold and brash question. "I don't quite know exactly, considering you're his son, but coming from me take probably as a warning." She continued. "Hide infiltrated the guild one time and their chief Xan nearly burned and broke my friend's spine once he swung her across the room to the lobby's fireplace. Maxine was hunched over for weeks on end. Hide members have the strength to kill, that's for sure."

I don't think they should have a notion of a utopia, especially if they're the ones slaughtering people and we wouldn't be a part of their plans anyways. Reiner was going against Hide as well as his perception of them. He was on the side of wizardry and fighting alongside his guildmates for the king's title. It would be a much bigger battle with Hide involved. "Why is he carrying you? Did you sprain an ankle?"

Vitallin leaned against the school building texting her friends back and forth looking between her phone and Reiner. "No, we were reenacting our wedding day." Elizabeth joked around. "Oh really?" Vitallin sent off an interesting smirk as she cocked an eyebrow. "Don't worry tinker bell he's all yours." The girl commented as she playfully pinched Vitallin's cheek. "Good morning class, please pass up your homework and open your books to page one hundred and ninety-five: Surface Area."

Mr. Mountgomery handed out the assignments. "If the work seems too hard don't be afraid to ask your classmates for help." The class was peaceful and concentrating on the task at hand. Some were struggling while others breezed through the row of questions. "Hey Vi, could you help me?" Megan asked as she turned around to look at the girl as Vitallin glanced up and looked at her.

Megan had a grunge, punk rock vibe to her. She had short ombre green hair cut into a messy bob, ear and tongue piercings, beautiful makeup, and tattoos; one most notably on her cheek: large dotted lines forming the shape of a heart. "Yeah Meg." Vitallin got up from her seat before getting interjected. "Aye yo, me too." A girl with a uniquely feminine voice called out to Vitallin as well, it was the adorably cute Chrissie, a contrast with Megan in personality.

She had a quirky and fun persona with her long messy brown hair, glowing dark skin and decorative ear piercings. "Yeah well why don't you join us then." The two grabbed a chair and huddled around Megan's desk. "Finding the surface area is easy," Vitallin explained as she showed off her notes. "The metric formula of a rectangular prism is two times length and width, plus two times length and height, plus two times height and width." (SA=2LW+2LH+2WH)

She continued. "The surface area for a triangular prism is two times the *area of base*, plus the *perimeter of the base* times height." (SA=2B+Ph) The girl leaned back in her chair hoping the two would understand. "Oh, I see now, thanks…" Megan knew. "This shit's annoying, I'm just wanting to get into Princeton University soon after all these courses are finished." Chrissie laid her head down on the girl's desk with disappointment.

"So Vi, what did you do over the last two weeks we were out?" "Not much really," She replied. "I finished painting cover designs for my author clients. I use acrylic and watercolors." "That's cool, so do you read any of your clients' books?" Chrissie questioned. "Yeah I've bought two of my clients books; one about a criminal syndicate, and the other is about a group of female spies being hunted down by foreign CIAs all over the world. It's a great thriller."

A few hours passed and class was over, the three went their separate ways as Vitallin dashed into the nearest restroom. "Look girls, it's the devil." A redheaded girl slapped Vitallin across the face then grabbed a fist full of her hair and bashed her face near the sink causing a black eye to swell up. "You guys have caused nothing but chaos to this school and I want you all *out*." She sternly talked in the girl's ear as she made her point across.

"Get the fuck off me!" Vitallin screamed as she managed to jab one of the girls in the eye with a pencil. "Help me!" The girl yelled as the group of delinquents dragged Vitallin to a stall and violently dunked her head in the toilet. "Let's see if a witch can drown in fucking piss!" *No!* Vitallin thought about her life and how it came to this. Why was she so hated and would she really want to protect these people? Vitallin just wished that once this tribulation was over, she could win the title to improve her own life as she would finally be in control.

The girl violently banged her hand on the steel sides of the stall hoping anyone would hear her outside. *Help me!* Luckily someone heard the commotion and dashed inside the restroom. "Hey get the fuck off her!" It was a tall muscular young man with the strength and aggression of a lion. "Well if it isn't the dauntingly emotionless cock sucking loner." The redhead girl laughed and mocked at the guy's expense when suddenly the young man grabbed her hair and bashed her face along the side of the stall causing her to release Vitallin.

"You piece of shit!" The other girls got mad and began fighting him. Vitallin noted this and grabbed a nearby broom. "Rot in hell!" The girl swung left and right causing damage to them anyway she could before using a reconstruction spell. "Akida." The curved part of the wooden broom handle ate away leaving it to become sharper than any stake. "Hey boy, step aside!" She warned as she hurled the broom straight at one of the girls stabbing her through the chest.

"Ahhhh!!" The pain gripped her voice as she fell down onto the porcelain white tiles dirtying it with blood. "Come on, follow me!" The man suddenly grabbed Vitallin's hand and sped downstairs to the nurses office. *Damn, she must be out…* The guy looked through the vertical window. It was dark inside yet he could see some light coming from one of the side rooms. "Try knocking some more." Vitallin suggested as she looked into the guy's steely blue eyes.

What a handsome face… She thought as she further examined him. *Strong jawline, dewy cool skin, black tousled hair…interesting.* The guy did as told and even jiggled the doorknob. Click-click! "It's open." The two walked through and turned on the lights. "No one's here, you should go sit down." The guy instructed as he went into another room to grab some cotton cloth rags and soap. Vitallin looked around the office then sat on a blue nursing bed.

"I guess you were the only one who heard me screaming." She tried laughing as she admits. "Yeah they were horrific," The young man placed the cleaning items beside her. "well at least you aren't dead." It hit her. Vitallin hugged the guy as tight as she could while holding back tears. She recalled all her previous "brush with death" moments and thought of how strong she really is, yet how worthless she was in the eyes of others. *Wow you reek of piss.* The guy embraced the girl before pushing away.

"What happened? Why did they do that to you?" He asks. "Do you know why school closed down the last two weeks?" "Yeah, there was a major fire on the second floor." He answered. "That fire was from magic vs. magic." She explained. "I'm not a devil but am a witch along with my friend Reiner who's a sorcerer." "You mean Reiner Strife? I knew that guy since middle school, who knew he'd pick Milford, it's so hard to get in."

He knows Reiner? The girl wondered about the boy's past school life. "So the kid's into witchcraft huh?" "Well it isn't necessarily like that, there's an entire world filled with sorcerers, witches and magic." Vitallin smiled, wiping the wet rag all over her face. "Seems fascinating, by the way what's your name?" The guy asks with a raspy voice. "Vitallin, and what is yours?" "Alex, Alex Hersh." He smiled, extending his hand for another greeting. "Thanks for helping me back there, you're a hero." Vitallin hugged the guy once more. "Come on, anyone seeing your situation would have stepped in."

Once school ended Reiner met up with Vitallin outside and gave the girl a slight embrace. "What's up?" He asks as she suddenly pushes him away, her gaze darting over to the side as she had a concerned expression planted on her face. "I got jumped in the restroom today." The girl said as Reiner's light brown eyes darkened with hatred. "Who was it?" He sternly asked.

"I don't really know, she's probably a junior. I've never seen her before but she had long wavy red hair and blooming rose tattoos up her neck, she was also with her group of friends." She went on to explain further. "They jumped me because I'm a witch and they didn't want their lives at risk as the school turned into a hotspot for chaos."

The girl couldn't get rid of one nagging thought. "Would we need to protect people like that? They won't change and may continue harming and killing others. Do people like that deserve a happy ending?" "You're right…" The young man thought about it. "But would you think having the other guilds win would make anything else better? We'd be controlled by a fascist or worse if all we know, plus since it's civilians all you have to do is prove to them that their lives will become better; we would be able to do whatever we want with them using the hope that fights despair."

Reiner continued his speech. "You can drive out hatred and misery with love and hope." He put his views on the matter. "Sorry if I'm coming off too philosophical." Reiner laughed. "Yeah, I guess you're right." "Did you try fighting them back?" The boy moved Vitallin's hair away from her face. "Yeah after some guy came in to help, they were dunking my head in fucking piss!" "Those fucking assholes." The young man was at a loss for words as a slight melancholic pause came between the two.

"The guy who helped me out apparently knows you, saying that he knew you a while back his name was Alex Hersh, ring a bell by any chance?" *Alex Hersh*…Reiner thought of a connection. "Oh that Alex, we were friends back in middle school. He was interesting and even smarter than me." "What does he do?" The girl was intrigued. "He was the ultimate chemist, particularly a chemical physicist." Reiner explained.

"He was a bigger nerd than me, spending hours in the school's lab doing tests and writing down notes as if he was submitting them to the UK's Royal Society of Chemistry." The kid laughed. "That's cool, what a talent." She was impressed.

CHAPTER XXII

Family Ties

Instead of the two going home, they decided to head over to Bates recreation center to relax and do homework. "I haven't been here in months." Vitallin took a whiff of the fresh cedar air as she swung her backpack onto the bleachers. There were a tolerable amount of people within the rec center as there were a few teenagers in the gym playing basketball.

"Did you know they built a bowling alley downstairs? It's probably better than the swimming pool." "Probably not, nothing can be better than seeing you in that red bikini." The boy smooth talked. "With those large tits you'd look good in anything." "Is that so? Pervert." Vitallin licked her hand and smeared it along the boy's cheek. "What's that about?" He laughed.

"Consider it a wet kiss for such a poor flirt." She smirked. "At least I tried." Reiner kissed the girl on the lips. "I need help with business english." "How come you do so well with annoying classes but need help in simple ones?" She tried wrapping her head around it. "Because I love solving things as *everything* has an answer and reason behind it." Reiner handed his textbook to her as she read a passage.

"A misplaced modifier is a modifier placed too far from the word or words it modifies, this makes the sentence sometimes awkward and even humorous." She continued with a test example. "Is this correct or incorrect: She wore a bicycle helmet on her head which was too large." "I'm…not quite sure. It sounds fine if you're adding a syntax for a complete sentence." He managed to make a point. "Dammit, you have a point but for the sake of the example it's wrong."

"I see." The young man had a wager. "How about I do your math homework, and you do my work?" "Sure." Between doing work and playing around the two talked about unchained familiars, fighting and the stolen Siren books. "Hey Vi, I wanna know what your fighting style is." Reiner wanted to train with her someday.

"Well I do know how to combine value to most spells." She told. "Like how?" "With the words you say you can manipulate its actions." She continued. "Say if you were to make your enemies blood literally boil you'd write down *vrazei aima* into a spellbook and combine them by smearing your blood on it, thus enhancing it with your magic." Reiner squinted his brows with unknowing interest as to how she'd know what to do.

"Who taught you that?" He asked. "I figured I'd teach myself." She smiled as if it was a discovery. "I believe that the human soul can achieve anything, especially since I have magic coursing through my veins." "How about showing me some moves then?" Reiner was pumped. "Alrighty then let's hit the tracks." After an hour of studying and homework the two head over to the outdoors track. With street lights on, the air was cool as the dark blue evening sky twinkled above.

The kids walked further and further behind the building and threw their stuff onto the snow laden grass. "Let's see what you're made of." They said to each other as they stepped onto the snowy track. "Ready, set…" Reiner counted down from the other end. Vitallin felt the adrenaline as her throat tightened, expecting him to go easy on her. "Go!" The boy dashed towards the girl as she took a stance.

"Mikos kymatos!" Vitallin remembered her flaming wind technique, Reiner quickly dodged only to have it chase after him. *That's sick!* He was impressed. "Xechasmeno asteri." Black stars appeared behind Vitallin's footsteps as she chased the young man around. They soon shot out purple chains entangling her ankles and legs together. "Shit, it hurts!" She gritted her teeth as she tried untangling them.

"Hurry up, they're poisonous." He said. *Really now…* She had an idea, a silly one. "I'll stop the match and give you an antidote from Reece if you forfeit." Reiner wagered as he walked closer to her. "Never, prisma!" *Very well then.* He stepped away from her before falling onto the ground. "What the heck?" Reiner felt a cold barrier against his hand as if there was an invisible wall preventing him from moving any further.

Prisma must mean prism. Before putting the two and two together, Reiner was already trapped within the glass prism unable to think of a plan of escape. *Fuck!* "Fotismos gyrou." Having Vitallin learn a thing or two in science paid off as she snapped her fingers together causing a poisonous light to enter through the prism when she suddenly fell to the ground.

"Oh no…" Reiner's whole body went numb as he felt nauseous and light headed. *Shit, I gotta escape somehow.* While reserving his strength, Reiner banged on the glass as hard as he could but it wouldn't budge. *This must be made out of quartz crystals.* "Shit!" In a moment, Reiner began hacking up blood but he was more concerned about escaping before it's too late. The kid placed his palm on the prism wall and thought about fusing it.

"Thryallida." He said in a low tone. The area began vibrating and soon melted from the inside out. "Vitallin!" The young man struggled to breath as he saw her helplessly on the ground. *I gotta get to Reece fast!* With strength depleting, Reiner armed their backpacks and hulled the girl up his back. With mental fortitude the boy power-walked home not caring about what happens to him, luckily they were thirteen minutes away.

"So this play thing can inhibit mana huh?" Meanwhile Reece was at home testing Nero out by squeezing its bunny ears. *What else does this thing do?* Nero began frantically kicking and squirming around urging the ram to let go. "Whoa." The floppy bunny then jumped from the headboard and used a notebook and ink pen from the floor to write down a greeting and foreknowing information.

Hello horned man, I'm sorry to say but Mr. Lucien Ladenhade would like to have a word with you. Nero made sure to get the ram's attention.

Hmm, you mean that damned capital leader in Betham? I wonder what situations he's been up to. This piqued the guy's interest as the bunny continued writing.

He's wanting to discuss alliances and even undertake you by teaming you up with some of his associate captains to eradicate a group of guilds and acquire a dead heart box along with bridging your regions together. "That's nice and all but out of all of the genius mages out there why me, our regions are barely close to each other and retrieving a *dead heart box* may cause problems." The ram reasoned to himself when suddenly the door swung open as Reiner burst through the room.

"Reece, give me your antidote Vitallin and I are poisoned." The young man couldn't hold her up much longer. "Yeah hold on a sec." Reece rummaged through his pouch and tossed the large bottle to the boy. Reiner sat the girl on his bed, her eyes cloudy as if she had cataracts. He took a gulp of the sour liquid then poured some into her mouth. The cloudiness of her eyes went away as for the boy's pain as well.

"Rei…ner, you're alive?" Vitallin proved her vitality as she fell back on the bed and rolled on her side. "Yeah, and you are too." He said as he kissed her cheek. "Your spells are insane." The kid applauded. "I'm sorry, I had a dumb idea of manipulating the poison in my blood once you used that attack. I thought it would make my magic more powerful."

Reiner shook his head. "Don't risk your life for power, your magic is already strong enough, believe me." He turned his head towards Reece. "By the way, what were you doing all this time?" "I've been figuring out this stuffed rabbit for a while and it gave out some useful information." He got to the point. "I'm going to one of the eastern regions of Novo Incipere, there's a certain guy in Betham who wants to see me."

"May I come with you?" Reiner exclaimed as he wanted to explore the many regions of the other world once he learned there were even more guilds out there. "Sure but I feel it's best if you stay behind and tend to your little girlfriend here." The guy had a point. "It's alright I'm fine, I can roll over without pain see?" The girl spoke up, clearing the concern.

"So who's this guy you're meeting up with?" Reiner asked. "He's one of the high commissioners of one of the eastern regions with many magic forces at his disposal." Reece explained. "They work alongside regional councils to bridge and discuss alliances and regions but I'm unsure why the man needs me." He leaned back in the rolling chair resting his case there. "That's important, they're probably wanting you to retrieve something like a crystal of some sort." The kid started assuming stuff.

"It probably has an ancient inside of it." Vitallin chimed in. "Well he does want me to find a dead heart box." "What's that?" The girl asked, lying down kicking her feet in the air. "It's a sacred box containing the heart of one of the first title holders." "The first holder?!" The kids blurted out in unison as Reece grabbed their attention. "Yeah, the one who was a part of the first previous generational war. I don't know who it is but I've heard their heart could create and curse a whole new category of magic altogether."

*The previous generational wars...*Reiner thought of the title's many capabilities. "Hey Reiner, could I spend the night over?" Vitallin asked yawning herself to sleep. "Sure, why not?"

He said as he threw a pillow at her. The night was peaceful all throughout the house. There was no sound, not even for a mouse in which Reece took this opportunity to disappear. "Kryfi porta." He opened a portal door to the other side, not trying to wake the others. Reece stepped into the night as the stars showed themselves amongst the colorful sky.

Our regions aren't really that close ya know… The ram griped as he headed out far east to the Betham region thinking about the future and Lucien. The weekend morning was cloudy and dreary. A certain female woke up lighting a specific question in her mind: *Would anything change if I see Anri again?* Erika pondered on her thoughts as she stared at the ceiling.

Reece, if whatever you said about Anri being alive is true, then make sure she remembers me. And about the other world… where did it come from? What's the outcome? Rei— "Erika! Come downstairs and eat your breakfast!" The girl's mother shouted, snapping her from her train of thought.

"Coming!" The spicy scent of sausages permeated the air as the dining table was set with eggs, french toast, sausage, cheese grits, and apples. The mood was vibrant yet typical as the t.v. was on in one room and radio music in another. "Good morning Erika." Her mother greeted flipping her black long wavy hair back. "Morning mother, father…" Erika pulled out a chair. "So dear, how's school going?" Her mother asked, reaching for the plate of french toast. "Pretty nice, I'm making all A's so yeah…" "How's Rinfer?"

Her suave father spoke up with his husky voice. He wore a gray slim fitted suit complementing his lean physique. "I'm monitoring two countries and my new supervisor isn't irritating though I don't know why they'd replace chief Conwell? He was good for many years." An interesting atmosphere soon hanged over the family. "You know tomorrow's your sister's birthday. Would you mind planting down some flowers at the cemetery?" Her father brought up a certain nagging topic.

"Anri isn't dead." Erika spoke up as her mother looked at her with a confused expression planted on her youthful face. "You're in denial." Mr. Marvel argued. "I'm not in denial, Reece knows where she is! He's been with her!" The girl listened to her words and was certain as she trusted him, not allowing her emotions to get in the way. "You mean Reece Eatherlove? The man who couldn't protect her and allowed her to get shot to death? How pathetic, he couldn't even be with her in the most dire times…what a piece of shit."

"Shut your fucking mouth! Again, Anri isn't dead and Reece loves her; he wouldn't break trust between family and not between me!" Erika yelled as she shed a painful tear. "None of you know how this makes me feel let alone care. I've been through dark places in my life and had to crawl out of them myself!" She continued her cry.

"All you guys ever do is turn a side eye and move on as if everything's fucking fine!" At that moment Erika got up and ran to her room sad yet rightfully angry. She thought of ways to simmer down but figured it would be best to leave the house so she took a shower, got dressed, and headed out. "Ten, eleven, twelve…" *He still looks cute.* Meanwhile Vitallin was awake facing towards the sleeping Reiner. "Hehehehe." The girl was coloring in the boy's many freckles with an ink pen before getting a mischievous idea to write on the side of his cheek.

"Good morning!" Vitallin smirked as she dropped the pen underneath the bed. "Hey, how'd you sleep?" Reiner woke up dazed and drowsy. "Like a baby, unlike you." She continued. "By the way, today's Saturday so we don't have classes and your familiar isn't here." "What?" Reiner took a look around the room. "Dammit he went to that other region without me." The guy was pretty disappointed. "So wouldn't the dead heart box be similar to ancients?"

"I don't know, what makes you say that?" Reiner questioned with interest. "Well there was an ancient trapped within a weapon Elizabeth had and they're like veterans of the previous generational war." Reiner sat up on the bed. "So ancients are similar to title holders?" He tried understanding. "I don't know, probably. I've trained with one and he was pretty helpful." "That's so cool, no wonder you're strong." He commented. "It would have explained that prism spell."

Ding-dong! The doorbell rang once Reiner looked out the window and saw a black jaguar parked on his driveway. *Could it be Erika's What would she want so early in the morning?* "I'm going to see who it is." Reiner said as Vitallin followed. "Stupid parents…Reece wouldn't abandon Anri like that!" Erika mumbled underneath her breath, trying her hopes up. "Hey Erika, why are you here?" Reiner asks while running his hand through his messy brown hair.

The girl gave the kid a concerned look then laughed underneath her breath. "What's so funny?" She held up her makeup mirror at him. *What the hell Vitallin!* He saw where she wrote "*I eat fresh shit*" on his cheek. He was annoyed. *Hopefully this shit washes off, that little…* "I'm wanting to speak with Reece, I got in an argument with my parents this morning and I've been having some pressing thoughts lately." "The guy's not here." Vitallin butted in as she peered her head out behind Reiner.

"Uh…hello Vitallin?" Erika was flabbergasted as she glanced at her then back at Reiner. *Are they…? No, don't tell me they just had sex!* The girl quickly looked off to the side as she wildly blushed, unable to look at the two. "Yeah apparently Reece isn't here, he's in another region within the other world." Reiner spoke. "You mean Novo Incipere, right?" Erika looked up at the young man wanting to know more clues about that world and her sister.

"Yeah apparently he's been called on a mission of some sort though he'd be out for a while." "Well do you…" Erika again looked at Reiner then towards Vitallin, cocking a smug yet annoyed brow at her. "Would you like to go on a trip?" She waited for a favorable reply. "Yeah sure but could Vitallin come too? It'll be interesting and she might learn a thing or two." He made sure to prank her back.

"Well," Vitallin stuck her tongue out at the girl dissing her and Reiner's relationship. "sure whatever." After Vitallin and Reiner took turns taking a shower they hopped into the car and drove to the Bright Stone trails: two thirty-seven mile forest and mountain trails which legend says if you run all the way through you'd gain light speed abilities.

CHAPTER XXIII

Revelations

The air was crisp as they hopped out the car. The forest was near them as the entrance sign was ahead. "So you wanted to go hiking? Not what I was expecting but great exercise anyways." Reiner commented. "Yeah, I'd figure you'd pick a movie theater or something." Vitallin had a hint of displeasure in her voice. "It's a beautiful trail made for exercising on such a cloudy day, something your lazy ass wouldn't understand." Erika replied to the girl underneath her breath.

"Anyways Reiner, could you lead the way?" "Sure." The three followed along the log fence making their way into the forest where they saw a few people ahead of them. "So Erika if you don't mind me asking, what were you and your parents arguing about?" He wondered. "It's about Anri." She continued. "They doubt the possibility she's alive and blames her life and supposed death on Reece."

"She's wanted within my region of Novo Incipere." Reiner told. "What did she do?" Erika was shocked. "She murdered a few allied guilds." *So she did kill someone…* "So about the other world, how did it come to be? I mean how come my sister's apart of it?" "I don't quite know exactly." He said. "Reece found me coming out of a box of marbles I was probably given when I was little but I'm assuming they were sorcerers and witches long before us and had their reasons for being inside that world in the first place."

Wow. Erika had an interesting view of Anri though it wasn't like her to keep secrets. *How come she's a witch anyways? I didn't expect them to be in our lineage.* The group curved around a few streams and up a hill to emerge from the woods, seeing a beautiful waterfall a few feets below. "Jeez, my feet are tired, when will it end?" Vitallin complained while crossing the bridge overlooking the forest waterfall. "It's called exercise, try to keep up." The young man motioned to her. "In my case, think of it as punishment for writing on my face." He was over it a while ago. "We are near the halfway mark."

Erika announced looking at the trail sign. "We can rest once we get there." "Yo Eric, how would you handle seeing your sister again?" Vitallin asked some personal questions. "I mean it's probably been years since she last saw you and would you still approve of her even though she's a wanted murderer?" *Thanks for caring bonehead.* She appreciated her forethought.

Erika would at least think Anri would remember her but wouldn't know what to expect given the fact that she's fighting within the portions of a dire universal war. "Uh…I'd respect her still. She would be fighting people out of self defense since people are probably setting her up…by the way Reiner what do you guys do? What's Novo Incipere about?" She looked his way. At that moment the boy thought of a clever compromise. *Since she works for Rinfer, would she know any connection with Hide and what they're associations are about? Who is that Shuttman guy?* He remembered his time at Marge's place.

"I have some questions for you too, and I won't talk if you don't." He said placing his hands on Erika's shoulders causing her to smile as she blushed. "What do you want to know?" "It's about Rinfer and Hide, does that name ring a bell?" He made sure to get to the point. "Yeah, most of the employees and associates had to watch a presentation about Hide during the first day." She explained.

"They're a parent company working with us to showcase discoveries and scientific tests. Some of our spies gather research intel on the experiments from foreign lands for us to reapply to our tests and advance the societies, technology, and weaponry of all nations." *That's a lot.* Reiner just couldn't understand their morals of ethics. They kill mages or anyone who has magic yet try to advance the human condition?

The trio reached the halfway mark where there was a bench and trail map sign. "Now you tell me about the other world, what's its meaning?" "To sum it up, a generational legacy." He told the girl. "Me and goldilocks here are fighting a war on the side of hope, the king's title has an ability to control all worlds and influences lives within them. Imagine having such heinous and evil people having that title, you'd have a recipe for disaster as all hope is gone for you, your friends and loved ones." Reiner explained to the girl resting his palms on the rough wooden surface of the bench.

"Polka dots here is right, this is a war of power along with hope." Vitallin elaborated. "It's a battle for everyone's future." "That's scary." Erika exclaimed, expressing her fear of the unknown. *We all might be enslaved, or tortured even...*"Yeah the pressure is immense, but that battle is years away yet seems like months as things will change." He made sure to keep caution till that day as he doesn't know what might happen till then. "Do you think Novo Incipere's a pretty place?" Reiner was given a straightforward question.

"By pretty you mean lively, then yeah some sort. Most of the cities are beautiful at night." After resting the three got up and finished the trail by sundown as they were amongst the few groups to finish the whole thing. "I call shotgun!" Vitallin said, hopping into the front seat of the car. The night went smoothly as the kids bonded. Family revelations were told and viewed.

As Erika drove up the driveway, she unlocked the car doors. "Thanks Eric, I've had a pretty fun day today." Vitallin commented. "Wait, why are you getting out? Are you two dating?" She felt the weight of those words as she was jealous. "What if we are? Are you jealous?" Vitallin smirks as Erika rolls her eyes. "She can walk home." Reiner interjected. "But I wanna play with your body some more." Vitallin jokingly laughed, causing Erika to turn tomato red.

"Where's your brain, idiot?" Reiner nervously laughed. "Well that's a shame." Erika commented as she drove away. Once the kid got inside he headed upstairs to his room passing his mother sleeping on the couch. Reiner crashed on his plaid blue bed sheets and looked around the room. *Hmm, the guy isn't back yet.* He rolled to his side thinking about the road ahead and where it'll lead him. Battles among wars, people's intentions in the end of it all. Yes the years seem long but it'll count down soon enough and conclude an unknown future. Misfortunes or hope, life as we know it will change forever.

Meanwhile after long hours of running and flying on end Reece made it to the outskirts of a city named Rhyme and into the border town of Andrea. He was finally in one of the eastern regions of Novo Incipere: Betham region. *Dammit Lucien, you better give me a good reward after all this.* Andrea town was seasonally beautiful with its spring feel as the sweet peas and cherry blossoms were blooming this time around. Reece was exhausted as the heat grazed his supple, pale skin. "Fuck!" The sun was so unbearable he collapsed onto the stone ground.

"Hey sir, are you okay?" A scrawny elderly man came out of his shop and rushed to the ram's side. "You should come inside and get out of the sun." He crouched down beside him. "This is…we…western Betham right?" Reece was out of breath and numbed from running. He looked around the busy, unusual town. "Yes, correct." The shop owner said slowly lifting the young man up to his hooves. "Tell me, do you know a man named Lucien Ladenhade?" Reece soon asks.

"Not exactly, where were you headed?" "To the Lutherian Capitol, central Betham." He replied. "The man's waiting for me there." The shop owner pointed upwards near a ginormous floating city within the sky. "You see that city up there? It's like an intersection of the entire Betham region." He explained.

"People sometimes use it as a landmark to know where they're going, central Betham should be far east."

The high floating city was full of large buildings and houses spanning kilometers upon kilometers all around. There were long black chains raining down from underneath it surviving as some sort of rope to climb down from. "Thank you." Once Reece felt steady he headed east towards a populated bridge around the floating city. "Get the hell off me!" A woman yelled as Reece witnessed a couple fighting nearby. A tall redheaded man began grabbing the woman by the neck leaning her against the wide stoned bridge railing above high waters.

Figuring that people were walking around them, anyone could have helped out. "Let go of me!" The woman snapped as she began kicking and slapping the man all over. "Hey stop!" Reece yelled but realized that wouldn't work so he placed his hand on the ground and quickly said a reconstruction spell. "Petrini proexochi!" As the man released his grip and stepped back, configured pillars of stone pushed him high into the air across the wide river.

"No, Anthony!" The woman yelled as she turned towards Reece with anger in her eyes. Most of the people turned the other way, or hurried across the bridge. "You! What did you do?!" "It was for your safe—" Before finishing his words Reece found himself pinned head first on the stoned bridge. *What the hell!* "I wish you hadn't said that spell, you would've lived at least." The clear, stern voice of a man echoed through the ram's ears.

Managing to look behind in his field of vision, he saw a fairly young man with brown mid length hair and a stubble beard. He was wearing a dark blue military uniform accessorized with badges and chains…a Hide uniform.

*He must be…*Fortunately Reece recognized that uniform and face. "There's no way in hell you're taking my blood!" He yelled, struggling to break free from the man's pin. "Let's see about that, you faun." "Astynomia!" The ram quickly poofed out of the man's grasp quick enough to not have a needle stuck in him as he twirled himself on the bridge railing. "You guys are all pathetic, not only do you go hunting our lives but degrade the bloodline within our veins for some selfish, damned experiment that will never advance anything or one!"

Reece was irritated. "What next? Kill your son as well?" "This isn't about him!" The man charged at Reece swinging his assault rifle from behind and firing shots. *You see Reiner, this is why trust and truth is important, you'll know soon enough just how heinous your father really is along with the two worlds.* Reece blocked the man's gun while jumping above to grapple him onto the hot stone ground.

"Afxisitis thermotitas!" The faun held his hands around the man's neck. "You deserve to burn!" The spell burnt through the skin leaving third degree burns across the person's neck as it was painfully hot and bloody. He then unraveled himself away from him. "My son isn't like you fiends!" The guy shot a hot bullet through Reece's knee then grabbed the thick needle from the ground and injected some weird purple fluid inside the ram's arm.

"AHHH!!" The pain was unbearable like pouring loads of salt into a raw, hacked gash wound. What was in that liquid? "That's another one down." The man taunted as he grabbed his rifle. "Stasi chronou!" In a split second time temporarily froze. Reece's mind raced all over being grateful for such a spell. Who knew if the guy was going to rapid fire him to death? He knew he had to use this time to make it to the other side of town near the floating city, and far away from Jeffery.

"Fuck!" Reece was in pain as blood ran down his leg. Knowing he had to escape somehow, he hopped his way to the other side of the bridge and into a nearby forest where he still managed to see the floating city from afar. "I'd gladly take down Hide along with the other guilds if I have too." Reece mumbled to himself as he climbed a tree overlooking Andrea town.

"If I wasn't working with your son I would've over killed your ass you good for nothing." *What were you doing in Betham anyways?* It would only make things more complicated for him. *Is all this really worth it Lucien? I should've brought the stuffed rabbit with me.* The guy thought about the real reason and pay off for following along with the mission. *Taking the dead heart box out of it's sacred place might cause another target on my back, hell even the entire region.*

Not wanting to sit all day. Reece jumped off the tree and wobbled his way through the forest trying to tend to his bullet wound. "Dammit, it hurts! Kryo…pagima." Reece rubbed his wound up and down yet no ice crystals were forming. *What's going on?* He figured it had something to do with that needle earlier so he resulted to pieces of regeneration candy.

After more hours of walking north he made his way into Bessington: the capital of Betham. *Great, so the capitol must be near.* It was near twilight hour, figuring the time spell would wear off Reece headed by a nearby inn further by the capitol. "I wonder what Anri's going through…hopefully not worse than me." He settled in as he let his mind wander.

CHAPTER XXIV

Relics

Meanwhile, the next morning came on fast as Reiner didn't want to wake up, nor go to school. "Yo Reiner, your food's ready. Hurry up and eat." Kareen shouted across the hallway. *Man…why must you be so loud?* Shuffling his sheets around, the kid slugged out of bed and put his black slides on while sniffing his gray tee-shirt. He knew he reeked. The scent of fried food and sweet bread filled the kitchen air as fried plantains, bacon, sweet bammy bread, peppered eggs, saltfish, and cups of hot chocolate was set at the kitchen table.

"This looks good mom, what's the occasion?" The boy guessed as he took a strip of bacon. "You found a better income sufficient job?" "Maybe~ I do have enough money to move into a better house." "I see, so could you pay rent on my apartment when I leave for college?" He was serious. "We'll see, if you make it into Evergreen state." She'd bet on it. "I will." "Anyways how's Reece treating you? Have you experienced the other regions yet?" Kareen smiled. "You've gone before? How do you know about the others?" He was wondering why Reece left without him.

"My mother showed me around Novo Incipere instead of a vacation to Europe." Kareen laughed. "Trust me it was much better than being on a cruise ship to Europe." "Must've been nice though Reece has been doing things without me lately, he left to go to another region before I even woke up." Reiner told as he scarfed down the plate of peppered eggs.

"Hey Reiner," Kareen stopped the boy to listen for a second. "Hmm? What's up?" "Did you know that some of our greatest, greatest ancestors created the king's title? And that Jeffery's great grandfather tried fighting one of the council members decades ago." She continued her story. "Even though their essence is eternal he still managed to tear their body down, having their brain hidden away somewhere."

That's similar to what the ram's finding. Reiner grew bored so he popped a question about Jeffery. "Did you know dad was in an affair?" At that moment Kareen spat out her hot chocolate and shuttered. "No…how the hell did you find out?" The woman gave a confused yet pissed off look as she arched a thick brow. "I used a stuffed toy from a friend of mine." "A stuffed toy?" She could ever wonder why. "Aren't you a little too old to play with stuffed animals son?" "Can't explain, class starts at ten and I have to get going."

Putting the plate down, Reiner hurried into the bathroom to brush his teeth and take a hot shower. "Good day class, hope you all had a wonderful weekend…" Mrs. Veiter greeted with a smile. "Let's finish this semester strong with a book reading session shall we? No related assignments, just reading." The woman explained as she handed out paperback books to the class. "This book is about a certain boy who makes decisions that stick with him and learns what good/bad choices make of him as he grows painful sores but great things happen around him." She made her point. "You could say it's a test of life."

Speaking of tests, Reiner looked around the classroom in search of Lance. *Where's that bastard, and what's he up to?* The classroom was cleaned up and painted over with white and red school paint as the shelves were arranged to cover up the charred walls and tiles. The windows were also boarded up with thick slabs of wood, only insulating the room with large carved out holes. Sad.

"Martin Cobbs was an intelligent, deviant kid who skipped school, lied, and saw flaws within life. One day a strange old man from shop gave Martin some strange juice that showcased his morals. It is a story about how what you do comes back around in any form like luck and consequences." The young man read out loud as he slumped on his desk waiting for class to be over.

"Hey Reiner, how's it going? I had fun hiking with you." Erika smiled, stopping him at his locker. "Hey Erika, what's up?" Reiner wrapped his arms around her, pushing the girl into his chest. She felt the warmth and care surrounding her. Erika pulled out a thick black designer scarf from her backpack along with four hundred dollars.

"Here, to keep you warm and fed in the winter." She then musters up the guts to kiss the boy on the lips before having him step back. "Thanks, you must have a lot of money to spare." "Well duh, you know I'm a wealthy baby." The girl pointed behind Reiner as she saw Elizabeth walking up to them. "Hey there loverboy, Xavier wants to talk to you so come by the guild once you're ready." Elizabeth looked over at Erika.

"Hmm, I take it she's a friend." Giving Reiner a smirk the girl slipped out the hallway and out the side door. "Would I ever get to see the other world?" "Probably not but you will be happy without knowing along with all of us." He placed his hand on her shoulder. "You wanna take me home short stuff?" Reiner jokes. "Whatever, and so have you know I'm five-foot five, an average height." She stuck out her tongue.

The drive home was tedious at best as there was no interesting chatter, just music between the two. "Reiner, could I visit your house sometimes? It's kind of boring and dreadful at my place." Erika spoke her thoughts out loud. "It's best not." He replied. "I go on missions sometimes and I know you and Vitallin don't quite see eye to eye." "Come on, you make it seem like we're rabid dogs or something. How come she's sleeping in your house?" She pouted with obvious questions.

"We're dating." The boy said as he heard Erika groan with annoyance. "Well forget about me asking, I wanted to just hang out with you and Reece after all…" She admits. "Well maybe I could visit your place sometimes." Reiner smiled as he hopped out of the car. "You can always text me if any problems arise." The two waved goodbye and parted ways.

"Kryfi porta." The boy opened a portal door to the other side. *He should be in Betham by now…*Feeling the cold updraft of wind, Reiner was falling from the sky into the western portion of Vidalia town a little further away from Crow's headquarters.

Where am I? Isn't this Vidalia town? He looked around his surroundings and saw forest houses far from the eye can see. *People live in the forest?* "Hello mister! I saw you falling from the sky, are you an angel?" A young boy came out of the house wanting to help Reiner up. "Who are you? Why did you fall from the sky? Where are you headed?" The young swarthy kid continued asking him the most random questions.

"I'm fine. I have something to take care of so…" Reiner looked at the boy's clothes. Blackstrap cargo pants, and a black and red striped tee. The boy looked to be around the age of twelve with a short curly afro. There was a valknut bracelet on the kid's wrist which seemed questionable to Reiner. "I see, so you aren't my angel. I guess I can't have it my way after all."

"What do you mean? What angel?" He was confused. "Every few days my guardian angel Raphael comes back to me with information on my parents and their kidnappers." The kid explained. "Your parents were kidnapped?" "Unfortunately, they were out together so yeah, he told me that the two men were wearing uniforms as if they were in the military." *Could it be Hide? Xan? Jeffery?*

"Uh kid, sorry to say but there's no chance of seeing them again." Reiner assumed the worst. "That may be true but there's a possibility. I haven't received word from Raphael yet." *Does he really have an angel?* "The name's Adrian Kuts, you are?" "Reiner Strife, hey listen I gotta go now someone's waiting for me but it's best if you stay inside for now." "No need to worry, I've learned dark magic from my parents. It'll come in handy if someone tries to fight me." The boy mentioned as he shook Reiners hand.

But would it defend you from Hide? "Stay safe Adrian!" He hurried off to Crow's base. *Considering the fact that his parents are magic users they better fight for their lives.* The young man knocked on the door. "Why hello Reiner, I see you're here alone." Rosie answered the door wearing a crew sweater and jeans. "Hey I heard Xavier wanted to see me, may I come in?" He greeted with a smile.

"Yeah, he's waiting upstairs in the library." "Thanks." Stepping inside the guild lobby the boy headed upstairs. "Xavier, you in there?!" He yelled as he walked through the really massive room. The place was brightly lit with natural lighting. There were loads and loads of books and book ladders everywhere but most noticeably there was a ginormous red oak tree within the center of the room sprawling all the way up towards the balcony.

"President, I'm here." The young man called out to him. The library was so empty he heard his own echo. "Hey Reiner, you came." The man leaped off the high balcony using magic to catch his fall. "Have a seat, I need to have a word with you." Xavier pointed to the blue couches. "About what?" "It's about your new gift, along with the other guilds. Here, take this." Xavier hands Reiner some sort of chained necklace with an odd pendant.

It was a circular pendant of a sun with a hexagon in the middle that had some sort of interlocking hebrew text surrounding it. *Interesting, but why?* The boy thought. "It's yours to keep." "What's this about?" The young man felt the silver, cold medallion between his fingers. "It negates deadmans and keeps unchained familiars away once you rip the pendant off." "What's a deadman?" Reiner was intrigued. "Deadman are similar to ancient children a couple eras ago." He explained. "One can even argue they are one of Novo Incipere's pioneers." He continued.

"They attract unchained familiars that hunt them for their hearts both physically and figuratively as their magic is more powerful than a Valkyrie and enough to bend reality and time itself." *I remember Reece telling me about them.* Reiner thought. "I'm giving the relic to you but don't lose it alright, unchains are dangerous to encounter." "Thank you, though I haven't seen any recently, there were some in the other world." Reiner was wondering about those unchained familiars and where they were coming from.

So a deadman huh… "Now as far as the guilds go, there's an additional law in the code of houses within Simmerton's book of law." Xavier explained. "Law number two hundred and forty-three: Guild leaders are allowed to set tasks for other guild members who are allies, friends, ect." "Hmm, so that would be like Reece assigning tasks for his wife." Reiner added an example.

"Correct. Speaking of which, how's he doing?" "He's at Betham, some commissioner wanted to speak to him." He told. "Really, huh? So he's taking on the chance to bridge regions?" *What a great opportunity to get well known across the world.* The man was impressed as he smiled, tying his hair to the side. Commissioner Ladenhade was a wealthy, intimidating man yet easy going around Reece and fellow comrades, but having him want to eradicate multiple guilds would be vindictive for reasons unknown.

*Great, just a few more miles to go…*It was finally dusk and the ram was now away from the floating city and within the capital of Betham. *So this is central Betham huh…*Bessington was amazing with stone streets, tall buildings, a gigantic ferris wheel, and a beautiful night life scene. The Lutherian capitol was at least thirty miles away, Reece had a hard time casting spells since Jeffery stuck him with that needle. He wanted to fly around as he was done with walking.

Finally. Once he reached the wide marbled capitol building he was relieved. "Hey Lucien, a man like yourself wouldn't need little ole me to do your dirty work so what's the catch?" Reece said as he paged in on the building buzzard. "Ahahaha motives, influences, and causes drives purpose within a man allowing him to see the bigger picture." Commissioner Ladenhade continued speaking through the intercom.

"Welcome to Betham Reece, as you may know I have tasks for you and my forces." At that moment the door opened, allowing Reece to walk through. The building was incredibly spacious yet compact with many rooms as many trolls and green funny looking goblins wearing suits were walking in and out the elevator and up and down the stairs signing and handing in papers, files, and interesting envelopes. This would've given Reece an inferiority complex as he stood out. "Excuse me sir, which floor is Lucien Ladenhade on?" "Uhh… sixth floor I think, room six hundred and nine?" The polite troll smiled as he was unsure.

"Thank you." He stepped onto the elevator and up to the sixth floor. The hallway was office-like with dark warm wood walls, pictures of managers, and windows overlooking the vast city. "Well what do we have here?" Reece greeted as he pointed around the marbled floor with interest.

The room was messy as there was blood, papers, file pictures, and potions scattered around the desk and floor. "I'm mixing my blood and ripping spells into potion bottles Reece, see it as an experiment for my forces." He explained. "Their blood and magic would become heightened with the scene of having my Valkyrian blood inside them." *That's right, you are an offspring of a valkyrian and an ancient, you might be stronger than Rosie and president Xavier…*

"That's hella powerful but why would you need a dead heart box?

What business would you have with the first title holder?" He elaborated. "I mean he's the title holder that can see through you." The strong, sturdy, fairly old man stepped towards Reece trying to not give away his true motives. "I have a few deals I'd like to make with him." He redirected his answer. "Anyways, you guys are gonna search for the box for me so play nice, and maybe I'll reward you Reece."

"Tobi and Anieta, please report to the sixth floor." Lucien paged in on his intercom. "It'll take them a while for them to get here so please have a seat." "Hey Lucien, I'd hate to break it to you but I can't really use my spells anymore." Reece explained to the man. "What happened? Did someone corrupt your blood?" He laughed. "Well yeah, that's the case. Some Hide bastard stuck some weird inhibitor inside me."

"My potions should help though your body should reset where your blood could produce magic again, maybe that liquid should wear off." He suggested that he take some along with him. "How long has it been since we last spoke? What kinds of situations are you covering up this time?" "Nothing drastic as before." He said. "I've made enemies with the guilds Clovermaid and Lionheart." "How come?" Reece wondered.

"So that they'd know who I am, and what I control within this region." *I see…*In a second the elevator door rang open. "Hello, commissioner Ladenhade." A curly haired woman greeted as she stepped out the elevator. "Good day to you miss Johnson, you already know the task but I'd like you to meet Reece." "Hey, let's make the best of this mission shall we?"

He greeted turning around in the chair before getting a look at her appearance. The woman wore a white blouse and black suspending overalls accentuating her curvaceous body and large breasts. "Hi, nice to meet you." Anieta gratefully shook Reece's hand. "She specializes in dark magic and early aged alchemy." He told. "One of the best witches of central Betham." "My former guild was Tigera, what's your guild?" The woman asked, wanting to form a conversation.

"Crow. I'm from the Orieden reg—" Ding-ding! Before he could get any words out, the elevator opened up to a young man with long brown hair eating a container of cake pops. "What's up Lucien? Long time no see." The young man waved at him before shifting his attention towards Reece. "You must be the guy Lucien talked about, how strong are you?" "Let's say I could give you a heart attack with only my thumb."

The ram replied to the kid with a smile. "The name's Reece." "Tobi Krammer, a Hawthorne member who's good at hand to hand combat." He boasts. "I see, then show me some moves once we get on the guild base." Reece challenged the guy as commissioner Ladenhade spoke. "Find the box, I believe it's within the area of Newhaven." *So it could be at the Dundrill tower.* Anieta thought to herself.

"Take the potion bottles with you and move out." "Rodger!" The two said as Reece gave a thumbs up.

CHAPTER XXV

Teamwork

Once outside the Lutherian Capitol they head north-east toward the city of Newhaven. "I'm sick of walking." "Want me to help?" Tobi obliged as he cast a spell on the faun's legs allowing him to fly. "Thanks." He was thankful. "So are you two ready for the day of kings?" Tobi soon asks. "Me? Absolutely…hopefully Crow shapes up though I need to teach them more things." He thought of training Reiner.

"Well hopefully Tigera's doing their best without me…I'm banned from ever returning after attempting to kill my leader." Anieta continued her story. "I was in on a deal with my lover and his guild allowing me to join while making me an assistant to their vice-president." "What a bold move." Reece commented. "Though you shouldn't be anywhere near the presidents and don't deserve to be apart of a guild at all."

Reece continued as he made a point. "A guild member shouldn't betray their family under any circumstances, they are chosen for a reason like how I guide my guild's fighting strategies and motivations, we each play our own part." "Wow, so you're a president?" Tobi wondered with interest. "Vice." He reassured.

"My president and I were apart of the king's tournament and we even shadowed their council during our placement procedures." *Ha, you presidents are all the same, annoying fucks…*Anieta was annoyed. "You all act so full of yourselves, patronizing team members without attributing their needs and wishes. I knew I should've killed that bastard."

"Look, Anieta right? I don't know what went on in your guild but there never needed to be a motive to attempt house murder." This statement alone made Anieta more irritated but Tobi interjected. "No time to argue, just focus on the task at hand Anieta you're out of that guild." He said. "Just bury the hatchet already, that's the past not the present." Resolving matters aside, within a few hours the group arrived at Newhaven, home of the distanced guilds Starlight, and Lionheart.

"Finally, the sooner I get that box the faster the six-figure paycheck." Tobi laughed. "What now?" Reece asked Anieta. "Lucien said it was at this place, maybe it's hidden away in one of those convention buildings?" "Well we do have to find it so let's split up." He suggested as Tobi agreed. "I guess since that's your plan, whoever's the strongest should be on their own." "I kind of get where you guys are coming from but what if we need back up?" She had a point. "Plus Lucien said to eradicate any associations."

"They really wouldn't need it since they're the strongest but we'll come back to help once we are finished searching and taking them down." Tobi reassured her. "What sacred place would hold such a box?" The ram sprung up a good question. "A hidden building, underground facility, or a church perhaps?" "Let's see…" Reece teamed up with Tobi as Anieta searched for hidden buildings far west.

"Okay Tobi, let's see what you're made of." He gave the guy a pep talk. "You'll see, my combats so fast I leave after images." "Bet on it!" Reece took a swig of the bitter potion as they headed to a nearby church. "That's suspicious, why is it chained?" The guys looked around the building. There were boarded up windows, missing bricks, and graffiti everywhere.

"It looks abandoned, some guild members probably hang out here." Tobi assumed. "What are the odds of having the box be here?" "If not here then somewhere, either way we gotta take care of any members inside." Reece placed his hand on the warm metal door. "Ekriktiki kinisi!"

The door exploded inwards as smoke lingered through the air. *Hopefully this potion stays in me.* He wanted his magical abilities back.

There were many levels and rooms in the church coupled with a mysterious ambience. The church's interior was fantastic yet worn out with its gold finished theme as well as the vast ceiling painting showcasing the events of the previous day of kings along with the current title holders. It was a mesmerizing view, but unfortunately they were spotted.

Alright, let's get this party started! "Nekrigi!" Tobi yelled, as the building shook the floorboards rotted away sinking some of the people in along with emanating a toxic odor. "Try to fight back!" At that moment the guy began attacking and flipping people over faster than a cheetah. "Damn, you're good." Reece was impressed.

In a blink of an eye, bodies fell to the ground. "I'll search any rooms visible and hidden, devise a diversion for any that may come my way." He said as he headed up stairs. The stairs creaked so much he thought he was gonna fall through. "Hey you, stop right there!" A large swarthy old man fought Reece up the stairs.

"No trespassers allowed!" Before the man attempted to headbutt him, Reecc grabbed his head and bashed it to the wall so hard that blood came out of his ears. "Now get out of my way!" He hurried up the floor and into a nearby room. *An office? It wouldn't be in here, would it?* The ram searched through desk drawers, behind the shelve, and underneath the old floorboards. Nothing.

*Maybe there's a hidden pathway…*He then got an idea to move the picture frames to feel around the walls, and underneath the desk. *There's got to be a button or a secret clue somewhere.* Placing his head against the wall, in a faint ear he heard muffled voices. *Strange…another hideout huh?* "Who are you, and what are you doing at our base?"

A pale young man with tousled brown hair and freckles stopped Reece in his tracks. *Interesting, his face looks similar to Reiner…*The kid pointed his sharp black wand at Reece taking a stance. "Tell me why you're here!" "Like hell I would, look kid I don't feel like fighting you but looks like I have no choice. Since you have the face of a friend I'll go easy on you." The ram said as he stabbed his arm with a pencil.

"Omichli aimatos." The air grew toxic as the kid felt lightheaded and crouched down to the floor. "Tychero paichnidi!" A die rolled out of the kid's sleeve. Once he shook and rolled a four, two large stakes formed from the floor and wall striking the ram's shoulders and hooves. "Your magic blows." He taunted as he couldn't feel the pain. *This valkyrie blood is amazing.*

"Antigrafo ekrixi." A mini ray shot out of Reece's mouth and caused hot gash wounds all around the boy. *I won't… let you kill us…* As the kid took his final breath, the pool of blood revealed a giant symbol of a snake coiling around a sun. *What's this?* Reece thought about clues to the symbol and what it meant before having his name called. "Reece!" Tobi yelled as he ran into the room huffing and puffing while quickly shutting the door from behind.

"I tried fending them off but got over-exerted, there's too many of them we have to search fast." His face showed as it was bruised and beaten. "They're home rebels." Reece glanced at the kid's forearm. There was a tattoo of a four headed infinity snake below a healed wound where his leader's name should be. *I see…* looking away from the symbol, he took the kid's wand.

"There's a secret pathway somewhere up this ceiling." He told Tobi. "Hurry before some of them wake up, I've killed a few though some are left unconscious." *The sun is referencing the ceiling so…* Reece pointed the wand upwards towards the golden dome and spun his wrist around. "Fidisia matia!" Suddenly, a python slithered up the walls and across the ceiling cracking the surface as ropes fell down from above.

"Let's climb." The two began climbing up through the ceiling. "There had to be reconstruction magic at play here." *An underground tunnel? There are rooms here too.* "The hole is gone." Tobi exclaimed. Looking around the dark area by the corner of their eyes they saw a faint light, moving closer towards it they spotted a few rebel members to which they hid in an alternate hole.

What are they doing? "The box must be here." The young man whispered trying not to get caught. The cloaked rebels were doing a transmutation sequence and talking amongst themselves. "We will see the days beyond this world." A woman continued speaking. "We will go above and beyond all title holders and prove their mistakes as *we are number one.*"

Four of the members placed their hands onto a magic hexagram circle while having another place the heart of the first title holder on the glowing middle symbol. "I see the heart…" Reece whispered as they thought of an ambush. "I'll devise a sneak attack while you fight and get the dead heart, alright?" He told his plans. "Ready?" Reece asked. "Yeah." "Adiexodo." The ground shook as gigantic, scaly creatures formed from the ground up and attacked the group of rebels.

The boy ran through and fought the group, attacking and pinning them down. "Psithyros tou anemou!" Violent gusts of wind came through the vicinity cutting everyone. Tobi took the box and put the heart back in. "Reece catch!" He tossed the dead heart box to the ram before casting an illusion. "Diakoptis eikonas!" The tunnel became twisted and morphed with severe hallucinations accompanied by trippy motions, horrid auditory, and headaches.

The rebels began attacking and killing each other from insanity. "Come on, let's get out of here!" As Tobi and Reece planned a portal outside the church the two reflected on their mission and how well they worked together. "Good job, this was a success!" Tobi said, patting him on the back. "All we have to do now is find Anieta."

"Yeah…what do you think those rebels were planning by transmuting with the dead heart? I know it's insanely valuable but what were they *thinking*?" He thought out loud as Tobi replied. "I don't know, they said they wanted to kill the title holders? They are house rebels so yeah." *Strange…*"Anyways, we have to find miss Johnson." The two asked strangers around the city before going their own way.

"Excuse me miss, have you seen a dark-skinned woman who's yay tall with curly hair, wearing black overalls and has large boobs?" Tobi showed her a photo. "Um, no?" The woman laughed with a confused expression. "Guys, I'm right here!" Anieta yelled running up the graveled road. "Where did you go?" "I was at Dundrill towers." She told. "I've fought a few guild members but no luck in finding the box."

"We have it." Reece said. "Turns out there was a secret place within that rebel church." "So they were rebels huh? Those crooks always find ways to get around Simmerton's laws." Anieta pulled out a gem from her pocket. "I managed to pickpocket an encrusted emerald though." She continued. "Mission success." "Come on, let's head back to Lucien." Once back at the Lutherian Capitol, the group headed inside the building.

"Thank you for your work. Tobi and Anieta, may you two step outside for a minute? I'll pay you guys later." "Yes sir." As the two stepped outside the room, Lucien and Reece began talking. "It was a pretty great chance of luck being hidden away within a church getting transmuted by rebels." He said as he placed the object on the man's desk. "For your cooperation, I'm giving you the aorta portion of the heart."

Lucien said as Reece smiled hard. *What the hell? Is this for real?* It was like christmas for him. "You're not such a bad guy Ladenhade, thanks!" "Your welcome now about alliances, hand this file over to Orieden's house of guilds. I believe they'd be willing to take up the offer." He was handed with another favor. "Sure thing."

Once the ram left the room feeling happier than ever commissioner Lucien poked a hole through the dead heart, smeared the blood on his desk spelling the letters M-A-R-K-O-V, then clasped his hands together. "Markov, there's a wager you can't refuse." He talked as the spirit of the first title holder appeared before him. He was a tall beautiful man (to which you wouldn't have thought he fought in a war) "I know what you want Lucien, the answer is no. I know what you do, how could you betray a fellow friend?"

"I apologize for not being honest in my approaches but I don't have much empathy. My plans to meddle with the other region is purely beneficial for me whether I cause casualties or not." The man said. "I don't think causing wars across regions is a good idea since you're going to blame your "allies" for the cause of it." The title holder rested his case as he wisped away into the unknown.

Reece took a swig of the potion thinking of a faster way to get to Orieden. *This should be more than enough to get me back, I wonder what the kid is doing.* He thought while taking flight. Meanwhile, Reiner was at home lying down reading a book called *The destruction after mankind by F. J. Waltz,* a classic story about a man attempting to time travel and solve his family and friends murder cases.

Time passed away as the clock ticked and tock. Suddenly the box of marbles rattled from within. *Reece…?* This reminded him of his first encounter with the ram. "Yo, I'm back." Reece greeted climbing out the box. "How was Betham?" "I've got a present!" He dug through his pouch and took out the aorta, while grossing the kid out in the process. "How did you get an aorta? Who did you kill?" "It's not who I killed, it belongs to Markov, he's one of the first title holders."

The boy's disgust turned into interest. "Well I have something too." Reiner pointed at the necklace on his desk. "Xavier gave it to me, it keeps away unchained familiars." *I see…* "I also bumped into your father Reiner, he stuck an inhibitor inside me so I couldn't use my magic." He told the kid. "You saw Jeffery?" Reiners heart was conflicted with a strange yearn and resentment as his mind was made up. "We fought and he nearly overkilled me."

"We should fight back harder, Hide has been kidnapping and killing random civilians of Novo. It's damning to me." Reiner sat back down on the bed. "All I know is that these years are gonna be a wild ride for you, I hope you're up for it." His familiar commented.